Gold Mine

WILBUR SMITH

Gold Mine

© *Wilbur A. Smith 1970*

*Published by Edito-Service S A., Geneva
by arrangement with William Heinemann Ltd.*

13-076-002 (0

This book is for

DANIELLE

I

It began in the time when the world was young, in the time before man, in the time before life itself had evolved upon this planet.

The crust of the earth was still thin and soft, distorted and riven by the enormous pressures from within.

What is now the flat, compacted shield of the African continent, stable and unchanging, was a series of alps. It was range upon range of mountains, thrown up and tumbled down by the movements of the magma at great depth. These were mountains such as man has never seen, so massive as to dwarf the Himalayas, mountains of steaming rock from whose clefts and gaping wounds the molten magma trickled.

It came up from the earth's centre along the fissures and weak places in the crust, bubbling and boiling, yet cooling steadily as it neared the surface so that the least volatile minerals were deposited deeper down, but those with a lower melting point were carried to the surface.

At one point in the measureless passage of time, another series of these fissures opened upon one of the nameless mountain ranges, but from them gushed rivers of molten gold. Some natural freak of temperature and chemical change had resulted in a crude but effective process of refinement during the journey to the earth's surface. The gold was in high concentration in the matrix, and it cooled and solidified at the surface.

If the mountains of that time were so massive as to challenge the imagination of man, then the storms of wind and rain that blew around them were of equal magnitude.

It was a hellish landscape in which the gold field was conceived, cruel mountains reaching stark and sheer into the clouds. Cloud banks dark with the sulphurous gases of the belching earth, so thick that the rays of the sun never penetrated them.

The atmosphere was laden with all the moisture that was to become the seas, so heavy with it that it rained in one perpetual wind-lashed storm upon the hot rock of the cooling earth, then the moisture rose in steam to condense and fall again.

As the years passed by their millions, so the wind and the rain whittled away at the nameless mountain range with its coating of gold-rich ore, grinding it loose and carrying it down in freshets and rivers and rushes of mud and rock into the valley between this range and the next.

Now as the country rock cooled, so the waters lay longer upon the earth before evaporating, and they accumulated in this valley to form a lake the size of an inland sea.

Into this lake poured the storm waters from the golden mountains, carrying with them tiny particles of the yellow metal which settled with other sand and quartz gravel upon the lake bed, to be compacted into a solid sheet.

In time all the gold was scoured from the mountains, transported and laid down upon the lake beds.

Then, as happened every ten million years or so, the earth entered another period of intense seismic activity. The earth shuddered and heaved as earthquake after mammoth earthquake convulsed it.

One fearsome paroxysm cracked the bed of the lake from end to end draining it and fracturing the sedimentary beds, scattering fragments haphazardly so that great sheets of rock many miles across tilted and reared on end.

Again and again the earthquakes gripped and shook the earth. The mountains tottered and collapsed, filling the valley where the lake had stood, burying some of the sheets of gold-rich rock, pulverizing others.

That cycle of seismic activity passed, and the ages wheeled on in their majesty. The floods and the great droughts came and receded. The miraculous spark of life was struck and burned up brightly, through the time of the monstrous reptiles, on through countless twists and turns of evolution until near the middle of the pleistocene age a man-ape – australopithecus – picked up the thigh bone of a buffalo from beside an outcrop of rock to use it as a weapon, a tool.

Australopithecus stood at the centre of a flat, sun-seared plateau that reached five hundred miles in each direction to the sea, for the mountains and the lake beds had long ago been flattened and buried.

Eight hundred thousand years later, one of australopithecus' distant but direct line stood at the same spot with a tool in his hand. The man's name was Harrison and the tool was more sophisticated than that of his ancestor, it was a prospector's pick of wood and metal.

Harrison stooped and chipped at the outcrop of rock that protruded from the dry brown African earth. He freed a piece of the stone and straightened with it in his hand.

He held it to catch the sun and grunted with disgust. It was a most uninteresting piece of stone, conglomerate, marbled black and grey. Without hope he held it to his mouth and licked it, wetting the surface before again holding it to the sun, an old prospectors' trick to highlight the metal in the ore.

His eyes narrowed in surprise as the tiny golden flecks in the rock sparkled back at him.

History remembers only his name, not his age nor his antecedents, not the colour of his eyes nor how he died, for within a month he had sold his claim for £10 and disappeared – in search, perhaps, of a really big strike.

He might have done better to retain his title to those claims.

In the eighty years since then an estimated five hundred million ounces of fine gold have been recovered from the fields of the Transvaal and Orange Free State. This is a fraction of that which remains, and which in time will be taken from the earth. For the men who mine the South African fields are the most patiently persistent, inventive and pig-headed of all Vulcan's brood.

This mass of precious metal is the foundation on which the prosperity of a vigorous young nation of eighteen million souls is based.

Yet the earth yields her treasure reluctantly – men must coax and wrest it from her.

Even with the electric fan blowing up a gale from the corner it was stinking hot in Rod Ironsides' office.

He reached for the silver Thermos of iced water at the edge of his desk, and arrested the movement as the jug began to dance before his finger tips touched it. The metal bottle skittered across the polished wooden surface; the desk itself shuddered, rustling the papers upon it. The walls of the room shook, so that the windows rattled in their frames. Four seconds the tremor lasted, and then it was still again.

'Christ!' said Rod, and snatched up one of the three telephones on his desk.

'This is the Underground Manager. Get me the rock mechanic's lab, honey, and snap it up, please.'

He drummed his fingers on the desk impatiently as he waited to be connected. The interleading door of his office opened and Dimitri put his head around the jamb.

'You feel that one, Rod? That was a bad one.'

'I felt it.' Then the telephone spoke into his ear.

'Dr Wessels here.'

'Peter, it's Rod. Did you read that one?'

'I haven't got a fix on it yet – can you hold on a minute?'

'I'll wait.' Rod curbed his impatience. He knew that Peter Wessels was the only person who could read the mass of complicated electronic equipment that filled the instrument room of the rock mechanic's laboratory. The laboratory was a joint research project by four of the major gold-mining companies; between them they had put up a quarter of a million Rand to finance an authoritative investigation of rock and seismic activity under stress. They had selected the Sonder Ditch Gold Mining Company's lease area as the site for the laboratory. Now Peter Wessels had his microphones sited thousands of feet down in the earth, and his tape recorders and stylus graphs ready to pin-point any underground disturbance.

Another minute ticked by, and Rod swivelled his chair and stared out of the plate glass window at the monstrous head gear of No. 1 shaft, tall as a ten-storey building.

'Come on, Peter, come on, boy,' he muttered to himself. 'I've got twelve thousand of my boys down there.'

With the telephone still pressed to his ear, he glanced at his watch.

'Two-thirty,' he muttered. 'The worst possible time. They'll still be in the stopes.'

He heard the receiver picked up on the other end, and Peter Wessels' voice was almost apologetic.

'Rod?'

'Yes.'

'I'm sorry, Rod, you've had a force seven pressure burst at 9,500 feet in sector Sugar seven Charlie two.'

'Christ!' said Rod and slammed down the receiver. He was up from his desk in one movement, his face set and angry.

'Dimitri,' he snapped at his assistant still in the doorway. 'We won't wait for them to call us, it's a top sequence emergency. That was a force seven bump, with its source plumb in the middle of our eastern longwall at 95 level.'

'Sweet Mary Mother,' said Dimitri, and darted back into his own office. He bent his glossy black head of curls over the telephone and Rod heard him start his top sequence calls.

'Mine hospital . . . emergency team . . . Chief Ventilation Officer . . . General Manager's office.'

Rod turned away, as the outer door of his office opened and Jimmy Paterson, his electrical engineer, came in.

'I felt it, Rod. How's it look?'

'Bad,' said Rod, then there were the other line managers crowding into his office talking quietly, lighting cigarettes, coughing and shuffling their feet, but all of them watching the white telephone on Rod's desk. The minutes crawled by like crippled insects.

'Dimitri,' Rod called out to break the tension. 'Have you got a cage held at the shaft head?'

'They're holding the Mary Anne for us.'

'I've got five men checking the high tension cable on 95 level,' said Jimmy Paterson, and they ignored him. They were watching the white phone.

'Have you located the boss yet, Dimitri?' Rod asked again, he was pacing in front of his desk. It was only when he stood close to other men that you saw how tall he was.

'He's underground, Rod. He went down at twelve-thirty.'

'Put in an all-stations call for him to contact me here.'

'I've done that already.'

The white phone rang.

Only once, a shrill note that ripped along Rod's nerve ends. Then he had the receiver up to his ear.

'Underground Manager,' he said. There was a long silence and he could hear the man breathing on the other end.

'Speak, man, what is it?'

'The whole bloody thing has come down,' said the voice. It was husky, rough with fear and dust.

'Where are you speaking from?' Rod asked.

'They're still in there,' said the voice. 'They're screaming in there. Under the rock. They're screaming.'

'What is your station?' Rod made his voice cold, hard, trying to reach the man through his shock.

'The whole stope fell in on them. The whole bloody thing.'

'God damn you! You stupid bastard!' Rod bellowed into the phone. 'Give me your station!'

There was stunned silence for a moment. Then the man's voice came back, steadier now, angry from the insult.

'95 level main haulage. Section 43. Eastern longwall.'

'We're coming.' Rod hung up, picked up his yellow fibreglass hard helmet and lamp from the desk.

'43 section. The hanging wall has come down,' he said to Dimitri.

'Fatals?' the little Greek asked.

'For sure. They've got squealers under the rock.'

Rod clapped on his hat.

'Take over on surface, Dimitri.'

3

Rod was still buttoning the front of his white overalls as he reached the shaft head. Automatically he read the sign above the entrance:

STAY ALERT.   STAY ALIVE.
WITH YOUR CO-OPERATION THIS MINE HAS WORKED
16 FATALITY FREE DAYS.

'We'll have to change the number again,' Rod thought with grim humour.

The Mary Anne was waiting. Into its heavily wired confines were crowded the first aid team and emergency squad. The Mary Anne was the small cage used for lowering and hoisting personnel, there were two much larger cages that could carry one hundred and twenty men at one trip, while the Mary Anne could handle only forty. But that was sufficient for now.

'Let's go,' said Rod as he stepped into the cage, and the onsetter slammed the steel roller doors closed. The bell rang once, twice, and the floor dropped away from under him as the Mary Anne started down. Rod's belly came up to press against his ribs. They went down in one long continuous rush in the darkness. The cage jarring and racketing, the air changing in smell and taste, becoming chemical and processed, the heat building up rapidly.

Rod stood hunch-shouldered, leaning against the metal screen of the cage. The head room was a mere six foot three, and with his helmet on Rod stood taller than that. *So today we get another butcher's bill*, he thought angrily.

He was always angry when the earth took its payment in mangled flesh and snapping bones. All the ingenuity of man and the experience gained in sixty years of deep mining on the Witwatersrand were used in trying to keep the price in blood as low as possible. But when you go down into the ultra-deep levels below eight thousand feet and from those depths you remove a quarter of a million tons of rock each month, mining on an inclined sheet of reef that leaves a vast low-roofed chamber thousands of feet across, then you must pay, for the stress builds up in the rock as the focal points of pressure change until the moment when it reaches breaking point and she bumps. That is when men die.

Rod's knees flexed under him as the cage braked and then yo-yoed to a halt at the brightly lit station on 66 level.

Here they must trans-ship to the sub-main shaft. The door rattled up and Rod left the cage, striding out down the main haulage the size of a railway tunnel; concreted and whitewashed, brightly lit by the bulbs that lined the roof, it curved gently away.

The emergency team followed Rod. Not running, but walking with the suppressed nervous energy of men going into danger. Rod led them towards the sub-main shaft.

There is a limit to the depth which you can sink a shaft into the earth and then equip it to carry men suspended on a steel cable in a tiny wire cage. The limit is about seven thousand feet.

At this depth you must start again, blast out a new headgear chamber from the living rock and below it sink your new shaft, the sub-main.

The sub-main Mary Anne was waiting for them, and Rod led them into it. They stood shoulder to shoulder, and the door rattled shut and again the stomach-swooping rush down into darkness.

Down, down, down.

Rod switched on his head lamp. Now there were tiny motes in the air – air that had been sterilely clean before.

Dust! One of the deadly enemies of the miner. Dust from the burst. As yet the ventilation system had been unable to clear it.

Endlessly they fell in darkness and now it was very hot, the humidity building up so the faces about him, both black and white, were shiny with sweat in the light of his head lamp.

The dust was thicker now, someone coughed. The brightly lit stations flashed past them – 76, 77, 78 – down, down. The dust was a fine mist now. 85, 86, 87. No one had spoken since entering the cage. 93, 94, 95. The deceleration and stop.

The door rattled up. They were 9,500 feet below the surface of the earth.

'Come on,' said Rod.

4

There were men cluttering the lobby of 95 station, a hundred and fifty, perhaps two hundred of them. Still filthy from their work in the stopes, clothing sodden with sweat, they were laughing and chattering with the abandon of men freshly released from frightful danger.

In a clear space in the centre of the lobby lay five stretchers, on two of them the bright red blankets were pulled up to cover the faces of the men upon them. The faces of the other three men looked as though they had been dusted with flour.

'Two' – grunted Rod – 'so far.'

The station was a shambles, with men milling aimlessly, each minute more of them came back down the haulages as they were pulled out of the undamaged stopes, which were now suspect.

Quickly Rod looked about him, recognizing the face of one of his mine captains.

'McGee,' he shouted. 'Take over here. Get them sitting down in lines ready to load. We'll start hauling the shift out immediately. Get onto the hoist room, tell them I want the stretcher cases out first.'

He paused long enough to watch McGee take control. He glanced at his watch. Two fifty-six. He realized with astonishment that only twenty-six minutes had passed since he felt the pressure burst in his office.

McGee had the station under a semblance of control. He was shouting into the hoist room telephone, on Rod's authority demanding priority to clear 95 station.

'Right,' said Rod. 'Come on.' And he led into the haulage.

The dust was thick. He coughed. The hanging wall was lower here. As he trudged on once more, Rod pondered the unfortunate choice of mining terminology that had named the roof of an excavation 'the hanging wall'. It made one think of a gallows, or at the best it emphasized the fact that there were millions of tons of rock *hanging* overhead.

The haulage branched, and unerringly Rod took the right

9

fork. In his head he carried an accurate three-dimensional map of the entire 176 miles of tunnels that comprised the Sonder Ditch's workings. The haulage came to a 'T' junction and the arms were lower and narrower. Right to 42 section, left to 43 section. The dust was so thick that visibility was down to ten feet. The dust hung in the air, sinking almost imperceptibly.

'Ventilations knocked out here,' he called over his shoulder. 'Van den Bergh!'

'Yes, sir.' The leader of the emergency squad came up behind him.

'I want air in this drive. Get it on. Use canvas piping if you have to.'

'Right.'

'Then I want pressure on the water hoses to lay this dust.'

'Right.'

Rod turned into the drive. Here the foot wall – the floor – was rough and the going slower. They came upon a line of steel trolleys filled with gold reef abandoned in the centre of the drive.

'Get these the hell out of the way,' ordered Rod, and went on.

Fifty paces and he stopped abruptly. He felt the hair on his forearms stand on end. He could never accustom himself to the sound, no matter how often he heard it.

In the deliberately callous slang of the miner they called them 'squealers'. It was the sound of a grown man, with his legs crushed under hundreds of tons of rock, perhaps his spine broken, dust suffocating him, his mind unhinged by the mortal horror of the situation in which he was trapped, calling for help, calling to his God, calling for his wife, his children, or his mother.

Rod started forward again, with the sound of it becoming louder, a terrifying sound, hardly human, sobbing and babbling into silence, only to start again with a blood-chilling scream.

Suddenly there were men ahead of Rod in the tunnel, dark shapes looming in the dust mist, their head lamps throwing shafts of yellow light, grotesque, distorted.

'Who is that?' Rod called, and they recognized his voice.

'Thank God. Thank God you've come, Mr Ironsides.'

'Who is that?'

'Barnard.' The 43 section shift boss.

'What's the damage?'

'The whole hanging wall of the stope came down.'

'How many men in the stope?'

'Forty-two.'

'How many still in?'

'So far we've got out sixteen unhurt, twelve slightly hurt, three stretcher cases and two dead 'uns.'

The squealer started again, but his voice was much weaker.

'Him?' asked Rod.

'He's got twenty ton of rock lying across his pelvis. I've hit him with two shots of morphine, but it won't stop him.'

'Can you get into the stope?'

'Yes, there is a crawling hole.' Barnard flashed his lamp over the pile of fractured blue quartzite that jammed the drive like a collapsed garden wall. On it was an aperture big enough for a fox terrier to run through. Reflected light showed from the hole, and faintly from within came the grating sounds of movement over loose rock and the muffled voices of men.

'How many men have you got working in there, Barnard?'

'I' – Barnard hesitated, 'I think about ten or twelve.'

And Rod grabbed a handful of his overall front and jerked him almost off his feet.

'You think!' In the head lamps Rod's face was white with fury. 'You've put men in there without recording their numbers? You've put twelve of my boys against the wall to try and save nine?' With a heave Rod lifted the shift boss off his feet and swung him against the side wall of the drive, pinning him there.

'You bastard, you know that most of those nine are chopped already. You know that stope is a bloody killing ground, and you send in *twelve* more to get the chop *and* you don't record their numbers. How the hell would we ever know who to look for if the hanging fell again?' He let the shift boss free, and stood back. 'Get them out of there, clear that stope.'

'But, Mr Ironsides, the General Manager is in there, Mr Lemmer is in there. He was doing an inspection in the stope.'

For a moment Rod was taken aback, then he snarled. 'I don't give a good damn if the State President is in there, clear the stope. We'll start again and this time we'll do it properly.'

Within minutes the rescuers had been recalled, they came squirming out of the aperture, white with dust like maggots wriggling from rotten cheese.

'Right,' said Rod, 'I'll risk four men at a time.'

Quickly he picked four of the floury figures, among them an enormous man on whose right shoulder was the brass badge of a boss boy.

'Big King – you here?' Rod spoke in fanikalo, the lingua franca of the mines which enabled men from a dozen ethnic groups to communicate.

'I am here,' answered Big King.

'You looking for more awards?' A month before, Big King had been lowered on a rope two hundred feet down a vertical orepass to retrieve the body of a white miner. The bravery award by the company had been 100 Rand.

'Who speaks of awards when the earth has eaten the flesh of men?' Big King rebuked Rod softly. 'But today is children's play only. Is the Nkosi coming into the stope?' It was a challenge.

Rod's place was not in the stope. He was the organizer, the co-ordinater. Yet, he could not ignore the challenge, no Bantu would believe that he had not stood back in fear and sent other men in to die.

'Yes,' said Rod, 'I'm coming into the stope.'

He led them in. The hole was only just big enough to admit the bulk of Rod's body. He found himself in a chamber, the size of an average room, but the roof was only three and a half feet high. He played his lamp quickly across the hanging wall, and it was wicked. The rock was cracked and ugly, 'a bunch of grapes' was the term.

'Very pretty,' he said, and dropped the beam of his lamp.

The squealer was within an arm's length of Rod. His body from the waist up protruded from under a piece of rock the size of a Cadillac. Someone had wrapped a red blanket around his upper body. He was quiet now, lying still. But as the beam of Rod's lamp fell upon him, he lifted his head. His eyes were crazed, unseeing, his face running with the sweat of terror and insanity. His mouth snapped open, wide and pink in the shiny blackness of his face. He began to scream, but suddenly the sound was drowned by a great red-black gout of blood that came gushing up his throat, and spurted from his mouth.

As Rod watched in horror, the Bantu posed like that, his head thrown back, his mouth gaping as though he were a gargoyle, the life blood pouring from him. Then slowly the head sagged forward, and flopped face downwards. Rod crawled to him, lifted his head and pillowed it on the red blanket.

There was blood on his hands and he wiped it on the front of his overalls.

'Three,' he said, 'so far.' And leaving the dying man he crawled on towards the broken face of the fall.

Big King crawled up beside him with two pinch bars. He handed one to Rod.

Within an hour it had become a contest, a trial of strength between the two men. Behind them the other three men were shoring up and passing back the rock that Rod and Big King loosened from the face. Rod knew he was being childish, he should have been back in the main haulage, not only directing the rescue, but also making all the other decisions and alternative arrangements that were needed now. The company paid him for his brains and his experience, not for his muscle.

'The hell with it,' he thought. 'Even if we miss the blast this evening, I'm staying here.' He glanced at Big King, and reached forward to get his hands onto a bigger piece of rock in the jam. He strained, using his arms first, then bringing the power of his whole body into it, the rock was solid. Big King placed huge black hands on the rock, and they pulled together. In a rush of smaller rock it came away, and they shoved it back between them, grinning at each other.

At seven o'clock Rod and Big King withdrew from the stope to rest and eat sandwiches, and drink Thermos coffee while Rod spoke to Dimitri over the field telephone that had been laid up to the face.

'We've pulled shift on both shafts, Rod, the workings are clear to blast. Except for your lot, there are fifty-eight men in your 43 section.' Dimitri's voice was reedy over the field telephone.

'Hold on.' Rod revolved the situation in his mind. He worked it out slower than usual, for he was tired, emotionally and physically drained. If he stopped the blast on both shafts for fear of bringing down more rock in 43 section, it would cost the Company a day's production, ten thousand tons of gold reef worth sixteen Rand a ton, the formidable sum of R160,000 or £80,000 or $200,000 whichever way you looked at it.

It was highly probable that every man in the stope was already dead, and the original pressure burst had de-stressed the rock above and around the 95 level, so there was little danger of further bumps.

And yet there might be someone alive in there, someone lying pinned in the womb-warm darkness of the stope with a bunch of loose grapes hanging over his unprotected body. When they hit all the blast buttons on the Sonder Ditch Mine, they fired eighteen tons of Dynagel. The kick was considerable, it would bring down those grapes.

'Dimitri,' Rod made his decision, 'burn all longwalls on No. 2 shaft at seven-thirty exactly.' No. 2 shaft was three miles away. That would save the Company R80,000. 'Then at precisely five minute intervals burn south, north and west longwalls here on No. 1 shaft.' Spreading the blast would reduce the disturbance, and that put another R60,000 in the shareholders' pockets. The total monetary loss inflicted by the disaster was around R20,000. Not too bad really, Rod thought sardonically, blood was cheap. You could buy it at three Rand a pint from the Central Blood Transfusion Service.

'All right,' he stood up, and flexed his aching shoulders, 'I'm pulling everybody back into the safety of the shaft pillar while we blast.'

5

After the successive earth tremors of the blast, Rod put them back into the stope, and at nine o'clock they uncovered the bodies of two machine boys crushed against the metal of their own rock drill. Ten feet further on they found the white miner, his body was unmarked, but his head was flattened.

At eleven o'clock they found two more machine boys. Rod was in the haulage when they dragged them out through the small opening. Neither of them were recognizable as human, they looked more like lumps of raw meat that had been rubbed in dirt.

A little after midnight Rod and Big King went into the stope again to take over from the team at the face, and twenty minutes later they holed through the wall of loose rock into another chamber that had been miraculously left standing.

The air in here was steamy with heat. Rod recoiled instinctively from the filthy moist gush of it against his face. Then he forced himself to crawl forward and peer into the opening.

Ten feet away lay Frank Lemmer, the General Manager of the Sonder Ditch Mine. He lay on his back. His helmet had been knocked from his head, and a deep gash split the skin above his eye. Blood from the gash had run back into his silver hair and clotted black. He opened his eyes and blinked owlishly in the dazzle of Rod's lamp. Quickly Rod averted the beam.

'Mr Lemmer,' he said.

'What the bloody hell are you doing with the rescue team?' growled Frank Lemmer. 'It's not your job. Haven't you learned a single goddamned thing in twenty years of mining?'

'Are you all right, sir?'

'Get a doctor in here,' replied Frank Lemmer. 'You're going to have to cut me loose from this lot.'

Rod wriggled up to where he lay, and then he saw what Frank Lemmer meant. From the elbow his arm was pinned under a solid slab of rock. Rod ran his hands over the slab, feeling it. Only explosive would shift that rock. As always Frank Lemmer was right.

Rod wriggled out of the opening and called over his shoulder.

'Get the telephone up here.'

After a few minutes delay he had the receiver, and was through to the station at 95 level which had been set up as an advance aid post and rest station for the rescuers.

'This is Ironsides, get me Doctor Stander.'

'Hold on.'

Then moments later, 'Hello, Rod, it's Dan.'

'Dan, we've found the old man.'

'How is he, conscious?'

'Yes, but he's pinned – you'll have to cut.'

'Are you sure?' Dan Stander asked.

'Of course I'm bloody well sure,' snapped Rod.

'Whoa, boy!' admonished Dan.

'Sorry.'

'Okay, where's he caught?'

'Arm. You'll have to cut above the elbow.'

'Charming!' said Dan.

15

'I'll wait here for you.'
'Right. I'll be up in five minutes.'

6

'It's funny, you see them chopped time and again, but you know it will never happen to you.' Frank Lemmer's voice was steady and even, the arm must be numb, Rod thought as he lay beside him in the stope.

Frank Lemmer rolled his head towards Rod. 'Why don't you go farming, boy?'

'You know why,' said Rod.

'Yes.' Lemmer smiled a little, just a twitching of the lips. With his free hand he wiped his mouth. 'You know, I had just three months more before I went on pension. I nearly made it. You'll end like this, boy, in the dirt with your bones crunched up.'

'It's not the end,' said Rod.

'Isn't it?' asked Frank Lemmer, and this time he chuckled. 'Isn't it?'

'What's the joke?' asked Dan Stander, poking his head into the tiny chamber.

'Christ, it took you long enough to get here,' growled Frank Lemmer.

'Give me a hand, Rod.' Dan passed his bag through, then as he crawled forward he spoke to Frank Lemmer.

'Union Steel closed at 98 cents tonight. I told you to buy.'

'Over-priced, over-capitalized,' snorted Frank Lemmer. Dan lay on his side in the dirt and laid out his instruments, and they argued stocks and shares. When Dan had the syringe full of pentathol and was swabbing Frank Lemmer's stringy old arm, Lemmer rolled his head towards Rod again.

'We made a good dig here, Rodney, you and I. I wish they'd give it to you now, but they won't. You're still too young. But whoever they put in my place, you keep an eye on him, you know the ground – don't let him balls it up.'

And the needle went in.

Dan cut through the arm in four and a half minutes, and twenty-seven minutes later Frank Lemmer died of shock and exposure in the Mary Anne on his way to the surface.

7

Once he had paid Patti's alimony there was not too much of Rod's salary left for extravagances, but one of these was the big cream Maserati. Although it was a 1967 model, and had done nearly thirty thousand miles when he bought it, yet the instalments still took a healthy bite out of his monthly pay cheque.

On mornings like this he reckoned the expense worthwhile. He came twisting down from the Kraalkop ridge, and when the national road flattened and straightened for the final run into Johannesburg he let the Maserati go. The car seemed to flatten against the ground like a running lion, and the exhaust note changed subtly, becoming deeper, more urgent.

Ordinarily, it was an hour's run from the Sonder Ditch Mine into the city of Johannesburg, but Rod could clip twenty minutes off that time.

It was Saturday morning, and Rod's mood was light and expectant.

Since the divorce Rod had lived a Jekyll and Hyde existence. Five days of the week he was the company man in top-line management, but on the last two days of the week he went into Johannesburg with his golf clubs in the boot of the Maserati, the keys to his luxury Hillbrow apartment in his pocket, and a chuckle on his lips.

Today the anticipation was keener than ever for, in addition to the twenty-two-year-old blonde model who was prepared to devote her evening to entertaining Rodney Ironsides, there was the mysterious summons from Dr Manfred Steyner to answer.

The summons had been delivered by a nameless female caller

describing herself as 'Dr Steyner's Secretary'. It had come the day after Frank Lemmer's funeral, and was for Saturday at 11 a.m.

Rod had never met Manfred Steyner, but he had, of course, heard of him. Anyone who worked for any of the fifty or sixty companies that comprised the Central Rand Consolidated Group must have heard of Manfred Steyner, and the Sonder Ditch Gold Company was just one of the Group.

Manfred Steyner had a bachelor's degree in Economics from Berlin University, and a Doctor's degree in Business Administration from Cornell. He had joined C.R.C. a mere twelve years previously at the age of thirty, and now he was the front runner. Hurry Hirschfeld could not live for ever, although he gave indications of doing so, and when he went down to make a takeover bid on Hades, the word was that Manfred Steyner would succeed him as Chairman of C.R.C.

Chairmanship of C.R.C. was an enviable position, the incumbent automatically became one of the five most powerful men in Africa, and that included heads of state.

The betting favoured Dr Steyner for a number of good reasons. He had a brain that had earned him the nickname of 'The Computer'; no one had yet been able to detect in him the slightest evidence of a human weakness, and more than this he had taken the trouble ten years previously to catch Hurry Hirschfeld's only granddaughter as she emerged from Cape Town University and marry her.

Dr Steyner was in a strong position, and Rod was intrigued with the prospect of meeting him.

The Maserati was registering 125 miles an hour as he went under the over-pass of the Kloof Gold Mining Company property.

'Johannesburg, here I come!' Rod laughed aloud.

It was ten minutes before eleven o'clock when Rod found the brass plaque reading 'Dr M. K. Steyner' in a secluded lane of the lush Johannesburg suburb of Sandown. The house was not visible from the road, and Rod let the Maserati roll gently in through the tall white gates, with their imitation Cape Dutch gables.

The gates, he decided, were a display of shocking taste but the gardens beyond them were paradise. Rod knew rock, but flowers were his weak suit. He recognized the massed banks of red and yellow against the green lawns as cannas, but after that he had no names for the blazing beauty spread about him.

'Wow!' he muttered in awe. 'Someone has done a hell of a lot of work around here.'

Around a curve in the macadamized drive lay the house. It also was Cape Dutch and Rod forgave Dr Steyner his gates.

'Wow!' he said again, and involuntarily braked the Maserati to a standstill.

Cape Dutch is one of the most difficult styles to copy effectively, where one line in a hundred out of place could spoil the effect; this particular example worked perfectly. It gave the feel of timelessness, of solidarity, and mixed it subtly with a grace and finesse of line. He guessed that the shutters and beams were genuine yellow wood and the windows hand-leaded.

Rod looked at it, and felt envy prickle and burn within him. He loved fine things, like his Maserati, but this was another concept in material possessions. He was jealous of the man that owned it, knowing that his own entire year's income would not be sufficient for a down payment on the land alone.

'So I've got my flat,' he grinned ruefully, and coasted down to park in front of the line of garages.

It was not clear which was the correct entrance to use, and he chose at random from a number of paved paths that all led in the general direction of the house.

Around a bend in this path he came on another spectacle. Though smaller it had, if anything, a more profound effect on Rod than the house had. It was a feminine posterior of equal grace and finesse of line, clad in Helanka stretch ski-pants, and protruding from a large and exotic bush.

Rod was captivated. He stood and watched as the bush shook and rustled, and the bottom wriggled and heaved.

Suddenly, in ladylike tones there issued from the bush a most unladylike oath and the bottom shot backwards and its owner straightened up with her forefinger in her mouth, sucking noisily.

'It bit me!' she mumbled around the finger. 'Damned stinkbug bit me!'

'Well, you shouldn't tease them,' said Rod.

And she spun round to face him. The first thing Rod noticed were her eyes, they were enormous, completely out of proportion to the rest of her face.

'I wasn't —' she started, and then stopped. The finger came out of her mouth. Instinctively one hand went to her hair, and the other began straightening her blouse and brushing off bits of vegetation that were clinging to her.

'Who are you?' she asked, and those huge eyes swept over him. This was fairly standard reaction for any woman between the ages of sixteen and sixty viewing Rodney Ironsides for the first time, and Rodney accepted it gracefully.

'My name is Rodney Ironsides. I've an appointment to see Dr Steyner.'

'Oh.' She was hurriedly tucking her shirt-tails into her slacks. 'My husband will be in his study.'

He had known who she was. He had seen her photographs fifty times in the Group newspaper; but in them she was usually in full-length evening dress and diamonds, not in a blouse with a tear in one sleeve nor pig-tails that were coming down. In the pictures her make-up was immaculate, now she had none at all and her face was flushed and dewed with perspiration.

'I must look a mess. I've been gardening,' said Theresa Steyner unnecessarily.

'Did you do this garden yourself?'

'Only a very little of the muscle work, but I planned it,' she answered. She decided he was big and ugly – no, not really ugly, but battered-looking.

'It's beautiful,' said Rod.

'Thank you.' No, not battered-looking, she changed her mind, tough-looking, and the chest hair curled out of the vee of his open neck shirt.

'This is a protea, isn't it?' He indicated the bush from which she had recently emerged. He was guessing.

'Nutans,' she said; he must be in his late thirties, there was greying at his temples.

'Oh, I thought it was a protea.'

'It is. "Nutans" is its proper name. There are over two hundred different varieties of proteas,' she answered seriously. His voice didn't fit his appearance at all, she decided. He looked like a prize fighter but spoke like a lawyer, probably was one. It was usually lawyers or business consultants who came calling on Manfred.

'Is that so? It's very pretty.' Rod touched one of the blooms.

'Yes, isn't it? I've got over fifty varieties growing here.'

And suddenly they were smiling at each other.

'I'll take you up to the house,' said Theresa Steyner.

8

'Mr Ironsides is here, Manfred.'

'Thank you.' He sat at the stinkwood desk in a room that smelled of wax polish. He made no effort to rise from his seat.

'Would you like a cup of coffee?' Theresa asked from the doorway. 'Or tea?'

'No, thank you,' answered Manfred Steyner without consulting Rod who stood beside her.

'I'll leave you to it, then,' she said.

'Thank you, Theresa.' And she turned away. Rod went on standing where he was, he was studying this man of whom he had heard so much.

Manfred Steyner appeared younger than his forty-two years. His hair was light brown, almost blond, and brushed straight back. He wore spectacles with heavy black frames, and his face was smooth and silky-looking, soft as a girl's with no beard shadow on his chin. His hands that lay on the polished desk top were hairless, smooth, so that Rod wondered if he had used a depilatory on them.

'Come in,' he said, and Rod moved to the desk. Steyner wore a white silk shirt in which the ironing creases still showed, the cloth was snowy white and over it he wore a Royal Johannesburg Golf Club tie, with onyx cuff links. Suddenly Rod realized that neither shirt nor tie had ever been worn before, that much was true of what he had heard then. Steyner ordered his shirts hand-made by the gross and wore each once only.

'Sit down, Ironsides.' Steyner slurred his vowels slightly, just a trace of a Teutonic accent.

'Dr Steyner,' said Rod softly, 'you have a choice. You may call me Rodney or *Mr* Ironsides.'

There was no change in Steyner's voice nor expression.

'I would like to go over your background, please, Mr Ironsides, as a preliminary to our discussion. You have no objection?'

'No, Dr Steyner.'

'You were born October 16th, 1931, at Butterworth in the Transkei. Your father was a native trader, your mother died January 1939. Your father was commissioned Captain in the Durban Light Infantry and died of wounds on the Po River in Italy during the winter of 1944. You were raised by your maternal uncle in East London. Matriculating from Queen's College, Grahamstown, in 1947, you were unsuccessful in obtaining a Chamber of Mines scholarship to Witwatersrand University for a B.Sc. (Mining Engineering) degree. You enrolled in the G.M.T.S. (Government Mining Training School) and obtained your blasting ticket during 1949. At which time you joined the Blyvooruitzicht Gold Mining Company Ltd as a learner miner.'

Dr Steyner stood up from his desk and crossing to the panelled wall he pressed a concealed switch and a portion of the panelling slid back to reveal a wash basin and towel rack. As he went on talking he began very meticulously to soap and wash his hands.

'In the same year you were promoted to miner and in 1952 to shift boss, 1954 to mine captain. You successfully completed the examination for the Mine Manager's ticket in 1959, and in 1962 you came to us as an Assistant Section Manager; in 1963, Section Manager, 1965, Assistant Underground Manager, and in 1968 you achieved your present position as Underground Manager.'

Dr Steyner began drying his hands on a snowy white towel.

'You've memorized my company record pretty thoroughly,' Rod admitted.

Dr Steyner crumpled the towel and dropped it into a bin below the wash basin. He pressed the button and the panelling slid closed, then he came back to the desk stepping precisely over the glossy polished wooden floor, and Rod realized that he was a small man, not more than five and a half feet tall, about the same height as his wife.

'This is something of an achievement,' Steyner went on. 'The next youngest Underground Manager in the entire Group is forty-six years of age, whereas you are not yet thirty-nine.'

Rod inclined his head in acknowledgement.

'Now,' said Dr Steyner as he reseated himself and laid his freshly washed hands on the desk top. 'I would like briefly to touch on your private life – you have no objections?'

Again Rod inclined his head.

'The reason that your application for the Chamber of Mines scholarship was refused, despite your straight A matriculation was the recommendation of your headmaster to the selection board in effect that you were of unstable and violent disposition.'

'How the hell did you know that?' ejaculated Rod.

'I have access to the board's records. It seems that once you had received your matric you immediately assaulted your former headmaster.'

'I beat the hell out of the bastard,' Rod agreed happily.

'An expensive indulgence, Mr Ironsides. It cost you a university degree.'

And Rod was silent.

'To continue: In 1959 you married Patricia Anne Harvey. Of the union was born a girl child in the same year, to be precise, seven and a half months after the wedding.'

Rod squirmed slightly in his chair, and Dr Steyner went on quietly.

'This marriage terminated in divorce in 1964. Your wife suing you on the grounds of adultery, and receiving custody of the child, alimony and maintenance in the sum of R450.00 monthly.

'What's all this about?' demanded Rod.

'I am attempting to establish an accurate picture of your present circumstances. It is necessary, I assure you.' Dr Steyner removed his spectacles and began polishing the lens on a clean white handkerchief. There were the marks of the frames on the bridge of his nose.

'Go on, then.' Despite himself, Rod was fascinated to learn just how much Steyner knew about him.

'In 1968 there was a paternity suit brought against you by a Miss Diane Johnson and judgement for R150.00 per month.'

Rod blinked, and was silent.

'I should mention two further actions against you for assault, both unsuccessful on the grounds of justification or self-defence.'

'Is that all?' asked Rod sarcastically.

'Almost,' admitted Dr Steyner. 'It is only necessary to note further recurrent expenditure in the form of a monthly payment of R150.00 on a continental sports car, and a further R100.00 per month rental on the premises 596 Glen Alpine Heights, Corner Lane, Hillbrow.'

Rod was furious, he had believed that no one in C.R.C. knew about the flat.

'Damn you! You've been prying into my affairs!'

'Yes,' agreed Dr Steyner levelly. 'I am guilty, but in good cause. If you bear with me, you'll see why.'

Suddenly Dr Steyner stood up from the desk, crossed the room to the concealed wash basin, and again began to wash his hands. As he dried them, he spoke again.

'Your monthly commitments are R850. Your salary, after deduction of tax, is less than one thousand Rand. You have no mining degree, and the chances of your taking the next step upwards to General Manager without it are remote. You are at your ceiling, Mr Ironsides. On your own ability you can go no further. In thirty years' time you will not be the youngest Underground Manager in the C.R.C. Group, but the oldest.' Dr Steyner paused. 'That is, provided that your rather expensive tastes have not landed you in a debtors' prison, and that neither the quickness and heat of your temper, nor the matching speed and temperature of your genitalia have gotten you into really serious trouble.'

Steyner dropped the towel in the bin and returned to his seat. They sat in absolute silence, regarding each other for a full minute.

'You got me all the way up here to tell me this?' asked Rod, his whole body was tense, his voice slightly husky, it needed only one ounce more of provocation to launch him across the desk at Steyner's throat.

'No.' Steyner shook his head. 'I got you up here to tell you that I will use all my influence, which I flatter myself is considerable, to secure your appointment – and I mean immediate appointment – to the position of General Manager of the Sonder Ditch Gold Mining Company Ltd.'

Rod recoiled in his chair as though Steyner had spat in his face. He stared at him aghast.

'Why?' he asked at last. 'What do you want in exchange?'

'Neither your friendship, nor your gratitude,' Dr Steyner told him. 'But your unquestioning obedience to my instructions. You will be my man – completely.'

Rod went on staring at him while his mind raced. Without Steyner's intervention he would wait at the very least ten years for this promotion, if it ever came. He wanted it, my God, how he wanted it. The achievement, the increase in income, the power that went with the job. His own mine! His own mine at the age of thirty-eight – and an additional ten thousand Rand per annum.

Yet Rod was not gullible enough to believe that Manfred Steyner's price would be cheap. When the instruction came that he was to follow with unquestioning obedience, he knew it would stink like a ten-day corpse. But once he had the job he could refuse the instruction. Get the job first, then decide once he received the instruction whether to follow it or not.

'I accept,' he said.

Manfred Steyner stood up from the desk.

'You will hear from me,' he said. 'Now you may go.'

9

Rod crossed the wide-flagged stoep without seeing or hearing, vaguely he wandered down across the lawns towards his car. His mind was harrying the recent conversation, tearing it to pieces like a pack of wild dogs on a carcass. He almost bumped into Theresa Steyner before he saw her, and abruptly his mind dropped the subject of the General Managership.

Theresa had changed her clothing, made up her face and eyes, and the pig-tails were concealed under a lime-coloured silk scarf, all this in the half hour since their last meeting. She was hovering over a flower bed with a flower basket on one arm, as bright and pleasing as a hummingbird.

Rod was amused and flattered, vain enough to realize that the change was in his honour, and connoisseur enough to appreciate the improvement.

'Hello.' She looked up, contriving successfully to look both surprised and artless. Her eyes were really enormous, and the make-up was designed to enhance their size.

'You are a busy little bee.' Rod ran a knowledgeable appraisal over the floral slack suit she wore, and saw the colour start in her cheeks as she felt his eyes.

'Did you have a successful meeting?'

'Very.'

'Are you a lawyer?'

'No. I work for your grandfather.'

'Doing what?'

'Mining his gold.'

'Which mine?'

'Sonder Ditch.'

'What's your position?'

'Well, if your husband is as good as his word, I'm the new General Manager.'

'You're too young,' she said.

'That's what I thought.'

'Pops will have something to say on the subject.'

'Pops?' he asked.

'My grandfather.' And Rod laughed before he could stop himself.

'What's so funny?'

'The Chairman of C.R.C. being called "Pops".'

'I'm the only one who calls him that.'

'I bet you are.' Rod laughed again. 'In fact I'd bet you'd get away with a lot of things no one else would dare.'

Suddenly the underlying sexuality of his last remark occurred to them both and they fell silent. Theresa looked down and carefully snipped the head off a flower.

'I didn't mean it that way,' apologized Rod.

'What way, Mr Ironsides?' She looked up and inquired with mischievous innocence, and they laughed together with the awkwardness gone again.

She walked beside him to the car, making it seem a completely natural thing to do, and as he slipped behind the steering-wheel she remarked:

'Manfred and I will be coming out to the Sonder Ditch next week. Manfred is to present long service and bravery awards to some of your men.' She had already refused the invitation to accompany Manfred, she must now see to it that she was re-invited. 'I shall probably see you then.'

'I look forward to it,' said Rod, and let in the clutch.

Rod glanced in the rear view mirror. She was a remarkably provocative and attractive woman. A careless man could drown in those eyes.

'Dr Manfred Steyner has got himself a big fat problem there,' he decided. 'Our Manfred is probably so busy soaping and scrubbing his equipment, that he never gets round to using it.'

10

Through the leaded windows Dr Steyner caught a glimpse of the Maserati as it disappeared around the curve in the driveway, and he listened as the throb of the engine dwindled into silence.

He lifted the receiver of the telephone and wiped it with the white handkerchief before putting it to his ear. He dialled and while it rang he inspected the nails of his free hand minutely.

'Steyner,' he said into the mouthpiece. 'Yes – yes.' He listened. 'Yes . . . He has just left . . . Yes, it is arranged . . . No, there will be no difficulty thère, I am sure.' As he spoke he was looking at the palm of his hand, he saw the tiny beads of perspiration appear on his skin and an expression of disgust tightened his lips.

'I am fully aware of the consequences. I tell you, I know.'

He closed his eyes and listened for another minute without moving as the receiver squawked and clacked, then he opened his eyes.

'It will be done in good time, I assure you. Goodbye.'

He hung up and went to wash his hands. Now, he thought, as he worked up lather, to get it past the old man.

11

He was old now, seventy-eight long hard years old. His hair and his eyebrows were creamy white. His skin was folded and creased, freckled and spotted, hanging in unexpected little pouches under his chin and eyes.

His body had dried out, so he stood gaunt and stooped like a tree that has taken a set before the prevailing winds; but there was still the underlying urgency in the way he held himself, the same urgency that had earned him the name of 'Hurry' Hirschfeld when first he bustled into the gold fields sixty years ago.

On this Monday morning he was standing before the full length windows of his penthouse office, looking down on the city of Johannesburg. Reef House stood shoulder to massive shoulder with the Schlesinger Building on the Braamfontein ridge above the city proper. From this height it seemed that Johannesburg cowered at Hurry Hirschfeld's feet, as well it should.

Long ago, even before the great depression of the 'thirties, he had ceased to measure his wealth in terms of money. He owned outright a little over a quarter of the issued share capital of Central Rand Consolidated. At the present market price of R120 per share, this was a staggering sum. In addition, through a complicated arrangement of trusts, proxy rights and interlocking directorates, he had control of a further massive block of twenty per cent of the company's voting rights.

The overhead intercom pinged softly into this room of soft fabrics and muted colours, and Hurry started slightly.

'Yes,' he said, without turning away from the window.

'Dr Steyner is here, Mr Hirschfeld,' his secretary's voice whispered, ghostly and disembodied into the luscious room.

'Send him in,' snapped Hurry. That goddamned intercom always gave him the creeps. The whole goddamned room gave him the creeps. It was, as Hurry had said often and loudly, like a fairy brothel.

For fifty-five years he had worked in a bleak uncarpeted office with a few yellowing photographs of men and machinery on its walls. Then they had moved him in here – he glanced around the room with the distaste that five years had not lulled. What did they think he was, a bloody ladies' hairdresser?

The panelling door slid noiselessly aside and Dr Manfred Steyner stepped neatly into the room.

'Good morning, Grandfather,' he said. For ten years, ever since Terry had been bird-brained enough to marry him, Manfred Steyner had called Hurry Hirschfeld that, and Hurry hated it. He remembered now that Manfred Steyner was also responsible for the design and decor of Reef House, and therefore the author of his recent irritation.

'What ever it is you want – No!' he said, and he moved across to the air-conditioning controls. The thermostat was already set at 'high', now Hurry turned it to 'highest'. Within minutes the room would be at the correct temperature for growing orchids.

'How are you this morning, Grandfather?' Manfred seemed not to have heard, his expression was bland and neutral as he moved to the desk and laid out his papers.

'Bloody awful,' said Hurry. It was impossible to disconcert the little prig, he thought, you might as well shout insults at an efficiently functioning piece of machinery.

'I am sorry to hear that.' Manfred took out his handkerchief and touched his chin and forehead. 'I have the weekly reports.'

Hurry capitulated and went across to the desk. This was business. He sat down and read quickly. His questions were abrupt, cutting and instantly answered, but Manfred's handkerchief was busy now, swabbing and dabbing. Twice he removed his spectacles and wiped steam from the lens.

'Can I turn the air-conditioning down a little, Grandfather?'

'You touch it and I'll kick your arse,' said Hurry without looking up.

Another five minutes and Manfred Steyner stood up suddenly.

'Excuse me, Grandfather.' And he shot across the office and disappeared into the adjoining bathroom suite. Hurry cocked his head to listen, and when he heard the taps hiss he grinned happily. The air-conditioning was the only method he had discovered of disconcerting Manfred Steyner, and for ten years he had been experimenting with various techniques.

'Don't use all the soap,' he shouted gleefully. 'You are the one always on about office expenses!'

It did not seem ludicrous to Hurry that one of the richest and most influential men in Africa should devote so much time and energy to baiting his personal assistant.

At eleven o'clock Manfred Steyner gathered his papers and began packing them carefully in his monogrammed pigskin briefcase.

'About the appointment of a new General Manager for the Sonder Ditch to replace Mr Lemmer. You will recall my memo regarding the appointment of younger men to key positions —'

'Never read the bloody thing,' lied Hurry Hirschfeld. They both knew he read everything, and remembered it.

'Well —' Manfred went on to enlarge his thesis for a minute, then ended, 'In view of this, my department, myself concurring entirely, urges the appointment of Rodney Barry Ironsides, the present Underground Manager, to the position. I hoped that you would initial the recommendation and we can put it through at Friday's meeting.'

Dextrously Manfred slid the yellow memo in front of Hurry Hirschfeld, unscrewed the cap of his pen and offered it to him. Hurry picked the memo up between thumb and forefinger as though it were someone's dirty handkerchief and dropped it into the waste-paper bin.

'Do you wish me to tell you in detail what you and your planning department can do?' he asked.

'Grandfather,' Manfred admonished him mildly, 'you cannot run the company as though you were a robber baron. You cannot ignore the team of highly trained men who are your advisers.'

'I've run it that way for fifty years. You show me who's going to change that.' Hurry leaned back in his chair with vast satisfaction and fished a powerful-looking cigar out of his inner pocket.

'Grandfather, that cigar! The doctor said —'

'And I said Fred Plummer gets the job as Manager of the Sonder Ditch.'

'He goes on pension next year,' protested Manfred Steyner.

'Yes,' Hurry nodded. 'But how does that alter the position?'

'He's an old dodderer,' Manfred tried again, there was a desperate edge to his voice. He had not anticipated one of the old man's whims cutting across his plans.

'He's twelve years younger than I am,' growled Hurry ominously. 'How's that make him an old dodderer?'

12

Now that the weekend was over, Rod found the apartment oppressive, and he longed to get out of it.

He shaved, standing naked before the mirror, and he caught a whiff of the reeking ashtrays and half-empty glasses in the lounge. The char would have her customary Monday-morning greeting when she came in later today. From Louis Botha Avenue the traffic noise was starting to build up and he glanced at his watch – six o'clock in the morning. A good time to examine your soul, he decided, and leaned forward to watch his own eyes in the mirror.

'You're too old for this type of living,' he told himself seriously. 'You've had four years of it now, four years since the divorce, and that's about enough. It would be nice now to go to bed with the same woman on two consecutive nights.'

He rinsed his razor, and turned on the taps in the shower cabinet.

'Might even be able to afford it, if our boy Manfred delivers the goods.' Rod had not allowed himself to believe too implicitly in Manfred Steyner's promise; but during the whole of these last two days the excitement had been there beneath the cynicism.

He stepped into the shower and soaped himself, then turned the cold tap full on. Gasping he shut it off and reached for his towel. Still drying himself, he went through and stood at the foot of the bed; as he towelled himself he examined the girl who lay among the tousled sheets.

She was tanned dark toffee brown so she appeared to be dressed in white transparent bra and panties where the skin was untouched by the sun. Her hair was a blonde-gold flurry across her face and the pillow, at odds with the jet black triangle of body hair. Her lips in sleep were fixed in a soft pink pout, and she looked disquietingly young. Rod had to make a conscious effort to remember her name, she was not the companion with whom he had begun the weekend.

'Lucille,' he said, sitting down beside her. 'Wake up. Time to roll.'

She opened her eyes.

'Good morning,' he said and kissed her gently.

'Mmm.' She blinked. 'What time is it? I don't want to get fired.'

'Six,' he told her.

'Oh, good. Plenty of time.' And she rolled over and snuggled down into the sheets.

'Like hell.' He slapped her bottom lightly. 'Move, girl, can you cook?'

31

'No —' She lifted her head. 'What's your name again?' she asked.

'Rod,' he told her.

'That's right – Piston Rod,' she giggled 'What a way to die! Are you sure you aren't powered by steam?'

'How old are you?' he asked.

'Nineteen. How old are you?'

'Thirty-eight.'

'Daddy, you're vintage!' she told him vehemently.

'Yes, sometimes I feel that way.' He stood up. 'Let's go.'

'You go. I'll lock up when I leave.'

'No sale,' he said, the last one he had left in the flat had cleaned it out – groceries, liquor, glasses, towels, even the ashtrays. 'Five minutes to dress.'

Fortunately she lived on his way. She directed him to a run-down block of flats under the mine dumps at Booysens.

'I'm putting three blind sisters through school. You want to help?' she asked as he parked the Maserati.

'Sure.' He eased a five-Rand note out of his wallet and handed it to her.

'Ta muchly.' And she slipped out of the red leather seat, closed the door and walked away. She did not look back before she disappeared into the block, and Rod felt an unaccountable wave of loneliness wash over him. It was so intense that he sat quies-cent for a full minute before he could throw it off, then he hit the gears and screeched away from the kerb.

'My little five-Rand friend,' he said. 'She really cares!'

He drove fast, so that as he topped the Kraalkop ridge the shadows were still long, and the dew lay silver on the grass. He pulled the Maserati into a layby and climbed out. Leaning against the bonnet he lit a cigarette, grimacing at the taste, and looked down at the valley.

There was no natural surface indication of the immense treasure house that lay below. It was like any of the other count-less grassy plains of the Transvaal. In the centre stood the town of Kitchenerville, which for half a century had rejoiced in the fact that Lord Kitchener had camped one night here in pursuit of the wily Boer: a collection of three dozen buildings which had expanded miraculously into three thousand, around a magnifi-cent town hall and shopping complex. Dressed in public lawns and gardens, wide streets and bright new houses, all of it paid for by the mining houses whose lease areas converged on the town.

Out of the bleak veld surrounding the town their headgears stood like colossal monuments to the gold hunger of man. Around the headgears clustered the plants and workshops. There were fourteen headgears in the valley. The field was divided into five lease areas, following the original farm titles, and was mined by five separate companies. Thornfontein Gold Mining, Blaauberg Gold Mining, West Tweefontein Mining, Deep Gold Levels, and the Sonder Ditch Gold Mining Company.

It was to this last that Rod naturally directed his attention.

'You beauty,' he whispered, for in his eyes the mountainous dumps of blue rock beside the shafts were truly beautiful. The complex but carefully thought out pattern of the works buildings, even the sulphur-yellow acres of the slimes dam, had a functional beauty.

'Get it for me, Manfred,' he spoke aloud. 'I want it. I want it badly.'

On the twenty-eight square miles of the Sonder Ditch's property lived fourteen thousand human beings, twelve thousand of them were Bantu who had been recruited from all over Southern Africa. They lived in the multi-storied hostels near the shaft heads, and each day they went down through two small holes in the ground to depths that were scarcely credible, and came up again out of those same two holes. Twelve thousand men down, twelve thousand up. That was not all: out of those two same holes came ten thousand tons of rock daily, and down them went timber and tools and piping and explosive, ton upon ton of material and equipment. It was an undertaking that must evoke pride in the men who accomplished it.

Rod glanced at his watch, 7.35 a.m. They were down already, all twelve thousand of them. They had started going down at three-thirty that morning and now it was accomplished. The shift was in. The Sonder Ditch was breaking rock, and bringing the stuff out.

Rod grinned happily. His loneliness and depression of an hour ago were gone, swallowed up in the immensity of his involvement. He watched the massive wheels of the headgears spinning, stopping briefly, and then spinning again.

Each of those shafts had cost fifty million Rand, the surface plant and works another fifty million. The Sonder Ditch represented an investment of one hundred and fifty million Rand, two hundred and twenty million dollars. It was big, and it would be his.

Rod flicked away the butt of his cigarette. As he drove down the ridge, his eyes moved eastward down the valley. All mining activity ceased abruptly along an imaginary north-south line, drawn arbitrarily across the open grassland. There was no surface indication why this should be so, but the reason was deep down.

On that line ran a geological freak, a dyke, a wall of hard serpentine rock that had been named 'the Big Dipper'. It cut through the field like an axe stroke, and beyond it was bad ground. The gold reef existed in the bad ground, they knew this; but not one of the five companies had gone after it. They had prospected it tentatively and then shied away from it, for the boreholes that they sank were frightening in their inconsistency.

A big percentage of the Sonder Ditch lease area lay on the far side of the Dipper, and there was a diamond-drilling team working there now. They had already completed five holes.

Rod could remember accurately the results:-

Borehole S.D. No. 1.	Abandoned in water at 4,000 ft.	
S.D. No. 2.	Abandoned in dry hole at 5,250 ft.	
S.D. No. 3.	Intersected carbon leader reef at 6,600 ft.	
Assay valve	27,323 inch penny-weights.	
First deflection	6,212 inch penny-weights.	
Second deflection	2,114 inch penny-weights.	
S.D. No. 4.	Abandoned in artesian water at 3,500 ft.	
S.D. No. 5.	Intersected carbon leader at 8,116 ft.	
Assay valve	562 inch penny-weights.	

And they were drilling the deflections on that one now.

The problem was to build up a picture from results like that. It looked like a mess of faulted and water-logged ground with the gold reef fragmented and fluky, showing unbelievably high values at one spot, and then more than likely pinching out fifty feet away.

They may mine it one day, thought Rod, but I hope to hell I'm on pension by the time they do.

In the distance beyond the slimes dam he could just make out the spidery triangle of the drilling rig against the grown grass.

'Go to it, boys,' he muttered. 'Whatever you find there won't make much difference to me.'

And he went in through the imposing gates at the entrance to the mine property, halting carefully at the stop sign where the railway line crossed the road and he forked two fingers at the traffic policeman lurking behind the gates.

The traffic cop grinned and waved, he had caught Rod the previous week, so he was still one up.

Rod drove down to his office.

13

That Monday morning Allen 'Popeye' Worth was preparing to drill his first deflection on the S.D. No. 5 borehole. Allen was a Texan – not a typical Texan. He stood five feet four inches tall, but was as tough as the steel drill with which he worked. Thirty years before he had started learning his trade on the oilfields around Odessa and he had learned it well.

Now he could start at the surface and drill a four-inch hole down thirteen thousand feet through the earth's crust, keeping the hole straight all the way, an almost impossible task if you took into account the whippiness and torque in a jointed rod of steel that long.

If, as happened occasionally, the steel snapped and broke off thousands of feet down, Allen could fit a fishing tool on the end of his rig, and patiently grope for the stump, find it, grapple it and pull it out of the borehole. When he hit the reef down there, he could purposely kick his drill off the line and pierce the reef again and again to sample it over an area of hundreds of feet. This was what was meant by deflecting.

Allen was one of the best. He could command his own salary and behave like a prima donna, and his bosses would still fawn on him, for the things he could do with a diamond drill were almost magical.

Now he was assessing the angle of his first deflection. The previous day he had lowered a long brass bottle to the end of his borehole and left it overnight. The bottle was half filled with concentrated sulphuric acid, and it had etched the brass of the bottle. By measuring the angle of the etching he knew just how his drill was branching off from his original hole.

In the tiny wood and iron building beside the drilling rig he finished his measurements and stood back from the work bench, grunting with satisfaction.

From his hip pocket he drew a corncob pipe and pouch. Once he had stuffed tobacco into the pipe and lit it, it became very clear as to why his nickname was 'Popeye'. He was a dead ringer for the cartoon character, aggressive jaw, button eyes, battered maritime cap and all.

He puffed contentedly, watching through the single window of the shack as his gang went about the tedious business of lowering the drilling bit down into the earth. Then he took the pipe from his mouth and spat accurately through the window, replaced the pipe and stooped to minutely check his measurements.

His foreman driller interrupted him from the doorway.

'On bottom, and ready to turn, boss.'

'Huh!' Popeye checked his watch. 'Two hours forty to get down, you don't reckon to rupture a gut do you?'

'That's not bad,' protested the foreman.

'And it sure as hell isn't good either! Okay, okay, cut the cackle and let's get her turning.' He bounced out of the shed and set off for the rig, darting quick beady little glances about him. The rig was a fifty-foot high tower of steel girders and within it the drill rod hung down until it disappeared into the collar. The twin two hundred-horsepower diesel engines throbbed expectantly, waiting to provide the power, their exhausts smoking blue in the early morning sunlight. Beside the rig lay a mountainous heap of drilling rods, beyond them the ten thousand-gallon puddling reservoir to provide water for the hole. Water was pumped into the hole continuously to cool and lubricate the tool as it cut into the rock.

'Stand by to turn her,' Popeye called to his gang, and they moved to their stations. Dressed in blue overalls, coloured fibreglass helmets, and leather gloves, they stood ready and tensed. This was an anxious moment for the whole team, power had to be applied with a lover's touch to the mile and a half length of rod, or it would buckle and snap.

Popeye climbed nimbly up onto the collar, and glanced about

him to make sure all was in readiness. The foreman driller was at the controls, watching Popeye with complete absorption, his hands resting on the levers.

'Power up!' shouted Popeye and made the circular motion with his right hand. The diesels bellowed harshly, and Popeye reached out to lay his left hand on the drilling rod. This was how he did it, feeling the rod with his bare hand as he brought in the power, judging the tension by ear and eye and touch.

His right hand gestured and the foreman delicately let in the clutch, the rod moved under Popeye's hand, he gestured again and it revolved slowly. He could feel it was near breaking point and he cut down the power instantly, then let it in again. His right hand moved eloquently, expressively as an orchestral conductor, and the foreman followed it, the junior member of a highly skilled team.

Slowly the tension of the gang relaxed as the revolutions of the drill built up steadily, until Popeye gave the clenched fist 'okay' and jumped down from the collar. They scattered casually to their other duties, while Popeye and the foreman strolled back to the shed, leaving the drill to grind away at a steady four hundred revolutions a minute.

'Got something for you,' said the foreman, as they entered the shed.

'What?' demanded Popeye.

'The latest *Playboy*.'

'You're kidding!' Popeye accused him delightedly, but the foreman fished the rolled magazine out of his lunch box.

'Hey, there!' Popeye snatched it from him and turned immediately to the coloured foldout.

'Isn't that something!' He whistled. 'This dolly could get a job in a stockyard beating the oxen to death with her boo-boos!'

The foreman joined the discussion of the young lady's anatomy, and so neither of them noticed the change in the sound of the drill until two minutes had passed. Then Popeye heard it through an erotic haze. He flung the magazine from him, and went through the door of the shed white-faced.

It was fifty yards from the shed to the rig, but even at that distance Popeye could see the vibration in the drilling rod. He could hear the labouring note of the diesels as they carried increased load, and he ran like a fox terrier, trying to reach the controls and shut off the engines before it happened.

He knew what it was. His drill had cut into one of the many fissures with which this badly faulted ground was criss-crossed. The puddling water from his borehole had drained away leaving the bit to run dry against dry rock. The friction heat had built up, the dust from the cut was not being washed away – and in consequence the rod had jammed. It was being held tightly at one end while at the other the two big diesels were straining to turn it. The whole rig was seconds away from a twist-off.

There should have been an operator at the controls to meet just such an emergency, but he was a hundred yards away, just emerging from the wood and iron latrine beyond the puddling dam. He was desperately trying to hoist his pants, clinch the buckle of his belt and run all at the same time.

'You whore's chamberpot!' roared Popeye, as he ran. 'What the hell you goofing off —'

The words choked off in his throat, for as he reached the door of the engine room there was a report like a cannon shot as the rod snapped, and immediately the diesels screamed into over-rev as they were relieved of the load. Just too late, Popeye punched the earth buttons on the magnetos, and the engines spluttered into silence.

In that silence Popeye was sobbing with exertion and frustration and anger.

'A twist-off,' he sobbed. 'A deep one. Oh no! God, no!' It might take two weeks to fish out the broken rod, pump cement into the fissure to seal it, and then start again.

He removed the cap from his head, and with all his strength hurled it on the engine room floor. He then proceeded to jump on it with both feet. This was standard procedure. Popeye jumped on his cap at least once a week, and the foreman knew that when he had finished doing that he would then assault anybody within range.

Quietly the foreman slipped behind the wheel of the Ford truck, and the rest of the gang scrambled aboard. They all bumped away down the rutted track. There was a roadhouse on the main road where they went for coffee at times like this. When the mists of rage had dispersed sufficiently from his mind for Popeye to start seeking a human sacrifice, he looked about to find the drilling area strangely still and deserted.

'Stupid bunch of yellow-bellied baboons!' he bellowed in

there each day, each to his own section and directed the actual assault on the rock.

While they chatted idly, waiting for the meeting to begin, Rod looked them over surreptitiously and was reminded of a remark that Hermann Koch of Anglo American had made to him once.

'Mining is a hard game, and it attracts a hard breed of men.'

These were men of the hard breed, physically and mentally tough, and Rod realized with a start that he was one of them. No, more than one of them. He was their leader, and with a fierce affection and pride he opened the meeting.

'Right, let's hear your gripes. Who is going to be first to break my heart?'

There are some men with a talent for controlling, and getting the very best results out of other men. Rod was one of them. It was more than his physical size, his compelling voice and hearty chuckle. It was a special magnetism, a personal charm and unerring sense of timing. Under his Chairmanship the meeting would erupt, voices crackle and snap, then subside into chuckles and nods as Rod spoke.

They knew he was as tough as they were, and they respected that. They knew that when he spoke it made sense, so they listened. They knew that when he promised, he delivered, so they were placated. And they knew that when he made a decision or judgement, he acted upon it, so every man knew exactly where he stood.

If asked, any one of these mine captains would have admitted grudgingly that 'there was no bulldust in Ironsides'. This was the equivalent of a presidential citation.

'Very well then.' Rod terminated the meeting. 'You have spent a good two hours of the company's time beating your gums. Now, will you kindly haul arse, go down there and start sending the stuff out.'

15

As these men planned the week's operation, so their men were at work in the earth below them.

On 87 level, Kowalski moved like a great bear down the dimly-lit drive. He had switched off the lamp on his helmet, and he moved without sound, lightly for a man of such bulk. He heard their voices ahead of him in the dimly-lit tunnel, and he paused, listening intently. There was no sound of shovel crunching into loose rock, and Kowalski's Neanderthal features convulsed into a fearsome scowl.

'Bastards!' he muttered softly. 'They think I am in stopes, hey? They think it all right if they sit on fat black bum, no move da bloody rock, hey?'

He started forward again, a bear on cat's feet.

'They find plenty different from what they bloody think, soon!' he threatened.

He stepped round the angle of the drive and flashed his lamp. There were three men Kowalski had put on lashing, shovelling the loose stuff from the footwall into waiting cocopans. Two of them sat against the cocopan, smoking contentedly while the third regaled them with an account of a beer drink he had attended the previous Christmas. Their shovels and sledge hammers leaned unemployed against the side wall of the drive.

All three of them froze into rigidity as the beam of Kowalski's lamp played over them.

'So!' The word burst explosively from Kowalski, and he snatched up a fourteen-pound hammer in one massive fist, reversed it and struck the butt of the handle against the foot wall. The steel head of the hammer fell off and Kowalski was left with a four foot length of selected hickory in his hand.

'You, boss boy!' he bellowed, and his free hand shot out and fastened on the throat of the nearest Bantu. With one heave he jerked him off his feet onto his knees and began dragging him away up the drive. Even in his rage, Kowalski was making sure there were no witnesses. The other two men sat where they were,

42

too horrified to move, while their companion's wails and cries receded into the darkness.

Then the first blow reverberated in the confined space of the drive, followed immediately by a shriek of pain.

The next blow, and another shriek.

The crack, thud, crack, thud, went on repeatedly, but the accompanying shrieks dwindled into moans and soft whimperings, then into complete silence.

Kowalski came back down the drive alone, he was sweating heavily in the lamp light, and the handle of the hammer in his hand was black and glistening with wet blood.

He threw it at their feet.

'Work!' he growled, and was gone, big and bearlike, into the shadows.

16

On 100 level, Joseph M'Kati was hosing down and sweeping the spillings from under the giant conveyor belt. Joseph had been on this job for five years, and he was a contented and happy man.

Joseph was a Shangaan approaching sixty years of age, the first frost was touching his hair. There were laughter lines around his eyes and at the corner of his mouth. He wore his helmet pushed to the back of his head, his overalls were hand-embroidered and ornamentally patched in blue and red, and he moved with a jaunty bounce and strut.

The conveyor was many hundreds of yards long. From all the levels above the shattered gold reef was scraped from the stopes and trammed back down the haulages in the cocopans. Then from the cocopans it was tipped into the mouths of the ore-passes. These were vertical shafts that dropped down to 100 level, hundreds of feet through the living rock to spew the reef out onto the conveyor belt. A system of steel doors regulated the flow of rock onto the conveyor, and the moving belt carried it down to the shaft and dumped it into enormous storage bins. From there it was fed automatically into the ore cage in fifteen-ton loads and carried at four-minute intervals to the surface.

Joseph worked on happily beneath the whining conveyor. The spillings were small, but important. Gold is strange in its behaviour, it moves downwards. Carried by its own high specific gravity it works its way down through almost any other material. It would find any crack or regularity in the floor and work its way into it. It would disappear into the solid earth itself if left long enough.

It was this behaviour of gold that accounted in some measure for Joseph M'Kati's contentment. He had worked his way to the end of the conveyor, washing and sweeping, and now he straightened, laid his bast broom aside and rubbed his kidneys with both hands, looking quickly around to make certain that there was no one else in the conveyor tunnel. Beside him was the ore storage bin into which the conveyor was emptying its load. The bin could hold many thousands of tons.

Satisfied that he was alone, Joseph dropped onto his hands and knees and crawled under the storage bin, ignoring the continuous roar of rock into the bin above him, working his way in until he reached the holes.

It had taken Joseph many months to chisel the heads off four of the rivets that held the seam in the bottom of the bin, but once he had done it, he had succeeded in constructing a simple but highly effective heavy media separator.

Free gold in the ore that was dumped into the storage bin immediately and rapidly worked its way down through the underlying rock, its journey accelerated by the vibration of the conveyor and bin as more reef was dropped. When the gold reached the floor of the bin, it sought an avenue through which to continue its downward journey, and it found Joseph's four rivet holes, beneath which he had spread a square of Polythene sheet.

The gold-rich fines made four conical piles on the sheet of polythene, looking exactly like powdered black soot.

Crouched beneath the bin, Joseph carefully transferred the black powder to his tobacco pouch, replaced the Polythene to catch the next filtering, stuffed the pouch into his hip pocket, and scrambled out from under the bin. Whistling a tribal planting tune Joseph picked up his broom and returned to the endless job of sweeping and hosing.

17

Johnny Delange was marking his shot holes. Lying on his side in the low stope of 27 section he was calculating by eye the angle and depth of a side cutter blast to straighten a slight bulge in his longwall.

In the Sonder Ditch they were on single blast. One daily, centrally fired, blast. Johnny was paid on *fathomage*, the cubic measure of rock broken and taken out of his stope. He must, therefore, position his shot holes to achieve the maximum disruption and blow-out from the face.

'So,' he grunted, and marked the position of the hole in red paint. 'And so.' With one bold stroke of the paint brush he set the angle on which his machine boy was to drill.

'Shaya, madoda!' Johnny clapped the shoulder of the black man beside him. 'Hit it, man.'

Machine boys were selected for stamina and physique, this one was a Greek sculpture in glistening ebony.

'Nkosi!' The machine boy grinned an acknowledgement, and with his assistant lugged his rock drill into position. The drill looked like a gargantuan version of a heavy calibre machine gun.

The noise as the big Bantu opened the drill was shattering in the low-roofed, constricted space of the stope. The compressed air roared and fluttered into the drill, buffeting the eardrums. Johnny made the clenched-fist gesture of approval, and for a second they smiled at each other in the companionship of shared labour. Then Johnny crawled on up the stope to mark the next shot hole.

Johnny Delange was twenty-seven years old, and he was top rock breaker on the Sonder Ditch. His gang of forty-eight men were a tightly-knit team of specialists. Men fought each other for a place on 27 section, for that's where the money was. Johnny could pick and choose, so each month when the surveyors came in and measured up, Johnny Delange was way out ahead in fathomage.

Here was the remarkable position where the man at the lowest

point of authority earned more than the man at the top. Johnny
Delange earned more than the General Manager of the Sonder
Ditch. Last year he had paid super-tax on an income of twenty-
two thousand Rand. Even a miner like Kowalski, who brutalized
and bullied his gang until he was left with the dregs of the mine,
would earn eight or nine thousand Rand a year, about the same
salary as an official of Rod Ironsides' rank.

Johnny reached the top of his longwall and painted in the last
shot holes. Down the inclined floor of the stope below him all
his drills were roaring, his machine boys lying or crouching
behind them. He lay there on one elbow, removed his helmet
and wiped his face, resting a moment.

Johnny was an extraordinary-looking young man. His long
jet black hair was swept back and tied with a leather thong
at the back of his head in a curlicue. His features were those of an
American Indian, gaunt and bony. He had cut the sleeves out of
his overalls to expose his arms – arms as muscular and sinuous as
pythons, tattooed below the elbows, immensely powerful but
supple. His body was the same, long and sinewy and powerful.

On his right hand he wore eight rings, two on each finger, and
it was clear from the design of the rings that they were not
merely ornamental. They were heavy gold rings with skull and
cross-bones, wolves' heads and other irregularities worked into
them, a mass of metal that formed a permanent knuckle-duster.
Of the big eyes in the one skull's head Rod Ironsides had once
asked: 'Are those real rubies, Johnny?' And Johnny had
replied seriously:

'If they aren't, then I've sure as hell been gypped out of three
Rand fifty, Mr Ironsides.'

Johnny Delange had been a really wild youngster, until eight
months ago. It was then he had met and married Hettie. Court-
ship and marriage occupying the space of one week. Now he was
settling down very well. It was all of ten days since he had last
fought anybody.

Lying in the stope he allowed himself five minutes to think
about Hettie. She was almost as tall as he was, with a wondrously
buxom body and chestnut red hair. Johnny adored her. He was
not the best speechmaker in Kitchenerville when it came to
expressing his affection, so he bought her things.

He bought her dresses and jewellery, he bought her a deep-
freezer *and* a fifteen cubic foot Frigidaire, he bought her a

Chrysler Monaco with leopard-skin upholstery and a Kenwood Chef. In fact, it was becoming difficult to enter the Delange household without tripping over at least one of Johnny's gifts to Hettie. The congestion was made more acute by the fact that living with them was Johnny's brother, Davy.

'Hell, man!' Happily Johnny shook his head. 'She's a bit of all-right, hey!'

There was an eye-level oven he had spotted in a furniture store in Kitchenerville the previous Saturday.

'She'll love that, man,' he muttered, 'and it's only four hundred Rand. I'll get it for her on pay day.'

The decision made, he clapped his helmet onto his head and began crawling out of the stope. It was time now to go up to the station and collect the explosives for the day's blast.

His boss boy should have been waiting for him in the drive, and Johnny was furious to find no sign of him nor the piccanin who was his assistant.

'Bastard!' he grunted, playing the beam of his lamp up and down the drive. 'He's been acting up like hell.'

The boss boy was a pock-marked Swazi, not a big man, but powerful for his size and highly intelligent. He was also a man of mean disposition, Johnny had never seen him smile, and for an extrovert like Johnny it was galling to work with someone so sullen and taciturn. He tolerated the Swazi because of his drive and reliability, but he was the only man in the gang that Johnny disliked.

'Bastard!' The drive was deserted, the roar of the rock drills was muted.

'Where the hell is he?' Johnny scowled impatiently. 'I'll skin him when I find him.'

Then he remembered the latrine.

'That's where he is!' Johnny set off down the drive. The latrine was a rock chamber cut into the side of the drive, a flap of canvas served as a door; beyond was a regular four-holer over sanitary buckets.

Johnny pulled the canvas aside and stepped into the cubicle. The boss boy and his assistant were there. Johnny stared in surprise, for a moment not understanding what they were doing. They were so absorbed they were unaware of Johnny's presence.

Suddenly realization dawned, and Johnny's face tightened with revulsion and disgust.

47

'You filthy —' Johnny snarled, and catching the boss boy by the shoulders pulled him backwards and pinned him against the wall. He lifted his heavily metalled fist and drew it back ready to hurl it into the boss boy's face.

'Strike me and you know what happens,' said the boss boy softly, his expression flat and neutral, looking steadily into Johnny's eyes. Johnny hesitated. He knew the Company rules, he knew the Government labour officers' attitude, he knew what the police would do. If he hit him, they would crucify him.

'You are a pig!' Johnny hissed at him.

'You have a wife,' said the boss boy. 'My wife is in Swaziland. Two years I have not seen her.'

Johnny lowered his fist. Twelve thousand men, and no women. It was a fact. The actuality sickened him, but he understood why it happened.

'Get dressed.' He stepped back, releasing the boss boy. 'Get dressed both of you. Come to the station. I will meet you there.'

18

For a week now, since the fall of hanging in 43 section, Big King had been out of the stopes.

Rod had ordered it that way. The excuse was that Big King's white miner had been killed in the fall and now he must await an allocation to another section. In reality Rod wanted to rest him. He had seen the strain both physical and emotional that Big King had undergone during the rescue. When together they had unearthed the miner's corpse, the man with whom Big King had worked and laughed, Rod had seen the tears roll unashamedly down Big King's cheeks as he picked up the body and held it easily against his chest.

'Hamba gahle, madoda,' Big King had muttered. 'Go in peace, man.'

Big King was a legend on the Sonder Ditch. They boasted about him; how much Bantu beer he could drink in a sitting, how much rock he could lash single-handed in a shift, how he could dance any other man off his feet. He had been awarded a total of over a thousand Rand in bravery awards. Big King set the pace, others tried to equal him.

Rod had put him in charge of a transport team. For the first few days Big King had enjoyed the opportunity of showing off his strength and socializing, for the transport team moved about the workings allowing Big King to visit most of his numerous friends during a shift. But now Big King was becoming bored. He wanted to get back into the stopes.

'This,' he told his transport team contemptuously, 'is work for old men and young women.' And with one snatch and lift he picked up a forty-four gallon drum of dieseline and unaided placed it on the platform of the loco.

A forty-four gallon drum of dieseline weighs a little over eight hundred pounds avoirdupois.

19

All this fuss for that, Davy Delange paused in his labour of tamping the Dynagel into the shot holes. He leaned forward to inspect the reef. In the face of the stope it was a black line, drawn against the blue quartz rock.

The Carbon Leader Reef, it was called. A thin layer of carbon never more than a few inches thick, more often half an inch. Black soot, that's what it was. Davy shook his head thoughtfully. You could not even see the gold in it.

Davy was two years older than his brother Johnny, and there was no physical or mental resemblance between the two of them. Davy's sandy hair was cropped into a conventional 'short back and sides'. He wore no personal jewellery, and his manner was quiet and reserved.

Johnny was tall and lean, Davy squat and muscular. Johnny was extravagant, Davy careful beyond the point of meanness. Their only common trait was that they were both first-class miners. If Johnny broke more rock than Davy, it was only because Davy was more careful than Johnny; he did not take the same chances, he observed all the safety procedures which Johnny frequently flouted.

Davy earned less money than Johnny, but saved every penny he could. It was for his farm. Davy was going to buy a farm one day. Already he had saved a little over R49,000 towards it. In five more years he would have enough. Then he could get himself a farm and a wife to help run it. Johnny, on the other hand, spent every penny he earned. He was usually in debt to Davy by the end of each month.

'Lend us a hundred 'till pay day, Davy.' Disapprovingly, Davy lent him the money. Davy disapproved of Johnny, his appearance, attire and habits.

Abandoning his microscopic inspection of the Carbon Leader Reef, Davy resumed tamping in the explosive, working carefully and precisely on this highly dangerous procedure. The sticks of explosive were charged with detonators and ready to burn. By law, nobody but the miner-in-charge could perform this operation, but Davy did it automatically while he thought about Johnny's latest trespass. He had raised Davy's rent.

'A hundred Rand a month!' Davy protested aloud. 'I've got a good mind to move out and find my own digs.'

But he knew he would do no such thing. Hettie's cooking was too good, and her presence too feminine and alluring. Davy would stay on with them.

20

'Rod.' Dan Stander's voice was serious and low. 'I've got a nasty one for you.'

'Thanks for nothing.' Rod made his own voice weary and resigned as he spoke into the telephone. 'I'm just going on my underground tour. Can't it wait?'

'No,' Dan assured him. 'Anyway, it's on your way. I'm speaking from the first-aid station at the shaft head. Come across.'

'What is it?'

'Assault. White on Bantu.'

'Christ.' Rod jerked upright in his chair. 'Bad?'

'Ugly. Worked him over with the handle of a fourteen-pound hammer. I've put in forty-seven stitches, but I am worried about a fracture of the skull.'

'Who did it?'

'Miner by the name of Kowalski.'

'Him!' Rod was breathing heavily. 'All right, Dan. Can he make a statement?'

'No. Not for a day or two.'

'I'll be there in a few minutes.'

Rod hung up the phone and crossed the office.

'Dimitri.'

'Boss?'

'Pull Kowalski out of the stopes. I want him in my office soonest. Put someone in to finish his shift.'

'Okay, Rod, what's the trouble?'

'He beat up one of his boys.'

Dimitri whistled softly, and Rod went on.

'Call personnel, get them onto the police.'

'Okay, Rod.'

'Have Kowalski here when I get back from my tour.'

Dan was waiting for him in the first-aid room.

'Take a look.' He indicated the figure on the stretcher. Rod knelt beside him, his mouth tightening into a thin pale line.

The catgut stitches lay neatly across the dark swollen gashes in the man's flesh. His one ear had been torn off, and Dan had sewn it back on. There was a black gap where teeth had been behind the swollen purple lips.

'You will be all right now.' Rod spoke gently, and the Bantu's eyes swivelled towards him. 'The man who did this will be punished.'

Rod stood up. 'Let me have a written report on his injuries, Dan.'

'I'll fix it. See you for a drink at the Club after work?'

'Sure,' said Rod, but underneath he was seething with anger, and it stayed with him during the whole of his underground tour.

21

Rod dropped straight down to 100 level. His first duty was to get the stuff out, and he wanted to check the reserve in the ore storage bins. He came into the long brightly-lit tunnel beneath the ore passes, and paused. The loaded conveyor belt whined monotonously, speeding the broken reef towards the bins.

The tunnel was deserted, except for the lonely figure of the sweeper at the far end. It was one of the phenomena of a well-run gold mine that in a tour through the workings you encountered so few human beings. Mile after mile of haulage and drive were silent and devoid of life, and yet there were twelve thousand men down here.

Rod set off towards the bins at the shaft end of the tunnel.

'Joseph,' he greeted the old sweeper with a smile.

'Nkosi.' Joseph ducked and bobbed with shy pleasure.

'All is well?' Rod asked. Joseph was one of Rod's favourites, he was always so cheerful, so uncomplaining, so patently honest and without guile. Rod always made a point of stopping to chat to him.

'It is well with me, Nkosi. Is it well with you?'

Rod's smile died suddenly, he had noticed the fine white powdering of dust on Joseph's upper lip.

'You old rogue!' he scolded him. 'How often must I tell you to hose down before you sweep? Water! You must use water!'

This was part of the ceaseless battle of the miner to keep down the dust.

'The dust will eat your lungs!'

Phthisis, the dread incurable occupational disease of the miner, caused by silica particles being drawn into the lungs and there solidifying.

Joseph grinned shamefaced, shifting from one foot to the other. He was always embarrassed by Rod's childish obsession with dust. In Joseph's opinion this was one of the few flaws in Rod Ironsides' character. Apart from this weird delusion that dust could hurt a man, he was a good boss.

'It is much harder to sweep wet dirt than dry dirt,' Joseph explained patiently. Rod never seemed to understand this self-evident fact, Joseph had to point it out to him every time they had this particular discussion.

'Listen to me, old man, without water the dust will enter your body.' Rod was exasperated. 'The dust will kill you!'

Joseph bobbed again, grinning at Rod to placate him.

'Very well, I will use plenty water.'

To prove it he picked up the hose and began spraying the floor with enthusiasm.

'That is good!' Rod encouraged him. 'Use plenty of water.' And Rod went on down to the storage bins.

When Rod was out of sight, Joseph turned off the hose and leaned on his broom.

'The dust will kill you!' he mimicked Rod, and chuckled merrily, shaking his head in wonder at the childishness of it.

'The dust will kill you!' he repeated, and burst into delighted laughter, slapping his thigh.

He did a few shuffling dance steps, it was so funny.

The dance steps were awkward, for under his trousers, strapped to the calves of both legs, were heavy polythene bags filled with gold fines from under the bins.

22

Rod stepped out of the Mary Anne at 85 level, and paused to watch Big King loading a baulk of timber onto the loco while his transport team stood back respectfully and watched him. Turning from his task Big King saw Rod standing on the station landing and marched up to him.

'I see you,' he greeted Rod. Big King was not one to make hasty judgements, it was only after the rescue operations in 43 section that he had decided Rod was a man. He was now ready to accept him as an equal.

'I see you also, King Nkulu.' Rod returned the greeting.

'Find me work with men. I sicken of this.'

'You will be back in the stopes before the week is ended,' Rod promised.

'You are my father,' Big King thanked him and went back to the transport team.

23

Johnny Delange saw the Underground Manager coming up the haulage towards him. There was no mistaking that tall wide-shouldered silhouette, nor the man's free swinging stride.

'Whee!' Johnny whistled with relief, grateful for the premonition that had warned him to pack the fifty-pound cardboard cartons of Dynagel into the explosives locker of the railway truck, rather than, as he usually did, pile them haphazard onto the platform in defiance of safety standards.

'Stop!' Johnny commanded the boss boy and his assistant who were pushing the truck, and it trundled to a halt beside Rod.

'Morning, Johnny.'

'Hello, Mr Ironsides.'

'How's it going?'

Johnny hesitated before replying, and immediately Rod was aware of the tension between the three men. He glanced at the two Swazis, they were sullen and apprehensive.

'There's been trouble,' he thought. 'Not like Johnny, he's too clever to let tension cut down his fathomage.'

'Well —' Johnny paused again. 'Look, Mr Ironsides, get rid of this bastard for me.' He jerked his thumb at the boss boy. 'Give me someone else.'

'What's the trouble?'

'No trouble, I just can't work with him.'

Rod raised an eyebrow in disbelief, but turned to the boss boy.

'Are you happy in this section, or do you want transfer?'

'I want transfer!' growled the boss boy.

'Right.' Rod was relieved, sometimes in a case like this the Swazi would refuse transfer. 'Tomorrow you will be told your new section.'

'Nkosi!' The boss boy glanced sideways at his assistant. 'It is the wish of my friend that he transfers with me.'

So that's it, Rod thought, the ever-present spectre which we must ignore because we can find no way to lay it. Johnny had probably caught them at it.

'Your friend shall go with you,' Rod nodded, telling himself that this was not condonation, but merely practical politics. If he separated them, the boss boy would pick on someone else who might not be receptive. Then there would be more trouble, stabbings, faction fighting.

'I'll get you a replacement,' he told Johnny, and then suddenly a thought occurred to him. My God, yes! What a team they would make!

'Johnny, how would you like Big King?'

'Big King!' Johnny's gaunt bony features split into a wide smile. 'Now you're talking, boss!'

24

At three o'clock Rod had finished his tour and was in the cage on the way to the surface. The cage was crowded, men pressed shoulder to shoulder, the stench of sweat almost overpowering. They were hauling shift now, the day's work was over, the stopes were scraped and washed down, the shot holes drilled and charged, the fuses connected into the electrical circuit.

The men were out of the stopes now, falling back in orderly companies and battalions along the haulages to the stations. There to wait patiently for their turn to enter the cages and be whisked to the surface.

Rod was mulling over the myriad problems he had encountered during the day, and the solutions he had dreamed up. He had opened a new section in the back pages of his notebook and headed it simply 'COSTS'.

Already there were two entries there. Let them give me the job, he thought fervently, just let me have it one month and I'll move the world.

'Mr Ironsides.' The man beside him spoke. Rod glanced down at him recognizing him.

'Hello, Davy.' It was remarkable how dissimilar the two brothers were.

'Mr Ironsides, my boss boy has worked his ticket. He's going home at the end of the month. Can you see that I get a good man to replace him?'

'Your brother's boss boy has asked for transfer. Will you take him?'

'Ja!' Davy Delange nodded. 'I know him, he's a good boy.'

And that takes care of one more detail, thought Rod, as he stepped out of the cage into a bright summer's afternoon and tasted the fresh sweet air with pleasure. Now there are only the butt ends of the day's work to tidy up. Then I can go and fetch the drink that Dan promised me.

Dimitri met him in the passage outside the office.

'I've got Kowalski in my office.'

'Good,' said Rod grimly. He went into his own office and sat on the edge of his desk.

'Send him in,' he called through to Dimitri.

Kowalski came through the door and stopped. He stood very still, his long arms hanging slackly at his side, his belly bulging out over his belt.

'You call me,' he muttered thickly, his English hardly intelligible. It was a peasant's face, coarse-featured, dull-eyed. He had not shaved, dirt from the stopes clung in the thick black stubble of beard.

'You beat a man today?' Rod asked softly.

'He no work,' Kowalski nodded. 'I beat him. Maybe next time his brothers they work. No bloody nonsense!'

'You're fired,' said Rod. 'Pull your time and get the hell off this property.'

'You fire?' Kowalski blinked in surprise.

'There will be criminal charges pressed against you by the company.' Rod went on. 'But in the meantime I want you off the property.'

'Police?' Kowalski growled. There was expression on his face now.

'Yes,' said Rod, 'police.'

The spade-sized hands at the end of Kowalski's arms balled slowly into massive fists.

'You call da bloody police!' He took a step towards the desk, big, menacing.

'Dimitri,' Rod called sharply, 'close the door.'

Dimitri had been listening intently, now he jumped up from his desk and closed the interleading door. He stood with his ear pressed to the panelling. For thirty seconds more there was the growl and mutter of voices, then suddenly a thud, a bellow, another thud and a shattering crash.

Dimitri winced theatrically.

'Dimitri!' Rod's voice, and he pushed the door open.

Rod sat on the edge of his desk, swinging one leg casually, he was sucking the knuckle of his right hand.

'Dimitri, tell them not to put so much polish on the floor. Our friend slipped and hit his jaw on the desk.'

Dimitri clucked sympathetically as he stood over the reclining hulk of the big Pole. Kowalski was snoring loudly through his mouth.

'Gave himself a nasty bump,' said Dimitri. 'Shame!'

25

Dr Steyner worked on quietly for the remainder of Monday morning. He favoured the use of a tape recorder, for this cut out human contact which Manfred found vaguely repellent. He disliked having to speak his thoughts to a female who sat opposite him with skirts up around her thighs, squirming her bottom and touching her hair. However, what he really could not abide was the odour. Manfred was very sensitive to smells, even his own body smell of perspiration disgusted him. Women, he found, had a peculiar cloying odour that he could detect beneath their perfume and cosmetics. It nauseated him. This was why he had insisted on separate bedrooms for Theresa and himself. Naturally he had not told her the reason, but had insisted instead that he was such a light sleeper that he could not share a room with another person.

His office was in white and ice-blue, the air clean and cold from the air-conditioning unit, his voice was crisp and impersonal, the whirr of the recorder subdued, and with the conscious portion of his mind Manfred was happily absorbed in his conjuring tricks with figures and money, past performance and future estimates, a three-dimensional structure of variables and contingencies which only a super-normal brain could visualize. But beneath it was a sense of disquiet, he was waiting, hanging in time, and the outward sign of his agitation was the way the fingers of his right hand ran up and down his thigh as he worked, a caressing narcissistic gesture.

A few minutes before noon the unlisted direct telephone on his desk rang, and the movement of his hand stilled. Only one caller could reach him here, only one caller had that number. For a few seconds he sat unmoving, delaying the moment, then deliberately he switched off the recorder and lifted the telephone.

'Dr Manfred Steyner.' He identified himself.

'You have got our man in?' the voice inquired.

'Not yet, Andrew.'

There was silence from the other end, a dangerous crackling silence.

'But there is no cause for alarm. It is nothing. A delay merely, not a setback.'

'How long?'

'Two days – at the latest by the end of the week.'

'You will be in Paris next week?'

'Yes.' Manfred was an adviser to the Government team which was to meet the French for gold price talks.

'He will meet you there. It would be best for you that your side of the bargain were completed by then. You understand?'

'I understand, Andrew.'

The discussion was ended, but Manfred interjected to prevent the caller from hanging up.

'Andrew!'

'Yes.'

'Will you ask him if —' Manfred's tone had changed almost imperceptively, there was an obsequious edge in it. 'Ask him if I may play tonight, please, Andrew.'

'Wait.'

The minutes drifted by, and then the voice came back on the line.

'Yes, you may play. Simon will inform you of your limits.'

'Thank you. Tell him, thank you.'

Manfred made no effort to conceal his relief as he cradled the receiver. He sat beaming at the ice-blue paper on the far wall of his office, even his spectacles seemed to sparkle.

26

There were five men in the opulently furnished room. One of the men was subservient to the others, he was younger than they, attentive to their moods and wishes. Clearly he was a servant. Of the remaining four, one was just as obviously the host. He was seated at the focus of all their attention. He was fat, but not excessively so, the fat of good living not of gluttony. He was speaking, addressing himself to his three guests.

'You have expressed doubts as to reliability of the tool I intend using in the coming venture. I have arranged a demonstration which I hope will convince you that your concern is groundless. That is the reason for the invitation that Andrew here conveyed to you this afternoon.'

The host turned to the younger man. 'Andrew, would you be good enough to go through and wait for Dr Steyner to arrive, as soon as that happens, please let Simon seat him while you come through and inform us.' He gave his orders with dignity and courtesy, a man accustomed to command.

'Now, gentlemen, while we wait may I offer you a drink?'

The conversation that sprang up between the four of them as they sipped their drinks was knowledgeable, and extraordinarily well informed. At its root was one subject: wealth. Mineral wealth, industrial wealth, the harvest of the land and the sea. Oil, steel, coal, fish, wheat and – gold.

There were clues to the stature of these men in the cut and quality of the cloth they wore, the sparkle of a stone on a finger, the tone of authority in a voice, the casual unaffected use of a high name.

'He is here, sir,' Andrew interrupted them from the doorway.

'Oh! Thank you, my boy.' The host stood up. 'Would you mind stepping this way, please, gentlemen.'

He crossed the room and drew aside one of the gold and maroon drapes. Behind it was a window.

The four men clustered about the window and looked through into the room beyond. It was a gaming room of an expensive gambling establishment. There were men and women sitting about a baccarat table, and none of them so much as glanced up at the window overlooking them.

'This is a one-way glass, gentlemen,' the host explained. 'So you need not worry about being seen in such a den of iniquity.'

They chuckled politely.

'What kind of profit does this place show you?' one of them asked.

'My dear Robert!' The host feigned shock. 'You don't for a moment believe that I would be in any way associated with an illegal undertaking?'

This time they chuckled with genuine amusement.

'Ha!' explained the host. 'Here he is.'

Across the gaming room Dr Manfred Steyner was being ushered to a seat at the table by a tall sallow-faced young man, who in his evening dress looked like an undertaker.

'I have asked Simon to place him so that you may watch his face as he plays.'

They were intent now, leaning forward slightly, scrutinizing the man as he arranged the plaques that Simon had stacked at his elbow.

Dr Manfred Steyner began to play. His face was completely devoid of expression, but the pallor was startling. Every few seconds the pink tip of his tongue slipped out between his lips, then disappeared again. In the intervals between each coup, there was a reptilian stillness about him, the stillness of a lizard or an iguana. Only a pulse beat steadily in his throat and his spectacles glittered like a snake's eyes.

'May I direct your attention to his right hand during the play of this coup,' the host murmured, and all their eyes flicked downwards.

Manfred's right hand lay open beside the pile of his chips, but as his card was laid before him so his fingers closed.

'*Carte*.' Soundlessly he mouthed the word, and now his hand was a fist, the knuckles whitened, the tension was so fierce that his fist trembled. Yet, still his face was neutral.

The banker flipped his card.

'*Sept!*' The croupier's mouth formed the number. He faced Manfred's card, then he swept Manfred's stake away. Manfred's hand flopped open and lay soft and hairless as a dead fish on the green baize.

'Let us leave him to his pleasures,' suggested the host and drew the curtains across the window. They returned to their chairs, and they were strangely subdued.

'Jesus,' muttered one of the guests. 'That was ugly. I felt like a peeping tom, like watching someone, you know, pulling his pudding.'

The host glanced at him quickly, surprised at his perception.

'In effect, that is exactly what you were watching,' he told him. 'You will excuse me playing the role of lecturer, but I know a little about this man. It cost me nearly four hundred Rand for an analytical report on him by one of our leading psychiatrists.'

The host paused, assuring himself of their complete attention.

'The reasons are obscure, probably arising from an event or series of events during the period in which Dr Steyner was an orphan wandering through the smoking ruins of war-torn Europe.' The host coughed, deprecating his own flight of oratory. 'Be that as it may. The results are there for all to see. Dr Manfred Kurt Steyner's intelligence quotient is a genius rating of 158. He neither smokes nor drinks. He has no hobbies, plays no sport, has never made so much as an improper remark to any woman other than his wife, and there is some doubt as to just how often or to what extent she is favoured by his attentions.' The host sipped his drink conscious of their intense interest. 'Mechanically, if that is the correct term, Dr Steyner is neither impotent nor deficient in his manhood. However, he finds all bodily contact, and especially the secretions that may arise from such contact, to be utterly loathsome. For arousal he relies on the baccarat cards, for release he might endure a brief contact with a member of the opposite sex, but more likely he would – oh, what was the expression you used, Robert?'

They absorbed this in silence.

'He is, to be precise, a compulsive gambler. He is also a compulsive loser.'

They stirred with disbelief.

'You mean he tries to lose?' demanded Robert incredulously.

'No.' The host shook his head. 'Not on the conscious level.

He believes he is trying to win, but he lays bets against odds that, with his magnificent brain, he must realize are suicidal. It is a deep-seated sub-conscious need to lose, to be humiliated. A form of masochism.'

The host opened a black leather notebook and checked its contents.

'During the period from 1958 to 1963 Dr Steyner lost the total sum of R227,000 at this table. In 1964 he was able to arrive at an arrangement with his sole creditor to discharge the debt plus the accumulated interest.'

You could see the faces change as they rapidly searched their memories for a set of circumstances which would fit the dates and principals. Robert reached the correct deduction first. In 1964 their host had sold his majority holdings in the North Maun Copper Co. to C.R.C. at a price that could only be considered advantageous. Just prior to this Dr Steyner had been made head of finance and planning at C.R.C.

'North Maun Copper,' said Robert with admiration. That is how he had done it, the cunning old fox! He had forced Steyner to buy well above market value.

The host smiled softly, deferentially, neither confirming nor denying.

'Since 1964 to the present Dr Steyner has continued to patronize this establishment. His gambling losses for this further period amount to —' he consulted his notebook again, pretending surprise at the figure, 'to a touch over R300,000.'

They sighed and moved restlessly. Even to these men it was a very large sum of money.

'I think we can rely on him.' The host closed his notebook with a snap, and smiled around at them.

27

Theresa lay in the dark. The night was warm, the stillness spoiled only by the klonking of a frog down at the fishpond. The moonlight came in through the window, playing shadow pictures through the branches of the Pride of India tree onto the wall of her bedroom.

She threw back the single sheet, and swung her legs off the bed. She could not sleep, it was too warm, her nightdress kept binding under her armpits. She stood up and on a sudden reckless impulse she drew the nightdress off over her head and tossed it through the open door of her dressing-room, then, naked, she walked out onto the wide veranda. Into the moonlight, with the cool stone flags under her bare feet, and the warm night air moving like the touch of fairy hands on her skin.

She felt suddenly devilish and daring, she wanted to run down across the lawns and to have someone catch her doing it. She giggled, uncertain of this mood. It was so far removed from Manfred's conception of a good German Hausfrau's behaviour.

'He'd be furious,' she whispered with wicked delight, and then she heard the motor of the car.

She froze with horror, the headlights flicked through the trees as the car came up the driveway and she darted back into her room; in panic she dropped to her knees and searched for her nightgown, found it and ran to the bed as she dragged it on over her head.

She lay in the darkness and listened to the car door slam. There was silence until she heard him pass her door. His heels clacked on the yellow wood floor, he was almost running. Theresa knew the symptoms, the late night return, the suppressed urgency, and she lay rigid in her bed, waiting.

The minutes passed slowly, and then the interleading door from Manfred's suite swung open silently.

'Manfred, is that you?' She sat up and reached for the switch of the bedside lamp.

'Don't put the light on.' His voice was breathless, slurred as though he had been drinking but there was no trace of liquor on his breath as he stooped over her and kissed her. His lips were dry and tightly closed, as he slipped off his dressing-gown.

Two and a half minutes later he stood up from the bed, turning his back to Theresa as he quickly shrugged into the silk dressing-gown.

'Excuse me a minute, Theresa.' The breathlessness was gone from his voice. He went through the door of his own suite, and seconds later she heard the hiss of the shower and the tinkling splash of water.

She lay on her back and her fingernails cut into the palms of her hands. Her body was trembling with a mixture of revulsion and desire, it had been so fleeting a contact – enough to stir her, but so swift as to leave her with a feeling of having been used and sullied. She knew that the rest of the night would pass infinitely slowly, with restless burning tension, remorse and self-pity alternating with wild elation and half-crazed erotic fantasy.

'Damn him,' she screamed silently within her skull. 'Damn him! Damn him!'

She heard the shower stop, and then Manfred returned to her room. He smelt of 4711 Eau de Cologne, and he sat down carefully on the end of the bed.

'You may turn on the light, Theresa.'

It required a conscious effort for her to unclench her hand and reach out for the lamp switch. Manfred blinked behind his spectacles at the flood of light. His hair was damp and freshly combed, his cheeks shone like ripe apples.

'I hope you had an enjoyable day?' he asked, and listened seriously to her reply. Despite her tension, Theresa found herself falling under the almost hypnotic influence he wielded over her. His voice precise, almost monotonous. The glitter of his spectacles, the reptilian stillness of his body and features.

As she had so many times before, she thought of herself as a warm fluffy rabbit sitting tense and fascinated before the cobra.

'It is late,' he said at last and he stood up.

Looking down at her as she lay cuddled into the white silk sheets, he asked with as little emphasis as if he were requesting her to pass the sugar: 'Theresa, could you raise three hundred thousand Rand without your grandfather knowing?'

'Three hundred thousand!' She sat up startled.

'Yes. Could you?'

'Good Lord, Manfred, that's a small fortune.' She truly saw nothing unusual in her choice of adjective. 'You know it's all in the Trust Fund, well, most of it. There is the farm and the — no, I couldn't find half of that without Pops knowing.'

'Pity,' murmured Manfred.

'Manfred, you aren't in – difficulties?'

'No. Good Lord, no. It was just a thought. Forget that I asked. Good night, Theresa, I hope you sleep well.'

Involuntarily she lifted her hands towards him in invitation.

'Good night, Manfred.'

He turned and left the room, she let her hands fall to her sides. For Theresa Steyner the long night had begun.

28

'Ladies and Gentlemen, it is customary for the General Manager to introduce the distinguished guest who presents our special service awards. Last week, in tragic circumstances our General Manager, Mr Frank Lemmer, was killed in the Company's service, a loss which we all bitterly regret, and I am sure you all join me in sincere condolence to Mrs Eileen Lemmer.' Rod paused for the acknowledging murmur from his audience. There were two hundred of them packed into the mine club hall. 'It falls upon me, therefore, as Acting General Manager, to introduce to you Dr Manfred Steyner who is a senior Director of Central Rand Consolidated, our parent company. He is also head of the Departments of Finance and Planning.'

Sitting beside her husband, Theresa Steyner had noticed Manfred's irritation at Rod's mention of Frank Lemmer. It was company policy not to draw public attention to accidental death or injury inflicted on employees by the Company's operation. She liked Rod the better for his small tribute to Frank Lemmer.

Theresa was wearing sunglasses, for her eyes were swollen and red. In the dawning, after a sleepless night, she had succumbed suddenly to a fit of bitter weeping. The tears were without cause, or reason, and had left her feeling strangely lightheaded and with a brittle sense of well-being. However, her enormous eyes always showed up badly for hours after she had wept.

She sat with her legs demurely crossed, immaculate in a suit of cream shantung, a black silk scarf catching her hair and then letting it fall in a dark glossy brown cascade onto her shoulders. She leaned forward in polite attention to the speaker, one elbow on her knee, her chin cupped in her palm, one long tapered finger lying against her cheek. A lady with diamonds on her fingers and pearls at her throat, smiling an acknowledgement at Rod's reference to 'the lovely granddaughter of our Chairman'.

Except for the slight incongruity of the sunglasses, she was the perfect image of the young matron. Polished, poised, cosseted, secure in her unassailable virtue and duty.

However, the thoughts that were running through Theresa Steyner's head, and the flutterings and sensations that were prickling and tickling her, had they been known, would have broken up the assembly in disorder. All the formless fantasy and emotional disturbance of the previous night were now directed at one target – Rodney Ironsides. Suddenly, with a start of amusement and alarm, she was aware of a phenomenon that she had last experienced many years ago. She moved quickly, shifting her seat for the cream shantung marked so easily with any moisture.

'Terry Steyner!' she thought, deliciously shocked at herself, and found with relief that Rod had finished speaking and Manfred was standing up to reply. She joined in the applause enthusiastically to distract her errant fancy.

Manfred briefly mentioned the six gentlemen sitting in the front row of seats whose courage and devotion to duty they had come to honour, he then went on into an exploration of the prospects of an increase in the price of gold. In measured, carefully considered terms, he set out the advantages and benefits that would accrue to the industry, the nation and the world at large. It was an erudite and convincing dissertation, and there was a large contingent of newspaper men to record it. The press had been alerted by the public relations department of C.R.C. to the text of Dr Steyner's speech and all the leading dailies, weeklies, financial gazettes and journals were represented.

At intervals a photographer would come to crouch below the platform and pop a flash bulb up at Dr Steyner. On the eve of the gold price talks with France this would make good copy, for Steyner was the boy genius in the South African team.

The six heroes sat uncomfortably, forlorn in their best suits, scrubbed like schoolboys at a prize-giving ceremony, staring up at the speaker, not understanding a single word of the foreign language, but maintaining expressions of grave dignity.

Rod caught Big King's eye and winked at him. Solemnly Big King's right eyelid drooped and rose in reply, and quickly Rod averted his gaze to prevent himself laughing out loud.

He looked straight into Theresa Steyner's face, taking her

completely off her guard. Not even the dark glasses could conceal her thoughts, they were as clear as if she had spoken them aloud. Before she could drop her eyes to examine the hem of her skirt, Rod knew with a stomach swoop of excitement how it could be if he chose.

With a new awareness he examined her from the corner of his eye, seeing her for the first time as an accessible woman, a highly desirable woman, but nevertheless still the granddaughter of Hurry Hirschfeld and the wife of Manfred Steyner. This made her as dangerous as a force ten pressure burst, he knew, but the desire and temptation was hard to deny, inflamed perhaps rather than dampened by the danger.

He saw that she was blushing now, her fingers picking nervously at the hem of her skirt. She was as agitated as a school-girl, she knew he was watching her. Rod Ironsides, who until five minutes before had been thinking of nothing but his speech, now found himself impelled into a completely new and exciting dimension.

After the awards had been made, tea had been drunk, biscuits consumed and the crowd had dispersed, Rod escorted the Steyners down across the vivid green lawns of Kikuyu grass to where the chauffeur was holding the Daimler.

'What a magnificent physique that Shangaan has, what was his name – King?' Terry was walking between the two men.

'King Nkulu. Big King, we call him.'

Rod found his speech unsteady, he had stuttered slightly. This thing between the two of them was suddenly overpowering, it hummed like a turbine, making the space between them crackle with tension. Unless he were deaf, Manfred Steyner must be aware of it.

'He is pretty special. There is nothing he can't do, and do it far and away better than his nearest rival. My God, you should see him dance.'

'Dance?' inquired Terry with interest.

'Tribal dancing, you know.'

'Of course.' Terry hoped the relief in her voice was not obvious, she had been racking her badly flustered brains for an excuse to visit the Sonder Ditch again or have Rod Ironsides come to Johannesburg. 'I have a friend who is absolutely mad keen on seeing the dances. She pesters me every time I see her.'

Quickly she selected a name from her list of friends, she must have one ready should Manfred ask.

'They dance every Saturday afternoon, bring her out any time.' Rod fielded the ball neatly.

'What about this Saturday?' Terry turned to her husband, 'Would that be all right, Manfred?'

'What's that?' Manfred looked at her vaguely, he had not been following the conversation. Manfred Steyner was a worried man, he was pondering his obligation to gain control of the management of the Sonder Ditch within two days.

'May we come out here on Saturday afternoon to watch the tribal dancing?' Terry repeated her request.

'Have you forgotten that I fly to Paris on Saturday morning, Theresa?'

'Oh, dear.' Terry bit her lip thoughtfully. 'It *had* slipped my mind. What a pity, I would have enjoyed it.'

Manfred frowned slightly, irritated.

'My dear Theresa, there is no reason why you shouldn't come out to the Sonder Ditch without me. I am sure you will be safe enough in Mr Ironsides' hands.'

His choice of words brought the colour to Terry's cheeks again.

29

After the award ceremony, Big King's first stop was the Recruiting Agency Office at the entrance to the No. 1 shaft hostel. There were men clustered about the counter, but they stood aside for Big King and he acknowledged the courtesy by slapping their backs indiscriminately and greeting them with:

'Kunjane, madoda. How is it, men?'

The clerk behind the counter hurried to serve him. Up at the Mine Club Big King might be a little out of his depth, but here he was treated like a reigning monarch.

In two neat bundles Big King placed the award money on the counter.

'Twenty-five Rand you will send to my senior wife.' He instructed the clerk. 'And twenty-five Rand you will put to my book.'

Big King was scrupulously fair. Half of all his earnings was remitted to the senior of his four wives, and half was added to the substantial sum already credited in his savings bank passbook.

The agency was the procurer of labour for the insatiably man-hungry gold mines of the Witwatersrand and Orange Free State. Its representatives operated across the southern half of the continent. From the swamps and fever lagoons along the great Zambesi, from among the palm groves fringing the Indian Ocean, out of those simmering plains that the bushmen called 'the big dry', down from the mountains of Basutoland and the grasslands of Swaziland and Zululand they gathered the Bantu, the men themselves completing the first fifty or sixty miles of the journey on foot. Individuals meeting on a footpath to become pairs, arriving at a little general dealer's store in the bleak scrub desert to find three or four others already waiting, the arrival of the recruiting truck with a dozen men and their luggage aboard, the long bumping grinding progress through the bush. The stops at which more men scrambled aboard, until a full truck load of fifty or sixty disembarked at a railway siding in the wilderness.

Here the tiny trickle of humanity joined a stream, and at the first major centre they trans-shipped and became part of the great flood that washed towards 'Goldi'.

However, once they had reached Johannesburg and been allocated to one of the sixty major gold mines, the Agency's obligations towards its recruits were not yet discharged. Between them the employing mine and the Agency must provide each man with employment, training, advice and comfort, maintain contact between him and his family, for very few of them could write, reassure him when he worried that his goats were sick or his wife unfaithful. They must provide a banking and savings service with a personal involvement unknown to any commercial banking institute. They had, in short, to make certain that a man taken from an environment that had not changed in a thousand years and deposited into the midst of a sophisticated and technological society would retain his health, happiness and sanity, so that at the end of his contract he would return to the place from which he had come and tell them all how wonderful it was at 'Goldi'. He would show them his hard helmet, and his new suitcase crammed with clothes, his transistor radio and the little blue book with its printed figures, inflaming them also with the desire to make the pilgrimage, and keep the flood washing towards 'Goldi'.

Big King completed his business transactions and went in through the gates of the hostel, he was going to take advantage of the fact that he had missed the shift and would be among the first at the ablutions and dining-hall.

He went down across the lawns to his block. Despite the size of an establishment that housed six thousand men, the Company had tried to make it as attractive as possible. The result was an unusual design, half-way between a motel and an advanced penitentiary.

As a senior boss boy, Big King rated a room of his own. An ordinary labourer would share with five others.

Carefully Big King brushed down his suit and hung it in the built-in cupboard, wiped down his glossy shoes and racked them, then with a towel around his waist he set off for the ablution block and was irritated to find it already filled with new recruits up from the acclimatization centre.

Big King ran an appraising eye over their naked bodies and judged that this batch must be nearing the completion of their eight-day acclimatization. They were sleek and shiny, the muscle definition showing clearly through the skin.

You could not take a man straight out of his village, probably suffering from malnutrition, and put him down a gold mine to lash and bar and drill in a dry bulb heat of 91° Fahrenheit and 84% relative humidity, without running a serious risk of killing him with heat stroke or exhaustion.

Every recruit judged medically fit to work underground went into acclimatization. For eight days, eight hours a day, he and hundreds of others stood with only a loin cloth about his middle in a vast barn-like hall stepping up onto and down from a platform. The height of the platform was carefully matched to the man's height and body weight, the speed of his movements was regulated by a flashing panel of lights, the temperature and humidity were controlled at 91° and 84%, every ten minutes he was given water and his body temperature was registered by the half dozen trained medical assistants in charge of the room.

At the end of the eighth day he emerged as fit as an olympic athlete, and quite able to perform heavy physical labour in conditions of high temperature and humidity without discomfort or danger.

'Gwedeni!' growled Big King, and the nearest recruit, still white with soap suds, hurriedly vacated his shower with a respectful 'Keshle!' in deference to Big King's rank and standing. Big King removed his towel and stepped under the shower, revelling as always in the rush of hot water over his skin, flexing the great muscles of his arms and chest.

The messenger found him there.

'King Nkulu, I have word for thee.' The man used Shangaan, not the bastard Fanikalo.

'Speak,' Big King invited, soaping his belly and buttocks.

'The Induna bids you call at his house after you have eaten the evening meal.'

'Tell him I will attend his wishes,' said Big King and held his face up into the rush of steaming water.

Dressed in a white open-neck shirt and blue slacks, Big King sauntered down to the kitchens. Again the recruits were ahead of him, queueing with bowls in hand outside the serving hatches. Big King walked past them through the door marked 'No Admittance – Staff only'.

The kitchens were cavernous, glistening with white porcelain tile and stainless steel cookers and bins that could serve eighteen thousand hot meals a day.

When Big King entered a room, even one as large as this, no one was unaware of his presence. One of the assistant cooks snatched up a bowl not much smaller than a baby's bath, and hurried across to the nearest stainless steel bin. He opened the lid and looked expectantly at Big King. Big King nodded and the cook ladled about two litres of steaming sugar beans into the bowl, before passing on to the next bin where he again looked for and obtained Big King's approval. He added an equal quantity of mixed vegetables to the bowl, slammed down the lid and scampered across to where a second assistant waited with a spade beside yet another bin.

The spade was the same as those used for lashing gold reef underground, but the blade of this one had been polished to gleaming cleanliness. The second cook dug into the bin and came up with a spadeful of white maize porridge, cooked stiff as cake, the smell of it as saliva-making as the smell of new bread. This was the staple of Bantu diet. He deposited the spadeful in the bowl.

'I am hungry.' Big King spoke for the first time, and the second cook dug out another spadeful and added it to the bowl. They passed on to the end of the kitchens, and at their approach another cook lifted the lid on a pressure cooker the size of a washing machine. From it rose a cloud of fragrant steam.

Apologetically the cook held out his hand and Big King produced his meat ticket. Meat was the only food that was rationed. Each man was limited to one pound of meat a day; the Company had long ago discovered to its astonishment and cost that a Bantu, offered unlimited supplies of fresh meat, was quite capable of eating his own weight of it monthly.

Having ascertained that Big King was entitled to his daily pound, the cook proceeded to ladle at least five pounds of it into the bowl.

'You are my brother,' Big King thanked him, and the little procession moved on to where yet another cook was filling a half-gallon jug of thick, gruel-like, mildly alcoholic Bantu beer from one of the multiple spiggots beneath the thousand-gallon tank.

The bowl and jug were ceremonially handed to Big King and he went out onto the covered terraces where benches and tables were set out for alfresco dining in mild weather.

While he ate, the terrace began to fill, for the shift was out of the mine now. Every man who passed his table greeted Big King, but only a few privileged persons took the liberty of seating themselves at the same table. One of them was Joseph M'Kati, the little old sweeper from 100 level.

'It has been a good week, King Nkulu.'

'You say so.' Big King was non-committal. 'I go now to a meeting with the Old One. Then we shall see.'

The Old One, the Shangaan Induna, lived in a Company house. A self-contained residence with lounge and dining-room, kitchen and bathroom. He was handsomely paid by the Company, provided with servants, food, furniture and all the other appurtenances of his rank and station.

He was the head of the Shangaan community on the Sonder Ditch. A chief of the blood, a greybeard and member of the tribal councils. In similar houses and with the same privileges and in equal style lived the Indunas of the other tribal groups that made up the labour force of the Sonder Ditch. They were the paternal figureheads, the tribal jurists, ruling and judging within the framework of law and custom. The Company could not hope to maintain harmony and order without the assistance of these men.

'Baba!' Big King greeted his Induna from the doorway of his house, touching the forehead in respect not only for the man but also for what he represented.

'My son.' The Induna smiled his greeting. 'Come and sit by me.' He gestured for his servants to leave the room, and Big King went to squat at the feet of the old man. 'Is it true you go now to work with the mad one?' That was Johnny Delange's nickname.

They talked, the Induna questioning him on fifty matters that affected the welfare of his people. For Big King this was a comforting and nostalgic experience, for the Induna stood in the place of his father.

At last, satisfied, the Induna went on to other matters.

'There is a parcel ready tonight. Crooked Leg waits for you.'

'I shall go for it.'

'Go in peace then, my son.'

On his way through the gates of the hostel Big King stopped to chat with the guards. These men had the right of search over any person entering or leaving the hostel. Particularly they were concerned with preventing either women disguised as men or bottles of spirits entering the premises, both of which tended to have a disruptive effect on the community. As an after-thought they were also instructed to look out for stolen property entering or leaving. Big King had to ensure that none of them would ever, under any circumstances, take it into his head to search Big King.

While he stood at the gates, the last glow of the sunset faded and the lights began to come on across the valley. The clusters of red aerial warning lights atop the headgears, the massed yellow squares of the hotels, the strings of street lamps and the isolated pinpricks of the residential areas up on the ridge.

When it was truly dark, Big King left the guards and sauntered down the main road, until a bend in the road took him out of their sight. Then Big King left the road and started up the slope. He moved like a night animal, swiftly and with certainty of the path he followed.

He passed the ranch-type split-levels of the line management officials with their wide lawns and swimming-pools, pausing only once when a dog yapped nearby, then moving on again until he was into the broken rock and rank grass of the upper ridge; he crossed the skyline and started down the far side until he made out the grass-covered mound of rubble in the moonlight. He slowed and moved cautiously forward until he found the rusty barbed wire fence that guarded the entrance. He vaulted it easily and went on into the black mouth of the tunnel.

Fifty years before, a long-defunct mining company had suspected the existence of a gold reef in this area and had driven prospecting addits into the side of the ridge, exhausting its funds in the process, and finally abandoning the network of tunnels in despair.

Big King paused long enough to draw an electric torch from his pocket before going on into the tunnel, flashing the beam ahead of him. Soon the air stank of bats and their wings swished about his head. Unperturbed, Big King went on deeper and deeper into the side of the hill, taking a turning and fork in the tunnel without hesitation. At last there was a faint glow of yellow light ahead and Big King switched off his torch.

'Crooked Leg!' he called, his voice bounced and boomed along the tunnel. There was no reply.

'It is I, Big King!' he shouted again, and immediately a shadow detached itself from the sidewall and limped towards him, sheathing a wicked-looking knife as it came.

'All is ready.' The little cripple came to greet him. 'Come, I have it here.'

Crooked Leg had earned his limp and his nickname in a rockfall a dozen years ago. Now he owned and operated the concession photographic studio on the mine property, a flourishing enterprise, for dearly the Bantu love their own image on film. Not, however, as profitable as his nocturnal activities in the abandoned workings beyond the ridge.

He led Big King into a small rock chamber lit by a suspended hurricane lantern. Mingled with the bat stench was the acrid reek of sulphuric acid in high concentration.

On a wooden trestle table that occupied most of the chamber were earthenware jars, heavy glass bowls, polythene bags, and a variety of shoddy and very obviously second-hand laboratory equipment. In a clear space amongst all this clutter stood a large screw-topped bottle. The bottle was filled with a dirty yellow powder.

'Ha!' Big King exclaimed his pleasure. 'Plenty!'

'Yes. It has been a good week,' Crooked Leg agreed.

Big King picked up the bottle, marvelling once again at the unbelievable weight of it. This was not pure gold, for Crooked Leg's acid reduction methods were crude, but it was at least sixteen carats fine.

The bottle represented the week's collection of fines and concentrates by men like Joseph M'Kati from a dozen vulnerable points along the line of production; in some cases carried out from the company reduction works itself under the noses of the heavily armed guards.

All the men involved in this surreptitious milking off of the company's gold were Shangaans, there was only one man in whom was vested sufficient authority and prestige to prevent the greed and hostility which gold breeds from destroying the whole operation. That was the Shangaan Induna. There was only one man with the physical presence and necessary command of the Portuguese language to negotiate the disposal of the gold. That was Big King.

Big King placed the bottle in his pocket. The weight pulled his clothing out of shape.

'Run like a gazelle, Crooked Leg.' He turned back into the dark tunnel.

'Hunt like a leopard, King Nkulu,' chuckled the little cripple, as he disappeared into the moving shadows.

30

'A packet of Boxer tobacco,' said Big King. The eyes of José Almeida, the Portuguese owner of the mine concession store and the local roadhouse, narrowed slightly. He took down the yellow four-ounce packet from the shelves and handed it across the counter, accepted Big King's payment and counted the change into his palm.

He watched as the giant Bantu wandered down between the loaded shelves and racks of merchandise to disappear through the front door of the store into the night.

'Take charge,' he muttered in Portuguese to his plump little wife with her silky dark moustache, and she nodded in understanding, moving into José's place in front of the cash register. José went through into his storerooms and living quarters behind the store.

Big King was waiting in the shadows. When the back door opened he slipped through and José closed the door behind him. José led him through into a cubicle of an office, and from a cupboard he took down a jeweller's balance. Under Big King's watchful eye he began to weigh the gold.

José Almeida purchased the gold from the unofficial outlets of each of the five major mines on the Kitchenerville field, paying five Rands an ounce and selling again for sixteen. He justified the large profit margin he allowed himself by the fact that mere possession of unregistered gold was a criminal offence in South Africa, punishable by up to five years' imprisonment.

Almeida was a man in his middle thirties with lank black hair that he continually pushed back from his forehead, bright brown inquisitive eyes and dirty fingernails. Despite his grubby and well-worn clothing and unkempt hair style, he was a man of substance.

He had been able to pay in cash the forty thousand Rand demanded by the Company for the monopoly concession to trade on the mine property. He had, therefore, an exclusive clientele of twelve thousand well-paid Bantu, and had recovered his forty thousand during his first year of trading. He did not really need to run the risk of illicit gold buying, but gold is strange material. It infects most men who touch it with a reckless greed.

'Two hundred and sixteen ounces,' said José. His scale was set to record a twenty per cent error – in José's favour.

'One thousand and eighty Rand,' agreed Big King in Portuguese, and José went to the big green safe in the corner.

31

Terry Steyner entered the 'Grape and Gable' bar of the President Hotel at 1.14 p.m. precisely, and as Hurry Hirschfeld stood to greet her he reflected that fourteen minutes was hardly late at all for a beautiful woman. Terry's grandmother would have considered herself to be early if she was only that late.

'You're late,' growled Hurry. No sense in letting her get away with it unscathed.

'And you are a big, cuddly, growly, lovable old bear,' said Terry and kissed him on the tip of his nose before he could duck. Hurry sat down quickly scowling thunderously with pleasure. He decided he didn't give a good damn if Marais and Hardy, who further down the bar were listening and trying to cover their grins, repeated the incident to the entire membership of the Rand Club.

'Good day, Mrs Steyner.' The scarlet-jacketed barman smiled his greeting. 'Can I mix you a Manhattan?'

'Don't tempt me, Thomas. I'm on a diet. I'll just have a glass of soda water.'

'Diet,' snorted Hurry. 'You're skinny enough as it is. Give her a Manhattan, Thomas, and put a cherry in it. Never was a Hirschfeld woman that looked like a boy, and you'll not be the first of them.' As an afterthought, he added; 'I've ordered your lunch also, you'll not starve yourself in my company.'

'You are a shocker, Pops,' said Terry fondly.

'Now, young lady, let's hear what you've been up to since I last saw you.'

They talked together as friends, very dear and trusted friends. The affection they felt for each other went beyond the natural duty of their blood tie. There was a kinship of the spirit as well as the flesh. They sat close, heads together, watching each other's face as they talked, completely lost in the pleasure of each other's company, the murmur of their voices interrupted by a tinkling burst of laughter or a deep chuckle.

They were so absorbed that Peter, the headwaiter, came through from the Transvaal Room to find them.

'Mr Hirschfeld, the chef is in tears.'

'Good Lord.' Hurry looked at the antique clock above the bar. 'It's almost two o'clock. Why didn't someone tell me?'

The oysters had been flown up from Mossel Bay that morning, and Terry sighed with pleasure after each of them.

'I was out at the Sonder Ditch with Manfred on Wednesday.'

'Yes, I saw the photograph in the paper.' Hurry engulfed his twelfth and final oyster.

'I must say I like your new General Manager.'

Hurry laid down his fork and a little flush of anger started in his withered old cheeks.

'You mean Fred Plummer?'

'Don't be silly, Pops, I mean Rodney Ironsides.'

'Has that cold fish of yours been briefing you?' Hurry demanded.

'Manfred?' She was genuinely puzzled by the question, Hurry could see that. 'What's he got to do with it?'

'All right, forget it.' Hurry dismissed Manfred with a shake of his head. 'Why do you like Ironsides?'

'Have you heard him speak?'

'No.'

'He's very good. I'm sure he must be a first-class mining man.'

'He is.' Hurry nodded, watchful and non-committal.

Peter whisked Terry's plate away, giving her the respite she needed to gather her resources. In the previous few seconds she had realized that Rodney Ironsides was not, as she had believed, a certainty for the job. In fact, Pops had already chosen old plum-faced Plummer for the General Managership. It took another moment for her to decide that she would use even the dirtiest in-fighting to see that Rod was not overlooked.

Peter laid plates of cold rock lobster in front of them, and when he had withdrawn Terry looked up at Hurry. She had perfected the trick of enlarging her already enormous eyes. By holding them open like this she could flood them with tears. The effect was devastating.

'Do you know, Pops, he reminds me so much of the photographs of Daddy.'

Colonel Bernard Hirschfeld, Terry's father, had burned to death in his tank at Sidi Rezegh. She saw Hurry Hirschfeld's expression crack with pain, and Terry felt a sick little flutter of guilt. Had it been necessary to use such a vicious weapon to achieve her ends?

Hurry pushed at the rock lobster with his fork, his head was bowed so she could not see his face. She reached out to touch his hand.

'Pops —' she whispered, and he looked up. There was a restrained excitement in Hurry's manner.

'You know, you're bloody well right! He does look a bit like

78

Bernie. Did I ever tell you about the time when your father and
I —'

Terry felt dizzy with relief. I didn't hurt him, she told herself,
he likes the idea, he really does. With a woman's instinct she had
chosen the only form of persuasion that could have moved Hurry
Hirschfeld from his decision.

32

Manfred Steyner fastened his safety belt and lay back in the seat
of the Boeing 707, feeling slightly nauseated with relief.

Ironsides was in, and he was safe. Hurry Hirschfeld had sent
for him two hours before to wish him farewell and good luck
with the talks. Manfred had stood before him, trying desperately
to think of some way in which he could bring up the subject
naturally. Hurry saved him the trouble.

'By the way, I'm giving Ironsides the Sonder Ditch. Reckon
it's about time we had some young blood in top management.'

It was as easy as that. Manfred had difficulty in persuading
himself that those threats which had kept him lying awake during
the past four nights were no longer of consequence. Ironsides
was in. He could go to Paris and tell them. *Ironsides is in. We are
ready to go.*

The note of the jets changed, and the Boeing began to
roll forward. Manfred twisted his head against the neck rest and
peered through the Perspex porthole. He could not distinguish
Terry's figure amongst the crowd on the observation balcony of
Jan Smuts Airport. They taxied past a Pan Am Boeing which cut
off his view and Manfred looked straight ahead. Instantly his
nostrils flared, he looked around quickly.

The passenger in the seat beside him had stripped to his shirt-
sleeves. He was a big beefy individual who very obviously did
not use deodorant. Almost in desperation Manfred looked about.
The aircraft was full, there would be little chance of changing
seats and beside him the beefy individual produced a pack of
cigarettes.

'You can't smoke,' cried Manfred. 'The light's on.' The combination of body odour and cigarette smoke would be unbearable.

'I'm not smoking,' said the man, 'yet.' And placed a cigarette between his lips, his lighter ready in the other hand.

Nearly two thousand miles to Nairobi, thought Manfred, with his stomach starting to heave.

33

'Terry darling, why on earth should I go all the way out to Kitchenerville to watch a lot of savages prancing around?'

'As a favour to me, Joy,' Terry pleaded into the telephone.

'It means mucking up my whole weekend. I've got rid of the kids to their grandmother, I've got a copy of *A Small Town in Germany* and I was going to have a lovely time reading and —'

'Please, Joy, you're my last hope.'

'What time will we be home?' Joy was weakening. Terry sensed her advantage and pressed forward ruthlessly.

'You might meet a lovely man out at the mine, and he'll sweep you —'

'No, thanks.' Joy had been divorced a little over a year ago, some people took longer than others to recover. 'I've had lovely men in big fat chunks.'

'Oh, Joy, you can't sit around moping for ever. Come on, I'll pick you up in half an hour.'

Joy sighed with resignation. 'Damn you, Terry Steyner.'

'Half an hour,' said Terry and hung up before she could change her mind.

*   *   *

'I'm playing golf. It's Saturday, and I'm playing golf,' said Doctor Daniel Stander stubbornly.

'You remember when I drove all the way to Bloemfontein to —' Rod began, and Dan interrupted quickly.

'All right, all right, I remember. You don't have to bring that up again.'

'You owe me plenty, Stander,' Rod reminded him. 'All I am asking is one of your lousy Saturday afternoons. Is that so much?'

'I can't let the boys down. It's a long-standing date.' Dan wriggled to escape.

'I've already phoned Ben. It will be a pleasure for him to take your place.'

There was a long gloomy silence, then Dan asked, 'What's this bird like?'

'She's a beautiful, rich nymphomaniac, and she owns a brewery.'

'Yeah! Yeah!' said Dan sarcastically. 'All right, I'll do it. But I hereby declare all my obligation and debts to you fully discharged.'

'I'll give you a written receipt,' Rod agreed.

Dan was still sulking when the Daimler came up the drive and parked at the front of the Mine Club. He and Rod were standing at the Ladies' Bar, watching for the arrival of their guests.

Dan had just ordered his third beer.

'Here they come,' said Rod.

'Is that them?' Dan's depression lifted magically as he peered through the coloured-glass windows. The chauffeur was letting the two ladies out of the Daimler. They were both in floral slack suits and dark glasses.

'That's them.'

'Jesus!' said Dan with rare approval. 'Which one is mine?'

'The blonde.'

'Ha!' Dan grinned for the first time since their meeting. 'Why the hell are we standing here?'

'Why indeed?' asked Rod, his stomach was tied up in knots that twisted tighter as he went down the front steps toward Terry.

'Mrs Steyner. I'm so glad you could come.' With a wild lift of elation he saw it was still there, he had not imagined it, it was there in her eyes and her smile.

'Thank you, Mr Ironsides.' She was like a schoolgirl again, uncertain of herself, flustered.

'I'd like you to meet Mrs Albright. Joy, this is Rodney Ironsides.'

'Hello.' He smiled at her as he clasped her hand. 'It's gin time, I think.'

Dan was waiting at the bar for them, and Rod made the introductions.

'Joy is so excited at the chance of watching the dancing,' said Terry as they sat down on the bar stools. 'She's been looking forward to it for days.' And for an instant Joy looked stunned.

'You'll love it,' agreed Dan moving in to take up a position at Joy's elbow. 'I wouldn't miss it for anything.'

Joy was a tall slim girl with long straight golden hair that hung to her shoulders, her eyes were cool green but her mouth when she smiled was soft and warm. She smiled now full into Dan's eyes.

'Nor would I,' she said, and with relief Rod knew he could devote all his attention to Terry Steyner. Joy Albright would be more than adequately looked after. He ordered drinks, and all four of them promptly lost further interest in tribal dancing.

At one stage Rod told Terry Steyner, 'I am going up to Johannesburg this evening. There is no point in having your unfortunate chauffeur sit around all afternoon. Let him go, and I'll take you home.'

'Good,' Terry agreed immediately. 'Would you tell him, please?'

The next time Rod looked at his watch it was half past three.

'Good Lord!' he exclaimed. 'If we don't hurry, it will be all over.' Reluctantly Joy and Dan, who had their heads close together, drew apart.

The overflow from the amphitheatre pressed about them, a merry jostling throng, all inhibitions long since evaporated in the primeval excitement of the dance, much like the crowd at a bull ring.

Rod and Dan ran interference for the girls, ploughing a path through the main gateway and down to their reserved seats in the front row. All four of them were laughing and flushed by the time they were seated, the excitement about them was infectious and the liquor had heightened their sensibilities.

An expectant hum of voices.

'The Shangaans!' And the audience craned towards the entrance from which pranced a dozen drummers, their long wooden drums hung on rawhide straps about their necks, they took up stations around the circular earthen stage.

Tap, tap. Tap, tap – from one of the drummers, and silence gripped the amphitheatre.

Tap, tap. Tap, tap. Naked, except for their brief loin cloths, stooped over the drums that they clasped between their knees, they began to lay down the rhythm of the dance. It was a broken, disturbing beat, that jerked and twitched like a severed nerve. A compelling, demanding sound, the pulse of a continent and a people.

Then came the dancers, shuffling, row upon row, head-dresses dipping and rustling, the animal tail kilts swirling, war rattles at the wrists and ankles, black muscles already oiled with the sweat of excitement, coming in slowly, rank upon majestic rank, moving as though the drums were pumping life into them.

A shrill blast on a duiker horn and the ranks whirled like dry leaves in a wind, they fell again into a new pattern, and through the opening in their midst came a single gigantic figure.

'Big King!' The name blew like a sigh through the audience, and immediately the drums changed their rhythm. Faster, demanding, and the dancers hissed in their throats a sound like storm surf rushing up a stony beach.

Big King flung his arms wide, braced on legs like black marble columns, his head thrown back. He sang a single word of command, shrilling it, and in instantaneous response every right knee was brought up to the level of the chest. Half a second's pause and then two hundred horny bare feet stamped down simultaneously with a crash that shook the amphitheatre to its foundations. The Shangaans began to dance, and reality was gone in the moving, charging, swirling, retreating ranks.

Once Rod tore his eyes from the spectacle. Terry Steyner was sitting forward on the bench, eyes sparkling, lips slightly parted, completely lost in the erotic turmoil and barbaric splendour of it.

Joy and Dan had a firm hold on each others' hands, their shoulders and the outside of their thighs were pressed tightly together, and Rod was stabbed by a painful thrust of envy.

*　　*　　*

Afterwards, back in the Ladies' Bar of the Club, there was very little conversation but they were all of them tensed up, restless, moved by strange undercurrents and interplays of primitive desires and social restraints.

'Well,' said Rod at last, 'if I am to get you two ladies back to Johannesburg at a decent hour —'

Dan and Joy spoke together.

'Don't worry, Rod, I'll —'

'Dan says he will —' Then they stopped and grinned at each other sheepishly.

'I take it that Dan has suddenly remembered that he has to go to Johannesburg this evening also, and he has offered to give you a lift?' asked Rod dryly, and they laughed in confirmation.

'It looks as though we are on our own, Mrs Steyner.' Rod turned to Terry.

'I'll trust you,' said Terry.

'If you do that, you're crazy,' said Dan.

*　　*　　*

Outside the Maserati, darkness was falling swiftly. The horizon blending into the black sky, isolated lights winking at them out of the surrounding veld.

Rod switched on the headlights, and the instrument panel glowed softly, turning the interior into a warm secluded place, isolating them from the world. The wind whispered, and the tyres and the engine hummed a gentle intimate refrain.

Terry Steyner sat with her legs curled up under her, cuddled into the soft maroon leather of the bucket seat. She was staring ahead down the path of the headlights, and she seemed withdrawn and yet very close. Every few minutes Rod would take his eyes from the road and study her profile briefly. He did so again, and this time she met his gaze frankly.

'You realize what is happening?' she asked.

'Yes,' he answered as frankly.

'You know how dangerous it could be for you?'

'And you.'

'No, not me. I am invulnerable. I am a Hirschfeld – but you, it could destroy you.'

Rod shrugged.

'If we counted the consequences before every action, nobody would do anything.'

'Have you thought that I might be a spoiled little rich girl amusing myself? I might do this all the time.'

'You might,' Rod agreed. They were silent for a long while, then Terry spoke again.

'Rod?' she used his given name for the first time.

'Yes?'

'I don't, you know. I really don't.'

'I guessed that.'

'Thank you.' She opened her bag. 'I need a cigarette. I feel as though I'm standing poised on the edge of a cliff and I've got this terrible compulsion to hurl myself over the edge.'

'Light me one, Terry.'

'You need one also?'

'Badly.'

They smoked in silence again, both of them staring ahead, then Terry rolled down the window and flicked the cigarette butt away.

'You've got the job, you know.' All day she had wanted to tell him, it had been bubbling inside her. Watching his face, she saw his lips stiffen, his eyes crease into slits.

'Did you hear me?' she asked at last, and he braked the Maserati, swinging it off onto the shoulder of the road. He pulled on the hand brake and turned to face her.

'Terry, what did you say?'

'I said, you've got the job.'

'What job?' he demanded harshly.

'Pops signed the instruction this morning. You'll receive it on Monday. You're the new General Manager of the Sonder Ditch.' She wanted to go on and say – *and I got it for you. I made Pops give it to you.*

I never will, she promised, I will never spoil it for him. He must believe he won it fairly, not as my gift.

34

It was Saturday night, the big night in Dump City.

The Blaauberg Mine was the oldest producer on the Kitchener-ville field. There were sections of its property which had been worked out completely, and the old waste dumps were now abandoned and overgrown. Among the scrub and head-high weed in the valleys between these man-made hills had grown up a shanty town. Dump City, the inhabitants had named it. The buildings were made of discarded galvanized iron sheets and flattened oil drums, there was no sanitation or running water.

Remote from the main roads, the residential communities of the neighbouring mines or the town of Kitchenerville, hidden among the dumps, accessible only to a man on foot, never visited by members of the South African Constabulary, it was ideally suited to the purposes for which its three hundred permanent inhabitants had chosen it.

Every one of the shacks was a shebeen, a clip joint where watered liquor was sold at inflated prices, where dagga* was freely obtainable and where men from the surrounding mines gathered to carouse.

They came not so much for the liquor. Each of the mine hostels had a bar where a full range of liquor was on sale at club prices. Very few of them came for the dagga. There was little addiction amongst these well-fed, hard-worked and contented men. What they came for were the women.

Five mines in the area, each employing ten or twelve thousand men. Here at Dump City were two hundred women, the only available women within twenty miles. It was not necessary for the young ladies of Dump City to solicit custom, even the fat, the withered, the toothless, could behave like queens.

Big King came down the path that skirted the mine dump. With him were two dozen of his fellow tribesmen, big Shangaans wearing their regalia, carrying their fighting sticks and still tensed up from the dancing. They came at a trot, Big King leading them. They were singing, not the gentle planting or courting melodies, not the work chant nor the song of welcome.

They were singing the fighting songs, those their forefathers had sung when they carried the spear in search of cattle and slaves. The driving inflammatory rhythm, the fiercely patriotic words wrought so mightily on the delicate susceptibilities of the average Shangaan that the company had found it necessary to ban the singing of these songs.

Like a Scot hearing the pipes, when a Shangaan began singing these warlike chants, he was ready for violence.

*Marijuana.

The song ended as Big King led them down to the nearest shanty, and pushed aside the sacking that acted as a door. He stooped through the opening, and his comrades crowded in behind him.

A brittle electric silence fell on the large room. The air was so thick with smoke, and the light from the suspended hurricane lamps so feeble, that it was impossible to see the far wall. The room was filled with men, forty or fifty of them, the smell of humanity and bad liquor was solid. Among this press of men were half a dozen bright spots of the girls' dresses, but with their curiosity aroused by the singing more girls were coming through from the interleading doorways at the back, some of them had men with them and were still shrugging into their clothing. When they saw Big King and his warriors in full war kit, they fell silent and watchful.

At Big King's shoulder one of his Shangaans whispered:

'Basutos! They are all Basutos!' He was right, Big King saw that they were all men of that mountainous little independent state.

Big King started forward, swaggering just enough to make his leopard tail kilt swing and swirl and the heron feathers of his headdress rustle. He reached the primitive bar counter.

'Flying Bird,' he told the crone who owned the house, and she placed a bottle of Eagle Brandy on the counter.

Big King half filled a tumbler, conscious that every eye was on him, and drained it.

Slowly he turned and surveyed the room.

'What is it,' he asked in a voice that carried to every corner, 'that sits on top of a mountain and scratches its fleas. Is it a baboon, or a Basuto?'

A roar of delight went up from his Shangaans.

'A Basuto!' they shouted, crowding forward to the bar, while a growl and mutter went up from the rest of the room.

'What is it,' shouted a Basuto jumping to his feet, 'that has feathers on its head and crows from a dungheap? Is it a rooster, or a Shangaan?'

Without seeming to move, Big King picked up the bottle of Eagle Brandy and hurled it. With a crack it burst against the Basuto's forehead and he went over backwards taking two of his companions with him.

The old crone snatched up her cash register and ran as the room exploded into violent movement.

There was not enough space in which to use the fighting sticks, Big King realized, so he lifted a section of the bar counter off its trestles and holding it in front of him like the blade of a bulldozer, he charged across the room, flattening all and everything before him.

The crash of breaking furniture and the yelp and squeal of men being struck down drove Big King beyond the frontiers of sanity into the red atavistic fury of the beserker.

Basuto is also one of the fighting tribes of the N'guni group. These wiry mountaineers rushed into the conflict with the same savage joy as the Shangaans, a conflict that raged and roared out of the single room to engulf the entire population of Dump City.

One of the girls, her dress ripped from her back so she was left with only a tattered pair of bloomers, had climbed on top of the remains of the bar counter from where, with her big melon breasts swinging in the lamp light, she shrilled that peculiar ululation that Bantu women used to goad their menfolk into battle frenzy. A dozen of the other girls joined in, trilling, squealing, and the sound was too much for Big King.

With the bar top held ahead of him he charged straight through the flimsy wall of the shack, bursting it open like a paper bag, the roof sagged down wearily, and Big King raged on unchecked down the narrow dirt street, striking down any man who crossed his path, scattering chickens and yelping dogs, roaring like a bull gorilla.

He turned at the end of the encampment and came back, his frustration mounting as he found the street deserted except for a few prostrate bodies, through the gaping hole in the wall he entered the Shebeen once more to find that here also the fighting had died down. A few of the participants were crawling, or moaning as they lay on a carpet of broken glass.

Big King glared about him, seeking a further outlet for his wrath.

'King Nkulu!' The girl was still on the trestle table, her eyes bright with excitement, her legs trembling with it.

Big King let out another roar, and hurled the bar top from him. It clattered against the far wall and Big King started towards her.

'You are a lion!' She shrieked encouragement at him, and she took one of her big black velvety breasts in each hand and pointed them at him, squeezing them together, shaking with excitement.

'Eat me!' she screamed, as Big King swept her off the table and lifting her high, ran with her out into the night. Carrying her into the scrub below the mine dumps, holding her easily with one arm, ripping the leopard-tail kilt from his own waist as he ran.

35

It was Saturday night in Paris also, but there were men who were still working, for there were lights burning in the upstairs rooms of one of the big Embassies in the rue Royale.

The fat man who had been the host in the gambling establishment in Johannesburg was now the guest. He sat at ease in a leather club easy, his corpulence and the steel-grey hair at his temples giving him dignity. His face heavy, tanned, intelligent. His eyes glittery and hard as the diamond on his finger.

He was listening intently to a man of about the same age as himself who stood before a projected image on a screen that covered one wall of the room. There was that in the man's bearing and manner that marked him as a scholar, he was speaking now, addressing himself directly to the listener in the easy chair, pointing with a marker to the screen beside him.

'You see here a plan of the working of the five producing gold mines of the Kitchenerville fields in relation to each other.' He touched the screen with a marker. 'Thornfontein, Blaauberg, Tweefontein, Deep Gold Levels and Sonder Ditch.'

The man in the chair nodded. 'I have seen and studied this diagram before.'

'Good, then you will know that the Sonder Ditch property sits in the centre of the field. It has common boundaries with the other four mines and here,' he tapped the screen again, 'it is intersected by the massive serpentine dyke which they call the Big Dipper.'

Again the fat man nodded.

'It is for these reasons we have selected the Sonder Ditch as the trigger point.' The lecturer touched a button on the wall panel and the image on the screen changed.

'Now, here is something you have not seen before.'

The man in the chair crouched forward.

'What is it?'

'It is an underground map based on the borehole results of the five companies who have been exploring the ground to the east of the Big Dipper. These results have been pooled and interpreted by some of the finest brains in the fields of geology and hydrophysics. You have here a carefully considered representation of exactly what lies on the far side of the Big Dipper fault.'

The big man moved uncomfortably in his chair.

'It's a monster!'

'Yes, a monster. Lying just beyond the fault is an underground lake, no, that is not the correct word. Let us call it an underground sea, the size of, say, Lake Eyrie. The water is held in a vast sponge of porous dolomite rock.'

'My God.' For the first time the fat man had lost his poise. 'If this is right, why don't the mining companies arrive at the same conclusion and keep well away from it?'

'Because,' the lecturer switched off the image and the overhead lights came on, 'because in their highly competitive attitudes none of them has access to the findings of the others. It is only when all the results are studied that the picture becomes clear.'

'How did your Government come to be in possession of *all* the results?' demanded the fat man.

'That is not important.' The lecturer was brusque, impatient of the interruption. 'We are also in possession of the findings of a certain Dr Peter Wessels who is at present head of a research team in Rock Mechanics based on the Sonder Ditch mine property. It is Company classified information and consists of a paper that Dr Wessels has written on the shatter patterns and stresses of rock. His researches are directly related to the Ventersdorp quartzites which comprise the country rock of the Sonder Ditch workings.'

The lecturer picked up a pamphlet from his desk.

'I will not weary you by asking you to wade through its highly technical findings. Instead I will give it to you in capsule form. Dr Wessels arrives at the conclusion that a column of

Ventersdorp quartzite 120 feet thick would shatter under a side pressure of 4000 pounds per square inch.'

The lecturer dropped the pamphlet back on the desk.

'As you know, by law, the gold mining companies are bound to leave a barrier of solid rock 120 feet thick along their boundaries. That is all that separates one mine's workings from another, just that wall of rock. You understand?'

'Of course. It is very simple.'

'Simple? Yes, it is simple! This Dr Steyner, over whom you have control, will instruct the new General Manager of the Sonder Ditch to drive a tunnel through the Big Dipper dyke. The drive will puncture the vast underground reservoir and the water will run back and flood the entire Sonder Ditch workings. Once they are flooded, the pressure delivered by a 6000-foot head of water at the lower levels will be in excess of 4000 pounds per square inch. That is sufficient to burst the rock walls, and flood the Thornfontein, the Blaauberg, Deep Gold Levels and Tweefontein gold mines.

'The entire Kitchenerville gold fields would be effectively and permanently put out of production. The consequences for the economy of the Republic of South Africa would be catastrophic.'

The fat man was visibly shaken.

'Why do you want to do it?' he asked, shaking his head in awe.

'My colleague here,' the lecturer indicated a man who was sitting quietly in one corner, 'will explain that to you presently.'

'But – people!' the fat man protested. 'There will be people down there when it bursts, thousands of them.'

The lecturer smiled, raising one eyebrow. 'If I were to tell you that six thousand men would drown, would you refuse to proceed, and forfeit the million-dollar payment my Government has offered you?'

The fat man looked down, embarrassed, and muttered barely audibly. 'No.'

The lecturer chuckled. 'Good! Good! However, you may salve your aching conscience by assuring yourself that we do not expect more than forty or fifty fatalities from the flooding. Naturally, those men actually working on the face will be killed. But that tremendous volume of water under immense pressure should make it a merciful death. For the rest of them, the mine can be evacuated swiftly enough to allow them excellent chances of survival. The surrounding mines will have days to evacuate before the water pressure builds up sufficiently to burst through the boundary walls.'

There was silence then in the room for nearly a minute.

'Have you any questions?'

The fat man shook his head.

'Very well, in that case I will leave it to my colleague to complete the briefing. He will explain the necessity for this operation, will arrange the terms of payment and conditions upon which you will proceed.' The lecturer gathered up the pamphlet and other papers from the desk. 'It remains only for me to wish you good luck.' He chuckled again and left the room quickly.

The little man who up until then had remained silent, suddenly bounced out of his chair and began pacing up and down the wall-to-wall carpeting. He spoke rapidly, shooting occasional sideways glances at his audience, his bald head shining in the fluorescent lighting, wriggling his moustache like rabbit whiskers, puffing nervously at his cigarette.

'Reasons first. I'll make it short and sweet, right? The South Africans and the Frogs have got together. They're here in Paris now cooking up mischief. We know what they're up to, they're going to launch an all-out attack on my Government's currency. Gold price increase, you know. Very complicated and very nasty for us, right? They might just be able to do it, South Africa is the world's biggest gold producer. With the Frogs helping her, they might just be able to force an increase.'

He stopped in front of the fat man and thrust out an accusing finger.

'Are we going to sit back and let them have a free run? No, sir! We are going to throw down our own curve ball! In three months time the Syndicate will be ready to attack. At that precise moment we will kick the chair out from under the South Africans by cutting their gold production in half. We will flood the Kitchenerville goldfields and the attack will fizzle out like a damp squib, right?'

'As simple as that?' asked the fat man.

'As simple as that!' The bald head nodded vigorously. 'Now, my next duty is to make clear to you that the agreed million dollars is *all* the reward you receive. Neither you nor your agents may indulge in any financial transactions that might, in retrospect, show that this was a planned operation, right?'

'Right.' The fat man nodded.

'You give your assurance that you will not deal in any of the shares of the companies involved?'

'You have my solemn word.' The fat man told him earnestly, and not for the first time in his life reflected how easily and painlessly a promise could be given.

With the assistance of the three men who had watched Manfred Steyner that night at the gambling club in Johannesburg, he intended launching a bear offensive on the stock exchanges of the world.

On the day that they drilled into the Big Dipper dyke he and his partners would sell millions of the shares of the five mining companies for one of the biggest financial killings in the history of money.

'We are agreed then.' The bald head bobbed. 'Now, as for this Dr Steyner, we have had a screening and personality analysis and we believe that, despite the secure hold you have on his loyalties, he would jib at giving the order to drive on the Big Dipper if he were aware of the consequences. Therefore we have prepared a second geological report,' he produced from his brief case a thick manila folder, 'incorporating those figures which he will recognize. In other words the drilling results of the C.R.C. exploration teams, but the other figures are fictitious. This report purports to prove the existence of a fabulously rich gold reef beyond the fault.' He crossed to the fat man and handed him the folder. 'Take it. It will help you convince Dr Steyner, and he in turn to convince the new General Manager of the Sonder Ditch gold mine.'

'You have been thorough,' said the fat man.

'We try to give a satisfactory service to our customers,' said the bald man.

36

The game was five card stud poker, and there were two big winners at the table, Manfred Steyner and the Algerian.

Manfred had timed his arrival in Paris to ensure himself an

uninterrupted weekend before the rest of the delegates came in on the Monday morning flight.

He had checked in at the Hotel George Cinq on Saturday afternoon, bathed and rested for three hours until eight in the evening, then he had set out for the Club Chat Noir by taxi.

He had been playing now for five hours, and a steady succession of strong cards had pushed his winnings up to a formidable sum. It lay piled in front of him, a fruit salad of garish French bank notes. Across the table sat the Algerian, a slim dark-skinned Arab with toffee eyes and a silky black moustache. His teeth were very white against the creamy brown skin. He wore a turtle-neck shirt in pink silk, and a linen jacket of baby blue. With long brown fingers he kept smoothing and stacking his own pile of bank notes.

A girl sat on the arm of his chair, an Arab girl in a skin-tight gold trouser suit. Her hair was shiny black and hung onto her shoulders, her eyes were disconcertingly level as she watched Manfred.

'Ten thousand.' Manfred's voice was explosive, like that of a teutonic drillmaster. He was betting on his fourth card which had just been dealt to him. He and the Algerian were the remaining players in the game. The others had folded their hands and were sitting back watching with the casual interest of men no longer involved.

The Algerian's eyes narrowed slightly and the girl leaned down to whisper softly in his ear. He shook his head, annoyed, and drew on his cigarette. He had a pair of queens and a six showing and he leaned forward to study Manfred's cards.

The dealer's voice prodded. 'The bet is ten thousand francs, from four, five, seven of clubs. Possible straight flush.'

'Bet or drop,' said one of the uncommitted players. 'You're wasting time.'

The Algerian flashed him a venomous glance.

'Bet,' he said, and counted out ten thousand-franc notes into the pool.

'*Carte.*' The dealer slid a card face down in front of each of them. Quickly the Algerian lifted one corner of his card with his thumb, glanced at it and then closed the face.

Manfred sat very still, the card lying inches from his right hand. His face was pale, calm, but he was seething internally. Far from a possible straight flush, Manfred was holding four, five, seven of clubs and the eight of hearts. A six was the only card that could improve his hand and one six was already showing among the Algerian's cards. His chances were remote.

His lower belly and loins were tight and hot with excitement, his chest constricted. He drew out the sensation, wanting it to last for ever.

'Pair of queens still to bet,' murmured the dealer.

'Ten thousand.' The Algerian pushed the notes forward.

'He has found another queen,' thought Manfred, 'but he is uncertain of my flush or straight.'

Manfred placed his smooth white hand over his fifth card, cupping it. He lifted it.

'Table,' said Manfred calmly, and there was a gasp and rustle from the watchers. The girl's hand tightened on the Algerian's sleeve, she stared with hatred into Manfred's face.

'The gentleman has made a table bet,' intoned the croupier. 'House rules. Any player may bet the entire stake he has upon the table.' He reached across and began to count the notes in front of Manfred.

Minutes later he announced the total. 'Two hundred and twelve thousand francs.' He looked across at the Algerian. 'It is now up to you to bet against the possible straight flush.'

The girl whispered urgently into the Arab's ear, but he snapped a single word at her and she recoiled. He looked about the room, as if seeking guidance, then he lifted and examined his hole cards again.

Suddenly his face hardened, and he looked steadily across at Manfred.

'Call!' he blurted, and Manfred's clenched right hand fell open upon the table.

The Arab faced his hand. Three queens. The whole room looked expectantly at Manfred.

He flicked over his last card. Two of diamonds. His hand was worthless.

With a birdlike cry of triumph the Algerian leaped from his seat and reaching across the table began raking Manfred's stake with both arms towards him.

Manfred stood up from the table, and the Arab girl grinned maliciously at him, taunting him in Arabic. He turned quickly away and almost ran down the steps that led to the cloakrooms.

Twenty minutes later, feeling weak and slightly dizzy, Manfred slipped into the back seat of a Citroen taxi cab.

'George Cinq,' he told the driver. As he entered the lobby of the hotel he saw a tall figure rise from one of the leather arm-chairs and follow him across to the lifts. Shoulder to shoulder they stepped into the lift and as the doors slid closed the tall man spoke.

'Welcome to Paris, Dr Steyner.'

'Thank you, Andrew. I presume you have come to give me my instructions?'

'That is correct. He wishes to see you tomorrow at ten o'clock. I will call for you.'

37

It was Saturday night in Kitchenerville and in the men's bar of the Lord Kitchener Hotel the daily-paid men from the five gold mines were bellying up to the counter three deep.

The public dance had been in progress for three hours. At tables along the veranda the women-folk sat primly sipping their port and lemonade. Although they all were admirably ignoring the absence of the men, yet a constant and merciless vigil was kept on the door to the men's bar. Most of the wives already had the automobile keys safely in their handbags.

In the dining-hall, cleared of its furniture and sprinkled liberally with french chalk, the local four-piece band who played under the unlikely name of the 'Wind Dogs' launched without preliminaries into a lively rendition of 'Die Ou Kraal Liedjie', and from the men's bar, in various stages of inebriation, answering the call to arms came the troops.

Many of them had shed their jackets, the knots of their ties had slipped, their voices were boisterous and legs were a little unsteady as they led their women onto the dance floor and immediately showed to which school of the dance they belonged.

There was the cavalry squadron which tucked partner under one arm, very much like a lance, and charged. At the other end of the scale were those who plodded grimly around the perimeter, looking neither left nor right, speaking to no one, not even their partners. Then there were the sociables who reeled about the floor, red in the face, their movements completely unrelated to the music, shouting to their friends and attempting to pinch any feminine posterior that came within range. Their unpredictable progress interfered with the evolutions of the dedicated.

The dedicated took up their positions in the centre of the floor and twisted. A half dozen years previously the twist had swept like an Asian 'flu epidemic through the world and then faded out. Gone, forgotten, except in places like Kitchenerville. Here it had been taken and firmly entrenched into the social culture of the community.

Even in this stronghold of the twist, there was one master. 'Johnny Delange? Gott man, but he can twist, hey!' they murmured with awe.

With the sinuous erotic movements of an erect cobra, Johnny was twisting with Hettie. His shiny rayon suit caught the light and the lace ruffles of his shirt fluttered at his throat. There was a fierce grin of pleasure on his hawk features, and the jewelled buckles of his pointed Italian shoes twinkled as he danced.

A big girl with copper hair and creamy skin, Hettie was light on her feet. She had a tiny waist and a swelling regal bottom under the emerald-green skirt. She laughed as she danced, a full healthy laugh to match her body.

The two of them moved with the expertise of a couple who have danced together often. Hettie anticipated each of Johnny's movements, and he grinned his approval at her.

From the veranda Davy Delange watched them. He stood in the shadows, clutching a tankard of beer, a squat, lonely figure. When another dancing couple cut off his view of Hettie's luscious revolving buttocks he would exclaim with irritation and move restlessly.

The music ended and the dancers spilled out onto the veranda, laughing and breathless, mopping streaming faces; girls squealing and giggling as the men led them to their seats, deposited them and then headed for the bar.

'See you.' Johnny left Hettie reluctantly, he would have liked to stay with her, but he was sensitive about what the boys would say if he spent the whole evening with his wife.

He was absorbed into the masculine crowd, to join their

banter and loud laughter. He was deeply involved in a discussion of the merits of the new Ford Mustang, which he was considering buying, when Davy nudged him.

'It's Constantine!' he whispered, and Johnny looked up quickly. Constantine was a Greek immigrant, a stoper on the Blaauberg Mine. He was a big strong black-haired individual with a broken nose. Johnny had broken his nose for him about ten months previously. As a bachelor Johnny would fight him on the average of once a month, nothing serious, just a semi-friendly punch-up.

However, Constantine could not understand that nowadays Johnny was forbidden by his brand new wife from indulging in casual exchanges of fisticuffs. He had developed the erroneous theory that Johnny Delange was afraid of him.

He was coming down the bar room now, holding his glass in his massive hairy right hand with the little finger extended genteely. On his hip rested his other hand and he minced along with a simpering smile on his blue-jowled granite-textured features. Stopping in front of the mirror to pat his hair into place, he winked at his cronies and then came on down to where Johnny stood. He paused and ogled Johnny heavily, fluttering his eyelids and wriggling his hips. His colleagues from the Blaauberg Mine were weak with laughter, gurgling merrily, hanging onto each other's shoulders.

Then with a bump and grind that raised another howl of laughter Constantine disappeared into the lavatories, to emerge minutes later and blow Johnny a kiss as he went back to join his friends. They plied liquor on the Greek in appreciation of his act. Johnny's smile was a little strained as he resumed the discussion on the Mustang's virtues.

Twenty minutes and half a dozen brandies later, Constantine repeated his little act again on the way to the latrine. His repertoire was limited.

'Hold it, Johnny,' whispered Davy. 'Let's go and sit on the veranda.'

'He's asking for it. I'm telling you!' Johnny's smile had disappeared.

'Come on, Johnny, man.'

'No, hell, they'll think I'm running. I can't go now.'

'You know what Hettie will say,' Davy warned him. For a moment longer Johnny hesitated.

'The hell with what Hettie says.' Johnny bunched his right fist with its array of gold rings as he moved down to Constantine and leaned beside him on the counter.

'Herby,' he called the barman, and when he had his attention he indicated the Greek. 'Please give the lady a port and lemonade.'

And the bystanders scattered for cover. Davy shot out of the door onto the veranda to report to Hettie.

'Johnny!' he gasped. 'He's fighting again.'

'Is he!' Hettie came to her feet like a red-headed Valkyrie. But her progress to the men's bar was delayed by the crowd of spectators that jammed the doorway and all the windows. The crowd was tiptoeing and climbing onto the chairs and tables for a better view, every thud or crash of breaking furniture was greeted with a roar of delight.

Hettie had her handbag clutched in her right hand, and like a jungle explorer hacking his way through the undergrowth with a machete, she opened a path for herself to the bar room door.

At the door she paused. The conflict had reached a critical stage. Among a litter of broken glass and shattered stools, Johnny and the Greek were circling each other warily, weaving and feinting, all their wits concentrated upon each other. Both of them were marked. The Greek was bleeding from his lip, a thin red ribbon of blood down his chin that dripped onto his shirt. Johnny had a shiny red swelling closing one eye. The crowd was silent, waiting.

'Johnny Delange!' Hettie's voice cracked like a mauser rifle fired from ambush. Johnny started guiltily, dropping his hands, half turning towards her as the Greek's fist crashed into the side of his head. Johnny spun from the blow, hit the wall and slid down quietly.

With a roar of triumph Constantine rushed forward to put the boots into Johnny's prostrate form, but he pitched forward to sprawl unconscious beside Johnny. Hettie had hit him with the water bottle snatched up from one of the table tops.

'Please help me get my husband to the car,' she appealed to the men around her, suddenly helpless and little-girlish.

She sat beside Davy in the front of the Monaco, fuming with anger.

Johnny lay at ease upon the back seat. He was snoring softly.

'Don't be angry, Hettie.' Davy was driving sedately.

'I've told him, not once, a hundred times.' Hettie's voice crackled like static. 'I told him I wouldn't put up with it.'

'It wasn't his fault. The Greek started it,' Davy explained softly and placed his hand on her leg.

'You stick up for him, just because he is your brother.'

'That's not true,' Davy soothed her, stroking her leg. 'You know how I feel about you, Hettie.'

'I don't believe you.' His hand was moving higher. 'You men are all the same. You all stick together.'

Her anger was fast solidifying into a burning resentment of Johnny Delange, one in which she was willing to take a calculated revenge. She knew that Davy's hand was no longer trying to comfort her and quench her anger. Before she married Johnny Delange, Hettie had had every opportunity to learn about men, and she had been an enthusiastic and receptive pupil. She placed no special importance on an act of the flesh, dispensing her favours as casually as someone might offer a cigarette-case around.

'Why not?' she thought. 'That will fix Mr Johnny Delange! Not all the way, of course, but just enough to get my own back on him.'

'No, Hettie. It's true – I tell you.' Davy's voice was husky, as he felt her knees fall apart under his hand. He touched the silky-smooth skin above her stocking top.

The Monaco slowed to almost walking pace, and it was ten minutes more before they reached the company-owned house on the outskirts of Kitchenerville.

In the back seat Johnny groaned. Immediately Davy's hand jerked back to the steering-wheel, and Hettie sat up in the seat, straightening her skirt.

'Help me get him inside,' she said, and her voice was shaky and her cheeks flushed. She was no longer angry.

They were both a little tipsy. They had stopped to celebrate Rod's promotion at the Sunnyside Hotel. They had sat side by side in one of the booths, drinking quickly, excitedly, laughing together, sitting close but not touching.

Terry Steyner could not remember when she had last behaved this way. It must have been all of ten years ago, her last term at Cape Town varsity, swigging draught beer in the 'Pig and Whistle' at Randall's Hotel and talking the most inane rubbish. All the matronly dignity that Manfred insisted she maintain was gone, she felt like a freshette on a first date with the captain of the rugby team.

'Let's get out of here,' Rod said suddenly, and she stood up unquestioningly. He took her arm down the stairs, and the light touch of his fingers tingled on her bare skin.

In the Maserati again she experienced the feeling of isolation from reality.

'How often do you see your daughter, Rod?' she asked as he settled into the seat beside her, and he glanced at her, surprised.

'Every Sunday.'

'Tomorrow?'

'Yes.'

'How old is she?'

'Nine next birthday.'

'What do you do with her?'

Rod pressed the starter.

'How do you mean?'

'Where do you take her, what do you do together?'

'We go rowing on Zoo Lake, or eat ice cream sundaes. If it's cold or raining we sit in the apartment and we play mah-jong.' He let in the clutch, and as they pulled away he added, 'She cheats.'

'The apartment?'

'I keep a hideaway in town.'

'Where?'

'I'll show you,' said Rod quietly.

*   *   *

She sat on the studio couch and looked about her with interest. She had not expected the obvious care that he had taken in furnishing the apartment. It was in wheatfield gold, chocolate brown and copper. There was a glorious glowing autumn landscape on the far wall that she recognized as a Dino Paravano.

She noticed a little ruefully how Rod stage-managed the lighting for full romantic effect, and then moved automatically to the liquor cabinet.

'Where is the bathroom?' Terry asked.

'Second left, down the passage.'

She lingered in the bathroom, opening the medicine cabinet like a thief. There were three toothbrushes hanging in the slots, and below them an aerosol can of 'Bidex'. Quickly she shut the cabinet. Feeling disturbed, not sure if it was jealousy or guilt at her own prying.

The bedroom door was open and so she could not help seeing the double bed as she went back to the lounge. She stood in front of the painting.

'I love his work,' she said.

'Not too photographic for your taste?'

'No. I love it.'

He gave her the drink and stood beside her, studying the painting. She tinkled the ice in her glass, and he turned towards her. The feeling of unreality was still holding Terry as she felt him take the glass from her hand.

She was conscious of his hands only, they were strong and very practised. They touched her shoulders, and then moved onto her back calmly. She felt a voluptuous shudder shake her whole body, and then his mouth came down over hers and the sense of unreality was complete. It was all warm and misty, and she let him take control.

She never knew how long afterwards she jerked back to complete, chilling reality. They were on the couch. She lay in his arms. The front of her slack suit was open to the waist and her bra was unhooked. His head was bowed over her and with a handful of his thick springy hair she was directing his lips in their quest. His mouth was warm and sucky on her breast.

'I must be mad!' she gasped, and struggled violently from his arms. She was trembling with fright, horrified with herself. Nothing like this had ever happened to her before.

'This is madness!' Her eyes were great dark pools in her pale face, and her fingers were frantic as she buttoned her blouse. As the last button slipped into its hole, anger replaced her fright.

'How many women have you seduced on that couch, Rodney Ironsides?'

Rod stood up, reaching out a hand to reassure her.

'Don't touch me!' She stepped back. 'I want to go home!'

'I'll take you home, Terry. Just calm down. Nothing happened.'

'That's not your fault,' she blazed.

'No, it's not,' he agreed.

'If you had your way, you'd have —' she bit it off.

'Yes, I would have.' Rod nodded. 'But only if you wanted the same thing.'

She stared at him, starting to recover her temper and her control.

'I shouldn't have come up here, I know. It was asking for trouble, but please take me home now.'

39

The telephone woke Rod. He checked his wrist watch as he tottered naked and half asleep through to the lounge. Eight o'clock.

'Ironsides!' He yawned into the mouthpiece, and then came fully awake as he recognized her voice.

'Good morning, Rodney. How's your hangover?'

He had not expected to hear from her again.

'Just bearable.'

'I called to thank you for an amusing and – instructive evening.'

'Hark at the girl!' He grinned and scratched his chest. 'She changes with the wind. Last night I expected a bullet between the eyes.'

'Last night I got one big fright,' she admitted. 'It comes as a bit of a shock to discover suddenly that you are quite capable of acting the wanton. Not all the names I called you were meant.'

'I am sorry for my contribution to your distress,' Rod said.

'Don't be, you were very impressive.' Then quickly, changing the subject, 'You are picking up your daughter today?'

'Yes.'

'I'd like to meet her.'

'That could be arranged.' Rod was cautious.

'Does she like horses?'

'She's crazy about them.'

'Would you like to take her and me out to my stud farm on the Vaal river?'

Rod hesitated. 'Is it safe? I mean, being seen together?'

'It's my reputation, I'll look after it.'

'Fine!' Rod agreed. 'We'd love to visit your farm.'

'I'll meet you at your apartment. When?'

'Half past nine!'

* * *

Patti was still in her dressing-gown and she offered Rod her cheek casually to be pecked. There were curlers in her hair and from her eyes he could tell she'd had a late night.

'Hello, you're getting thin. Melly is dressing. Do you want some coffee? Your maintenance cheque was late again this month.' And she took a swipe at the spaniel pup as it squatted on the carpet. 'Damn dog pees all over the place. *Melanie.*' She raised her voice. 'Hurry up! Your Papa is here.'

'Hello, Daddy!' Melanie's voice shrieked delightedly from the interior of the apartment.

'Hello, baby.'

'You can't come in, Daddy, I haven't got any clothes on.'

'Well hurry up! I've come a million miles to see you.'

'Not a *million!*' You couldn't fool Melanie Ironsides.

'Did you say you wanted coffee? It's no trouble, it's made already.' Pattie led him through into the sitting-room.

'Thanks.'

'How are things?' she asked as she filled a cup and gave it to him.

'They've made me General Manager of the Sonder Ditch.' He could not prevent himself, it was too good. He had to boast.

Patti looked at him, startled.

'You're joking!' she accused, and then he saw her mind beginning to work like a cash register.

He almost laughed out loud. 'No. It's true.'

'God!' She sat down limply. 'It will nearly *double* your salary.'

He looked at her dispassionately, and not for the first time felt a great wash of relief as he realized he was no longer shackled to her.

'It's usual to offer congratulations,' he prompted her.

'You don't deserve it.' She was angry now. 'You are a selfish, philandering bastard, Rodney Ironsides, you don't deserve the good things that keep happening to you.' He had cheated her. She could have been the General Manager's wife, first lady of the goldfields. Now she was a divorcée, stuck with a miserable four fifty a month. It had seemed good before, but not now.

'I hope you will have enough conscience to make a suitable adjustment for Melanie and me. We are entitled to a share.'

The door burst open and Melanie Ironsides arrived at a gallop to wrap herself around Rod's neck. She had long blonde hair and green eyes.

'I got nine out of ten for spelling!'

'You're not clever, you're a genius. Also you're beautiful.'

'Will you carry me down to the car, Daddy?'

'What's wrong? Your legs in plaster?'

'Please, please, pretty please times three.'

Patti interrupted the love feast.

'Have you got your jersey, young lady?' And Melanie flew.

'I'll have her back before seven,' said Rod.

'You haven't answered my question.' Patti was surly. 'Do we get a share?'

'Yes, of course,' said Rod. 'The same big juicy four fifty you've had all along.'

*   *   *

They had been in Rod's apartment ten minutes when the door-bell announced Terry's arrival. She was in jeans and a checked

shirt with her hair in a plait, and she greeted Rod self-consciously.
When he introduced her to Melanie, she did not look much
older than his daughter.

The two girls summed each other up solemnly. Melanie
suddenly very demure and refined, and Rod was relieved to see
that Terry had the good sense not to gush over the child.

They were in the Maserati and half way to the village of Parys
on the Vaal River before Melanie had completed her microscopic scrutiny of Terry.

'Can I come up front and sit on your lap?' she asked at last.

'Yes, of course.' Terry was hard put to conceal her relief and
pleasure. Melanie scrambled over the seat and settled on Terry's
lap.

'You are pretty,' Melanie gave her considered opinion.

'Thank you. So are you.'

'Are you Daddy's girl friend?' Melanie demanded. Terry
glanced across at Rod, then burst out laughing.

'Almost,' she gurgled, and then all three of them were
laughing.

They laughed often that day. It was a day of sunshine and
laughter.

Terry and Rod walked together with fingers almost touching
through the green paddocks along the willow-lined bank of the
Vaal. Melanie ran ahead of them shrieking with glee at the antics
of the foals.

They went up to the stables where Melanie fed sugar lumps to
a winner of the Cape Metropolitan Handicap and then kissed his
velvety muzzle.

They swam in the pool beside the elegant white-washed homestead, laughter mingling with the splashes, and when they drove
back to Johannesburg in the evening Melanie curled in exhausted slumber on Terry's lap, her head cushioned on Terry's
bosom.

Terry waited in the Maserati while Rod carried the sleeping
child up to her mother, and when he returned and slipped into
the driver's seat, Terry murmured, 'My car is at your apartment.
You'll have to take me with you.'

Neither of them spoke until they were back in Rod's sitting-
room. Then he said, 'Thank you for a wonderful day.' And he
took her to his chest and kissed her.

In the darkness she lay pressed to his sleeping body, clinging to him, as though he might be taken from her. She had never felt such intensity of emotion before, it was a compound of awed wonder and gratitude. She had just been admitted to a new level of human experience she had never suspected existed.

The sheets were still damp. She felt bruised internally, aching, a slow voluptuous pulse of pain that she cherished.

Lightly she touched his body, not wanting to wake him, running her fingertips through the coarse curls that covered his chest, marvelling still at the infinity that separated this from what she had known before.

She shuddered with almost unbearable pleasure as she remembered his voice describing her body to her, making her proud of it for the first time in her life. She remembered the words he had used to tell her exactly what they were doing together, and the feel of his hands, so gentle, sure, so lovingly possessive upon her.

He was so unashamed, taking such obvious joy in her, that the reserves which the barren years of her marriage had placed in her mind were swept away and she was able to go with Rodney Ironsides beyond the storm into that tranquil state where mind and body are completely at peace.

She became aware of him awakening beside her, and she touched his face, his lips and his eyes with her fingertips.

'Thank you,' she whispered, and he seemed to understand, for he took her head and drew it gently down into the hollow of his shoulder.

'Sleep now,' he told her softly, and she closed her eyes and lay very still and quiet beside him, but she did not sleep. She would not miss one moment of this experience.

40

Rod's letter of appointment lay on his desk when he arrived at his office at seven-thirty on the Monday morning.

He sat down and lit a cigarette. Then he began to read it slowly, savouring each word.

'Duly instructed by the Board of Directors,' it began, and ended, 'it remains only to tender the congratulations of the Board, and to voice their confidence in your ability.'

Dimitri came through from his office, distracted.

'Hey! Rod! Christ what a start to the week! We've got a fault in the main high voltage cable on 90 level, and —'

'Don't come squealing to me,' Rod cut him short. 'I'm not the Underground Manager.'

Dimitri gaped at him, taken by surprise.

'What the hell, have they fired you?'

'Next best thing,' said Rod and flipped the letter across the desk. 'Look what the bastards have done to me.'

Dimitri read and then whooped;

'My God, Rod! My God!' He shot down the passage to carry the news to the other line managers. Then they were all in his office, shaking his hand. He judged most of their reactions as favourable, though occasionally he detected a false note. A twinge of envy here, one there who had recently had his ears burned by the Ironsides tongue, and an incompetent who knew his job was now in danger. The phone rang. Rod answered it, his expression changed and he cleared his office with a peremptory wave.

'Hirschfeld here.'

'Morning, Mr Hirschfeld.'

'Well, you've got your chance, Ironsides.'

'I'm grateful for it.'

'I want to see you. I'll give you today to sort yourself out. Tomorrow morning at nine o'clock, my office at Reef Buildings.'

'I'll be there.'

'Good.'

Rod hung up, and the day dissolved into a welter of activity and reorganization, constantly interrupted by a stream of well-wishers. He was still running the Underground Manager's job in addition to the General Manager's. It would be some considerable time before a new Underground Manager was transferred in from one of the other group mines. He was trying to arrange his move to the big office in the main Administrative Block up on the ridge, when he had another visitor, Frank Lemmer's secretary, Miss Lily Jordan, in a severe grey flannel suit looking like a wardress from Ravensbruck.

'Mr Ironsides, you and I have not seen eye to eye in the past.'

This was the understatement of the year. 'It is unlikely that we will in the future. Therefore, I have come to tender my resignation. I have made arrangements.'

The phone rang. Dan Stander's voice, breezy and carefree.

'Rod, I'm in love.'

'Oh Christ, no!' Rod groaned. 'Not this morning.'

'I've got to thank you for introducing me to her. She's the most wonderful —'

'Yeah, yeah!' Rod cut him short. 'Look, Dan, I'm rather busy. Some other time, all right?'

'Oh yes, I forgot. You are the new General Manager they tell me. Congratulations. You can buy me a drink at the Club. Six o'clock.'

'Right. By then I'll need one.' Rod hung up, and faced the hanging-judge expression of Miss Lily Jordan.

'Miss Jordan, in the past our interests have conflicted. In future they will not. You are the best private secretary within a hundred miles of the Sonder Ditch. I need you, the Company needs you.'

That was the magic word. Miss Jordan had twenty-five years' service with the Company. She wavered visibly.

'Please, Miss Jordan, give me a chance.' Shamelessly Rod switched on his most engaging smile. Miss Jordan's femininity was not so completely atrophied that she could resist that smile.

'Very well, then, Mr Ironsides. I'll stay on initially until the end of the month. We'll see after that.' She stood up. 'Now, I'll get your things moved up to the new office.'

'Thank you, Miss Jordan.' With relief he let her take over, and tackled the problems that were piling up on his desk. One man, two jobs. Now he was responsible for surface operation as well as underground. The phone rang, men queued up in the passage, memos kept coming through from Dimitri's office. There was no lunch hour, and by the time she rang he was exhausted.

'Hello,' she said. 'Do I see you tonight?' Her voice was as refreshing as a wet cloth on the brow of a prizefighter between rounds.

'Terry.' He simply spoke her name in reply.

'Yes or no. If it's *no*, I intend jumping off the top of Reef Building.'

'Yes,' he said. 'Pops has summoned me to a meeting at nine

tomorrow morning, so I'll be staying overnight at the apartment. I'll call you as soon as I get in.'

'Goody! Goody!' said she.

*   *   *

At five-thirty Dimitri stuck his head around the door.

'I'm going down to No. 1 shaft to supervise the shoot, Rod.'

'My God, what time is it?' Rod checked his watch. 'So late already.'

'It gets late early around here,' Dimitri agreed. 'I'm off.'

'Wait!' Rod stopped him. 'I'll shoot her.'

'No trouble.' Dimitri demurred. Company standard procedure laid down that each day's blast must be supervised by either the Underground Manager or his Assistant.

'I'll do it,' Rod repeated. Dimitri opened his mouth to protest further, then he saw that expression on Rod's face and changed his mind quickly.

'Okay then. See you tomorrow.' And he was gone.

Rod grinned at his own sentimentality. The Sonder Ditch was his now and, by God, he was going to shoot his own first blast on her.

They were waiting for him at the steel door of the blast control room at the shaft head. It was a small concrete room like a wartime pillbox, and there were only two keys to the door. Dimitri had one, Rod the other.

The duty mine captain and the foreman electrician added their congratulations to the hundreds he had received during the day, and Rod opened the door and they went into the tiny room.

'Check her out,' Rod instructed, and the mine captain began his calls to the shaft overseers at both No. 1 and No. 2 for their confirmation that the workings of the Sonder Ditch were deserted, that every human being who had gone down that morning had come out again this evening.

Meanwhile, the foreman electrician was busy at the electrical control board. He looked up at Rod.

'Ready to close the circuits, Mr Ironsides.'

'Go ahead,' Rod nodded and the man touched a switch. A green light showed up on the board.

'No. 1 north longwall closed and green.'

'Lock her in,' Rod instructed and the electrician touched another switch.

'No.1 east longwall closed and green.'

'Lock her in.'

The green light showed that the firing circuit was intact. A red light would indicate a fault and the faulty circuit would not be locked into the blast pattern.

Circuit after circuit was readied until finally the foreman stood back from the control board.

'All green and locked in.'

Rod glanced at the mine captain.

'All levels clear, Mr Ironsides. She's ready to burn.'

'Cheesa!' said Rod, the traditional command that had come down from the days when each fuse had been individually lit by a hand-held igniter stick.

'Cheesa' was the Bantu word for 'burn'.

The mine captain crossed to the control board and opened the cage that guarded a large red button.

'Cheesa!' echoed the mine captain and hit the button with the heel of his hand.

Immediately the row of green lights on the control board were extinguished, and in their place showed a row of red lights. Every circuit had been broken by the explosions.

The ground under their feet began to tremble. Throughout the workings the shots were firing. In the stopes the head charges fired at the top of the inclines, then in succession the other shots went off behind them. Each charge taking a ten-ton bite of rock and reef out of the face.

At the end of the development drives, a more complicated pattern was shooting. First a row of *cutters* went off down the middle of the oval face. Then the *shoulder charges* at the top corners, followed by the *knee charges* at the bottom corners. A moment's respite with the dust and nitrous fumes swirling back down the drive, then a roar as the *easers* on each side shaped the hole. Another respite and then the *lifters* along the bottom picked up the heap of broken rock and threw it back from the face.

Rod could imagine it clearly. Though no human eye had ever witnessed the blast, he knew exactly what was taking place down there.

The last tremor died away.

'That's it. A full blast,' said the mine captain.

'Thank you.' Rod felt tired suddenly. He wanted that drink, even though their brief exchange that morning had warned him that Dan would probably be insufferable. He could guess the conversation would revolve around Dan's new-found love.

Then he smiled as he thought about what waited for him in Johannesburg later that night, and suddenly he wasn't all that tired.

41

They sat facing each other.

'Only three things worry me,' Terry told Rod.

'What are they?' Rod rubbed soap into the face flannel.

'Firstly, your legs are too long for this bath.'

Rod rearranged his limbs, and Terry shot half out of the water with a squeak.

'Rodney Ironsides, would you be good enough to take a bit more care where you put your toes!'

'Forgive me.' He leaned forward to kiss her. 'Tell me what else worries you.'

'Well, the second thing that worries me is that I'm not worried.'

'What part of Ireland did you say you were from?' Rod asked. 'County Cork?'

'I mean, it's terrible but I'm not even a little conscience-stricken. Once I believed that if it ever happened to me I would never be able to look another human being in the eyes, I'd be so ashamed.' She took the flannel from his hands and began soaping his chest and shoulders. 'But, far from being ashamed, I'd like to stand in the middle of Eloff Street at rush hour and shout "Rodney Ironsides is my lover".'

'Let's drink to that.' Rodney rinsed the soap from his hands and reached over the side of the bath to pick up the two wine glasses from the floor. He gave one to Terry and they clinked them together, the sparkling Cape Burgundy glowed ruby red.

'Rodney Ironsides is my lover!' she toasted him.

'Rodney Ironsides is your lover,' he agreed and they drank.

'Now, I give *you* a toast,' he said.

'What is it?' She held her glass ready, and Rod leaned forward and poured the red wine from the crystal glass between her breasts. It ran like blood down her white skin and he intoned solemnly:

'Bless this ship and all who sail in her!'

Terry gurgled with delight.

'To her Captain. May he keep a firm hand on the rudder!'

'May her bottom never hit the reef!'

'May she be torpedoed regularly!'

'Terry Steyner, you are terrible.'

'Yes, aren't I?' And they drained their glasses.

'Now,' Rod asked, 'what is your third worry?'

'Manfred will be home on Saturday.'

They stopped laughing, Rod reached down for the Burgundy bottle and refilled the glasses.

'We still have five days,' he said.

42

It had been a week of personal triumph for Manfred Steyner. His address to the conference had been the foundation of the entire talks, all discussion had revolved upon it. He had been called upon to speak at the closing banquet which General de Gaulle had attended in person, and afterwards the General had asked Manfred to take coffee and brandy with him in one of the anterooms. The General had been gracious, had asked questions and listened attentively to the answers. Twice he had called his finance minister's attention to Manfred's replies.

Their farewells had been cordial, with a hint of state recognition for Manfred, a decoration. In common with most Germans, Manfred had a weakness for uniforms and decorations. He imagined how a star and ribbon might look on the snowy front of his dress shirt.

There had been a wonderful press both in France and at home. Even a bad-tempered quarter column in *Time* Magazine, with a picture, De Gaulle stooping over the diminutive Manfred solicitously, one hand on his shoulder. The caption read:

'The huntsman and the hawk. To catch a dollar?'

Now standing in the tiny cloakroom in the tail of the South African Airways Boeing, Manfred was whistling softly as he stripped his shirt and vest, crumpled them into a ball and dropped them into the waste bin.

Naked to the waist, he wiped his upper body with a wet cloth and then rubbed 4711 Eau de Cologne into his skin. From the briefcase he took an electric razor. The whistling stopped as he contorted his face for the razor.

Through his mind ran page after page of the report that Andrew had delivered that morning to his hotel room. Manfred had total recall when it came to written material. Although the report was in the briefcase beside him, in his mind's eye he could review it word for word, figure for figure.

It was a stupendous piece of work. How the authors had gained access to the drilling and exploration reports of the five Kitchenerville field companies he could not even guess, for the gold mining companies' security was as tight as that of any national intelligence agency. But the figures were genuine. He had checked those purporting to be from C.R.C. carefully. They were correct. So therefore the other four must also be genuine.

The names of the authors of the report were legend. They were the top men in the field. Their opinions were the best in Harley Street. The conclusion that they reached was completely convincing. In effect it was this:

If a haulage was driven from 66 level of the Sonder Ditch No. 1 shaft through the Big Dipper dyke, it would pass *under* the limestone water-bearing formations, and just beyond the fault it would intersect a reef of almost unbelievable value.

It had not needed the lecture that Manfred had received from his corpulent creditor to show him the possibilities. The man who gave the order to drive through the Big Dipper would receive the credit. He would certainly be elected to the Chairmanship of the Group when that office fell vacant.

There was another possibility. A person who purchased a big packet of Sonder Ditch shares immediately before the reef was intersected would be a very rich man when he came to sell those shares later. He would be so rich that he would no longer be dependent on his wife for the means to live the kind of life he wanted, and indulge his own special tastes.

Manfred blew the hairs from his razor and returned it to his brief case. Then as he took out a fresh shirt and vest, he began to sing the words to the tune:

'Heute ist der schönste Tag
In meinem Leben.'

He would telephone Ironsides from Jan Smuts Airport as soon as he had passed through customs. Ironsides would come up to the house on Sunday morning and receive his orders.

As he knotted the silk of his tie Manfred knew that he stood at the threshold of a whole new world, the events of the next few months would lift him high above the level of ordinary men.

It was the chance for which he had worked and waited all these years.

43

Circumstances had changed completely since his last visit, Rod reflected, as he took the Maserati up the drive towards the Dutch gabled house.

He parked the car and switched off the ignition, sitting a while, reluctant to face the man who had sponsored his career and whom Rod in return had presented with a fine pair of horns.

'Courage, Ironsides!' he muttered and climbed out of the Maserati and went up the path across the lawns.

Terry was on the veranda in a gay print dress, with her hair loose, sprawled in a canvas chair with the Sunday papers scattered about her.

'Good morning, Mr Ironsides,' she greeted him as he came up the steps. 'My husband is in his study. You know the way, don't you?'

'Thank you, Mrs Steyner.' Rod kept his voice friendly but

disinterested, then as he passed her chair he growled softly, 'I could eat you without salt.'

'Don't waste it, you gorgeous beast,' Terry murmured and ran the tip of her tongue over her lips.

Fifteen minutes later, Rod sat stony-faced and internally chilled before Manfred Steyner's desk. When at last he forced himself to speak, it felt as though the skin on his lips would tear with the effort.

'You want me to drive through the Big Dipper,' he croaked.

'More than that, Mr Ironsides. I want you to complete the drive within three months, and I want a complete security blanket on the development,' Manfred told him primly. Despite the fact that it was Sunday he was formally dressed, white shirt and dark suit. 'You will commence the drive from No. 1 shaft 66 level and make an intersect on reef at 6,600 feet with the S.D. No. 3 borehole 250 feet beyond the calculated extremity of the serpentine intrusion of the Big Dipper.'

'No,' Rod shook his head. 'You can't go through that. No one can take the chance. God alone knows what is on the other side, we only know that it is bad ground. Stinking rotten ground.'

'How do you know that?' Manfred asked softly.

'Everybody on the Kitchenerville field knows it.'

'How?'

'Little things.' Rod found it hard to put into words. 'You get a feeling, the signs are there and when you've been in the game long enough you have a sixth sense that warns you when —'

'Nonsense,' Manfred interrupted brusquely. 'We no longer live in the days of witchcraft.'

'Not witchcraft, experience,' Rod snapped angrily. 'You've seen the drilling results from the other side of the fault?'

'Of course,' Manfred nodded. 'S.D. No. 3 found values of thousands of penny-weights.'

'And the other holes went dry and twisted off, or had water squirting out of them like a pissing horse!'

Manfred flushed fiercely. 'You will be good enough not to employ bar-room terminology in this house.'

Rod was taken off balance, and before he could answer Manfred went on.

'Would you put the considered opinions of,' Manfred named three men, 'before your own vague intuitions?'

'They are the best in the business,' Rod conceded reluctantly.

'Read that,' snapped Manfred. He tossed a manila folder onto the desk top, then stood up and went to wash his hands at the concealed basin.

Rod picked up the folder, opened it and was immediately engrossed. Ten minutes later, without looking up from the report, he fumbled a pack of cigarettes from his pocket.

'Please do not smoke!' Manfred stopped him sharply.

Three-quarters of an hour later, Rod closed the folder. During that time Manfred Steyner had sat with reptilian stillness behind his desk, with the glitter of his eyes the only signs of life.

'How the hell did you get hold of those figures and reports?' Rod asked with wonder.

'That does not concern you.' Manfred retrieved the folder from him, his first movement in forty-five minutes.

'So that's it!' muttered Rod. 'The water is in the lime stone near the surface. We go in under it!' He stood up from the chair abruptly and began to pace up and down in front of Manfred's desk.

'Are you convinced?' Manfred asked, and Rod did not answer.

'I have promoted you above older and more experienced men" said Manfred softly. 'If I tear you down again, and tell the world you were not man enough for the job, then, Rodney Ironsides, you are finished. No one else would take a chance on you again, ever!'

It was true. Rod knew it.

'However, if you were to follow my instructions and we intersected this highly enriched reef, then part of the glory would rub off on you.'

That was also true. Rod stopped pacing, he stood with shoulders hunched, in an agony of indecision. Could he trust that report beyond his own deep intuition? When he thought about that ground beyond the dyke, his skin tickled with goose-flesh. He almost had the stink of it in his nostrils. Yet he could be wrong, and the weight of the opposition was heavy. The eminent names on the report, the threats which he knew Manfred would not hesitate to put into effect.

'Will you give me a written instruction?' Rod demanded harshly.

'What effect would that have?' Manfred asked mildly. 'As General Manager, the decision to work certain ground or not to work it is technically yours. In the very unlikely event that you encountered trouble beyond the fault, it would be no defence to produce a written instruction from me. Just as if you murdered my wife you could not defend yourself by producing a written instruction from me to do so.'

This again was true. Rod knew he was trapped. He could refuse, and wreck his career. Or he could comply and take the consequences whatever they may be.

'No,' said Manfred, 'I will not give you a written instruction.'

'You bastard,' Rod said softly.

Manfred answered as gently. 'I warned you that you would not be able to refuse to obey me.'

And the last twinge of remorse that Rod felt for his association with Terry Steyner faded and was gone.

'You've given me three months to hit the Big Dipper. All right, Steyner. You've got it!'

Rod turned on his heel and walked out of the room.

*   *   *

Terry was waiting for him among the protea plants on the bottom lawn. She saw his face and dropped all pretence. She went to meet him.

'Rod, what is it?' Her hand on his arm, looking up into his eyes.

'Careful!' he warned her, and she dropped her hand and stood back.

'What is it?'

'That bloody Gestapo bastard,' Rod snarled, and then, 'I'm sorry, Terry, he's your husband.'

'What has he done?'

'I can't tell you here. When can I see you?'

'I'll find an excuse to get away later today. Wait for me at your apartment.'

Later she sat on the couch below the Paravano painting and listened while he told her about it. All of it, the report, the threat and the order to pierce the Big Dipper.

She listened but expressed neither approval nor disapproval of his decision.

*   *   *

Manfred turned away from the window and went back to his desk. Even at that distance there had been no doubt about his wife's gesture. The hand outstretched, the face turned up, the lips parted in anxious inquiry, and then the guilty start and withdrawal.

He sat down at his desk, and laid his hands neatly in front of him. For the first time he was thinking of Rodney Ironsides as a man and not a tool.

He thought how big he was, tall and as wide across the shoulders as a gallow. Any reprisal on Ironsides could not be physical, and it could not be immediate. It must be after the drive to the Big Dipper.

I can wait, he thought coldly, there is time for everything in this life.

44

Johnny and Davy Delange sat in the two chairs before Rod's desk. They were both awkward and uncomfortable up here in the big office with picture windows looking out over the Kitchenerville valley.

I don't blame them, Rod thought, even I am not accustomed to it yet. Wall-to-wall carpeting, air-conditioning, original paintings on the wood-panelled walls.

'I have sent for you because you two are the best rock breakers on the Sonder Ditch,' Rod began.

'Tin ribs wants something,' thought Davy, with all the suspicion of the union man for management.

'We will now have a few words from our sponsor,' Johnny grinned to himself. 'Before we start the programme.'

Rod looked at their faces and knew exactly what they were thinking. He had been on daily pay himself once. Cut out the compliments, Ironsides – he advised himself – these are two tough cookies and they are not impressed.

'I am pulling you out of the stopes and putting you onto a special development end. You will take it in turns to work day and night shift. You will be directly responsible to me and there will be a security blanket on your activity.'

They watched him without reaction, their expressions guarded. Johnny broke the short silence.

'One end, one blast a day?' He was thinking of his pay. Calculated on the amount of rock broken, he would earn little more than basic salary with a blast on one small face daily.

'No.' Rod shook his head. 'Ultra-fast, multi-blast, and shaft sinkers' rates.'

And both the Delange brothers sat forward in their chairs.

'Multi-blast?' Davy asked. That meant that they could shoot just as soon as they were ready. A good team could blast three – maybe four times a shift.

'Ultra-fast?' Johnny demanded. That was language Johnny understood. It was a term employed only in emergency, as when driving in to rescue trapped men after a fall. It was tacit approval from management to waive standard safety procedure in favour of speed. Christ, Johnny exulted, I can shoot her four – maybe five times a shift.

'Shaft sinkers' rates?' they asked together. That was a 20 per cent bonus on stopers' rates. It was a fortune they were being offered.

Rod nodded affirmative to their questions, and waited for the reaction which he knew would follow. It came immediately.

The Delange brothers now began to look for the catch. They sat stolidly turning the deal over in their minds, like two cautious housewives examining a tomato for blemishes because the price was too cheap.

'How long is this drive?' Johnny asked. If the drive was short, a few hundred feet, then it was worth nothing. They would hardly get into their stride before it was completed.

'Close on six thousand feet,' Rod assured him. They looked relieved.

'Where is it headed?' Davy discovered the rub.

'We are going to drive through the Big Dipper to intersect on reef at 6,000 feet.'

'Jesus!' said Johnny. 'The Big Dipper!' He was awed but unafraid. It excited him, the danger, the challenge. Had he been born earlier, Johnny Delange would have made a fine spitfire pilot.

'The Big Dipper,' Davy murmured, his mind was racing.

Nothing in this world or beyond would entice Davy Delange to drive through the Big Dipper. He had an almost religious fear of it. The name alone conjured up all sorts of hidden menace and unspeakable horror. Water. Gas. Friable ground, faults. Mud-rushes. All a miner's nightmare.

There was no question of him doing it, yet the money was too good to pass up. He could net ten or eleven thousand Rand on those terms.

'All right, Mr Ironsides,' he said. 'I'll take the first night shifts. Johnny can start the day shifts.'

Davy Delange had made his decision. He would work until his drills hit the greenish-black serpentine rock of the dyke. He would then walk out of the drive and quit. He would go up to, but not beyond the dyke.

Afterwards, any of the other mines would snap him up, he had an impeccable record and he would force Johnny to follow him.

'Hey, Davy!' Johnny was delighted, he had expected Davy to turn the deal down flat.

Now he would be able to buy the Mustang for certain – and perhaps an MGB GT for Hettie – and take a holiday to Durban over Christmas, and . . .

Rod was puzzled by Davy's easy agreement. He studied him a moment and decided that he had ferrety eyes. He's a sneaky little bastard, Rod decided, I'll have to watch him.

45

It took one shift only to prepare for the development. Rod selected the starting point. The main haulage curved away from the shaft on 66 level. Three hundred feet along this tunnel there was a chamber that had been cut out as a loco repair station but which was now out of use. Two large batwing ventilation doors were fitted to the opening of the chamber to provide privacy and behind them the chief underground surveyor set up his instruments and marked out the head of the tunnel that would fly arrow straight a mile and more through the living rock to strike through the Big Dipper into the unknown.

The area surrounding the head chamber was roped off and sign-posted with warnings.

'DANGER
INDEPENDENT BLASTING'

The mine captains were instructed to keep their men well away, and all loco traffic was rerouted through a secondary haulage.

On the doors of the chamber another notice was fixed.

'FIERY MINE PROCEDURE IN FORCE
NO NAKED LIGHTS BEYOND THIS POINT.'

Owing to small deposits of coal and other organic substance in the upper stratas of rock, the Sonder Ditch was classed as a fiery mine and subject to the Government legislation covering this subject. No matches, lighters or other spark-generating devices were allowed into a new development end, because the presence of methane gas was always suspected.

Colourless, odourless, tasteless, detectable only by test with a safety lamp, it was a real and terrifying danger. A nine per cent concentration in air was highly explosive. Stringent precautions were taken against accidental triggering of methane that may have oozed out of a fissure or cavity in the rock.

From the main compressed air-pipes running down the corners of the shaft were taken leads to air tanks in the haulage, ensuring that sixty pounds per square inch of pressure was available for the rock drills. Then drills, pinchbars, hammers, shovels, and the other tools were unloaded from the cage at 66 level and stored at the shaft head.

Lastly, explosive was placed in the red lockers at the head of the development, and on the evening of October 23rd 1968, thirty minutes after the main blast, Davy Delange and his gang disembarked from the cage and went to the disused loco shop.

Davy, with the surly little Swazi boss boy beside him, stood before the rock wall on which the surveyor had marked the outline of the tunnel. Behind him his gang had fallen unbidden to their labour, each man knowing exactly what was expected of him.

Already the machine boys and their assistants were lugging their ungainly tools forward.

'You! You! You! You!' Davy indicated to each of them the hole on which he was to begin and then stepped back.

'Shaya!' he commanded. 'Hit it!' And with a fluttering bellow that buffeted the eardrums the drive began.

The drilling ceased and Davy charged the holes. The fuses hung like the tails of white mice from their holes. Each length carefully cut to ensure correct firing sequence.

'Clear the drive!' The boss boy's whistle shrilled, the tramp of heavy boots receded until silence hung heavy in the chemically cleaned air.

'Cheesa!' Davy and the boss boy, with the igniters burning like children's fireworks in their right hands, touched them to the hanging tails until the chamber was lit by the fierce blue light of the burning fuses. The shadows of the two men flickered gigantic and distorted upon the walls.

'All burning. Let's go!' And the two men walked quickly back to where the gang waited along the haulage.

The detonations sucked at their ears, and thrust against their lungs, so that afterwards the silence was stunning.

Davy checked his wristwatch. By law there was a mandatory thirty minutes' wait before anyone could go back to the face. There may be a hang-fire waiting to blow the eyes out of someone's head. Even if there were not, there was still the cloud of poisonous nitrous fumes that would destroy the hair follicles in a man's nostrils and render him still more vulnerable to the fine particles of rock dust that would seek to enter his lungs.

Davy waited those thirty minutes, by which time the ventilation had sucked away the fumes and dust.

Then, alone, he went up the haulage. With him he carried his safety lamp, its tiny blue flame burning behind the screen of fine brass wire mesh. That mesh was flash proof and insulated the flame from any methane in the air.

Standing before the raw circular wound in the rock wall, Davy tested for methane gas. Watching the blue flame for the tell-tale cap. There was no sign of it, and satisfied he extinguished the lamp.

'Boss boy!' he yelled, and the Swazi came up uncoiling the hose behind him.

'Water down!'

Only when the rock face and all the loose rubble below it was glistening and dripping with water was Davy satisfied that the dust was laid sufficiently to bring up his gang.

'Bar boys!' he yelled, and they came up, carrying the twelve-foot long pinchbars, a tool like a giant crowbar.

'Bar down. Make safe!' And the bar boys attacked the bunches of loose rock that were flaking and crumbling from the hanging wall. Two of them manipulating one bar between them, with the steel point striking sparks from the rock. The dislodged fragments rained down, heavily at first and then less and less until the rock above their heads was solid and clean.

Only then did Davy scramble over the pile of rubble to reach the face and begin marking in the shot holes.

Behind him his gang were lashing the stuff into the waiting coco pans, and his machine boys were dragging the drills up to the face.

Davy's gang made three blasts that first night. As he rode up in the cage into a pink, sweet-smelling dawn, Davy was satisfied.

'Perhaps tonight we will get in four blasts,' he thought.

In the Company change house he showered, running the water steaming hot so his skin turned dull angry red, and he worked up a fat white lather of soap suds over his head and at his armpits and crotch.

He rubbed down with a rough thick towel and dressed quickly. Crossing the parking lot to his battered old Ford Anglia he felt happy and good-tired; hungry and ready for bed.

He drove into Kitchenerville at a steady forty miles an hour, and by this time the sun was just showing over the Kraalkop ridge. The dawn was misty rose, with long shadows against the earth, and he thought that this was how it would be in the early mornings on the farm.

On the outskirts of the town Johnny's Monaco roared past him going in the opposite direction. Johnny waved and blew the horn, shouting something that was lost in the howl of wind and motor.

'They'll catch him yet.' Davy shook his head in disapproval. 'The speed limit is forty-five along here.'

He parked the Anglia in the garage and let himself in through the kitchen door. The Bantu maid was busy over the stove.

'Three eggs,' he told her and went through to his bedroom. He shrugged off his jacket and threw it on the bed. Then he returned to the door and glanced quickly up and down the passage. It was deserted, and there was no sound besides the clatter of the maid in the kitchen.

Davy sidled into the passage. The door to Johnny's bedroom was ajar, and Davy moved quietly down to it. His heart was pounding in his throat, his breathing was stifled by his guilt and excitement.

He peered around the edge of the door and gasped aloud. This morning it was better than usual.

Hettie was a sound sleeper. Johnny always maintained it would take a shot of Dynagel to wake her. She never wore night clothes and she never rose before ten-thirty in the morning. She lay on her stomach, hugging a pillow to her chest, her hair a joyous tangle of flaming red against the green sheets. The morning was warm and her blankets had been kicked aside.

Davy stood in the passage. A nerve in his eyelid began to twitch, and under his shirt a drop of perspiration slid from his armpit down along his flank.

On the bed Hettie mumbled unintelligibly in her sleep, drew her knees up and rolled slowly onto her back. One arm came up and flopped limply over her face, her eyes were covered by the crook of her elbow.

She sighed deeply. The twin mounds of her bosom were pulled out of shape by their own weight and the angle of her arm. The hair in her armpit and at the base of her belly was bright shiny red-gold. She was long and smooth and silky white, crowned and tipped with flame.

She moved her body languorously, voluptuously, and then settled once more into slumber.

'Breakfast ready, master,' the maid called from the kitchen. Davy started guiltily, then retreated down the passage.

He found with surprise that he was panting, as though he had run a long way.

46

Johnny Delange leaned against the sidewall of the haulage, his hard helmet tilted at a jaunty angle and a cigarette dangling from his lips.

Down at the face the shots began to fire. Johnny recognized each detonation, and when the last dull jar disrupted the air about them, he pushed himself away from the wall with his shoulder.

'That was the *lifters*,' he announced. 'Come on Big King!'

Not for Johnny Delange a thirty-minute waste of time. As he and Big King set off down the haulage together they were binding scarves over their noses and mouths. Ahead of them a bluey-white fog of dust and fumes filled the tunnel, and Big King had the hose going, using a fine mist spray to absorb the fumes and particles.

They pushed on up to the face, Johnny stooping over the safety lamp. Even he had a healthy respect for methane gas.

'Bar boys!' he bellowed, not waiting for Big King to finish watering down. They came up like ghosts in the fog. Hard behind them the machine boys hovered with their drills.

Taking calculated risks Johnny had his drills roaring forty-five minutes sooner than Davy Delange would have in the same circumstances.

When he came back to the face from cutting fuses and priming his explosives, he found his lashing gang struggling with a massive slab of rock that had been blown intact from the face. Five of them were beating on it with fourteen-pound hammers in an attempt to crack it into manageable pieces. As Johnny reached them, Big King was berating them mercilessly.

'You look like a bunch of virgins grinding millet.'

The hammers clanged and struck sparks from the slab. Sweat oozed from every pore of the hammer boys' skin, greasing their bodies, flying from their heads in sparkling droplets with each blow.

'Shaya!' Big King goaded them on. 'Between you all you wouldn't crack the shell of an egg. Hit it, man! Hit it!'

One by one the men fell back exhausted, their chests heaving, gulping air through gaping mouths, blinded by their own sweat.

'All right,' Johnny intervened. The rock was holding up the whole blast. It warranted drastic measures to break it up.

'I'll pop her,' he said, and any government inspector or mine safety officer would have paled at those words.

'Stand far back and turn your faces away,' Big King instructed his gang. From the forehead of one of his men he took a pair of wire mesh goggles, designed to shield the eyes from flying splinters and rock fragments. He handed them to Johnny who placed them over his eyes.

From the canvas carrying bag he took out a stick of Dynagel. It looked like a candle wrapped in yellow greased paper.

'Give me your knife.' Big King opened a large clasp knife and handed it to Johnny.

Carefully Johnny cut a coin-shaped sliver of explosive from one end of the stick, a piece twice as thick as a penny. He returned the remains of the stick to the bag and handed it to Big King.

'Get back,' he said and Big King moved away.

Johnny eyed the slab of rock thoughtfully and then placed the fragment of Dynagel in the centre of it. He adjusted the goggles over his eyes, and picked up one of the fourteen-pound hammers.

'Turn your eyes away,' he warned and took deliberate aim. Then with a smooth overhead two-handed swing he brought the hammer down on the Dynagel.

The explosion was painful in the confined space of the drive, and afterwards Johnny's ears hummed with it. A tiny drop of blood ran down his cheek from the scratch inflicted by a flying splinter. His wrists ached from the jolt of the hammer in his hands.

'Gwenyama!' grunted Big King in admiration. 'The man is a lion.'

The explosion had cracked the slab into three wedge-shaped segments. Johnny pushed the goggles onto his forehead and wiped the blood from his cheek with the back of his hand.

'Get it the hell out of here,' he grinned, then he turned to Big King.

'Come.' He jerked his head towards the end of the tunnel. 'Help me charge the holes.'

The two of them worked quickly, sliding the sticks of Dynagel into the shot holes and tamping them home with the charging sticks.

For anyone who was not in possession of a blasting licence, to charge up was an offence punishable by a fine of one hundred Rand or two months' imprisonment, or both. Big King had no licence, but his assistance saved fifteen minutes on the operation.

Johnny and his gang blew the face five times that day, but as they rode up in the cage into the cool evening air he was not satisfied.

'Tomorrow we'll shoot her six times,' he told Big King.

'Maybe seven,' said Big King.

*   *   *

Hettie was waiting for him in the lounge when he got home. She flew to him and threw her arms about his neck.

'Did you bring me a present?' she asked with her lips against his ear, and Johnny laughed tantalizingly. It was very seldom that he did not have a gift for her.

'You did!' she exclaimed, and began to run her hands over his pockets.

'There!' She thrust her hand into the inside pocket of his jacket, and brought out the little white jeweller's box.

'Oh!' She opened it, and then her expression changed slightly.

'You don't like them?' Johnny asked anxiously.

'How much did they cost?' she inquired as she examined the porcelain and lacquer earrings, representing two vividly coloured parrots.

'Well,' Johnny looked shamefaced, 'you see, Hettie, it's the end of the month, you see, and well, like I'm a bit short till pay day, you see, so I couldn't —'

'How much?'

'Well, you see,' he took a breath, 'two Rand fifty.'

'Oh,' said Hettie, 'they're nice.' And she promptly lost interest in them. She tossed the box carelessly onto the crowded mantel-piece and set off for the kitchen.

'Hey, Hettie,' Johnny called after her. 'How about we go across to Fochville? There's a dance there tonight. We go and twist, hey?'

Hettie turned back, her expression alive again.

'Gee, yes, man!' she enthused. 'Let's do that. I'll go and change, hey!' And she ran up the passage.

Davy came out of his bedroom, on his way to work.

'Hey, Davy.' Johnny stopped him. 'You got any money on you?'

'Are you broke again?'

'Just 'till pay day.'

'Hell, man, Johnny, you got a cheque for eleven hundred the beginning of the month. You spent it all?'

'Next month,' Johnny winked, 'I'm going to get a cheque for two or three thousand. Then watch me go! Come, Davy, lend me fifty. I'm taking Hettie dancing.'

47

For Rod the days flicked past like telegraph poles viewed from a speeding automobile. Each day he gained confidence in his own ability. He had never doubted that he could handle the underground operation and now he found that he had a firm grasp on the surface as well. He knew that his campaign to reduce working costs was having effect, but its full harvest would only be apparent when the quarterly reports were drafted.

Yet he lay awake in the big Manager's residence on the ridge in which he and his few sticks of furniture seemed lost and lonely, and he worried. There were always myriad nagging little problems, but there were others more serious.

This morning Lily Jordan had come through into his office.

'Mr Innes is coming up to see you at nine.'

'What's he want?' Herbert Innes was the Manager of the Sonder Ditch Reduction works.

'He wouldn't tell me,' Lily answered. The end of the month had come and gone and Lily was still with him. Rod presumed that he had been approved.

Herby Innes, burly and red-faced, sat down and drank the cup of tea that Lily provided, while he regaled Rod with a stroke by stroke account of his Sunday afternoon golf round. Rod interrupted him after he had hit a nine-iron short at the third, and shanked his chip.

'Okay, Herby. What's the problem?'

'We've got a leak, Rod.'

'Bad?'

'Bad enough,' Herby grunted. To him the loss of a single ounce of gold during the process of recovery and refinement was catastrophic.

'What do you reckon?'

'Between the wash and the pour we are losing a couple hundred ounces a week.'

'Yes,' Rod agreed. 'That is bad enough.'

Twenty thousand Rand a month, one hundred twenty thousand a year.

'Have you any ideas?'

'It's been going on for some time, even in Frank Lemmer's day. We have tried everything.'

Rod was a little hazy about the workings of the reduction plant, not that he would admit that, but he was. He knew that the ore was weighted and sampled when it reached the surface, from this a fairly accurate estimate of gold content was made and compared with actual recovery. Any discrepancy had to be investigated and traced.

'What is your recovery rate for the last quarter?'

'Ninety-six point seven-three.'

'That's pretty good,' Rod admitted. It was impossible to recover all the gold in the ore that was surfaced but Herby was getting most of it out. 96.73 per cent of it, to be precise. Which meant that very little of the missing two hundred ounces was being lost into the dumps and the slimes dam.

'I tell you what, Herby,' Rod decided. 'I'll come down to the plant this afternoon. We'll go over it together, perhaps a fresh eye may be able to spot the trouble.'

'May do.' Herby was sceptical. 'We've tried everything else. We are pouring this afternoon. What time shall I expect you?'

'Two o'clock.'

They started at the shaft head, where the ore cage, the copie, arrived at the surface every four minutes with its cargo of rock which it dumped into a concrete shute. Each load was classified as either 'reef' or 'waste'.

The reef was dropped into the massive storage bins, while the waste was carried off on a conveyor to the wash house to be sluiced down before going to the dump. Tiny particles of gold sticking to the waste rock were gathered in this way.

Herby put his lips close to Rod's ear to make himself heard above the rumbling roar of rock rolling down the chute.

'I'm not worried about this end. It's all bulk here and very little shine.' Herby used the reduction plant slang for gold. 'The closer we get to the end, the more dangerous it is.'

Rod nodded and followed Herby down the steel ladder until they reached a door below the storage bins. They went through into a long underground tunnel very similar to the ore tunnel on 100 level.

Again there was a massive conveyor belt moving steadily along the tunnel while ore from the bins above was fed onto it. Rod and Herby walked along beside the belt until it passed under a massive electro magnet. Here they paused for a while. The magnet was extracting from the ore all those pieces of metal which had found their way into the ore passes and bins.

'How much you picking up?' Rod asked.

'Last week fourteen tons,' Herby answered, and taking Rod's arm led him through the door beside them. They were in an open yard that looked like a scrap-metal merchant's premises. A mountain of pinch bars, jumper bits, shovels, steel wire rope, snatch blocks, chain, spanners, fourteen-pound hammers, and other twisted and unrecognizable pieces of metal filled the yard. All of it was rusted, much of it unusable. It had been separated from the ore by the magnet.

Rod's mouth tightened. Here he was presented with indisputable evidence of the carelessness and it-belongs-to-the-company attitude of his men. This pile of scrap represented a waste that would total hundreds of thousands of Rand annually.

'We will see about that!' he muttered.

'If one of those hammers got into my jaw mills it would smash it to pieces,' Herby told him dolefully and led him back into the conveyor tunnel.

The belt angled upwards sharply and they followed the cat-walk beside it. They climbed steadily for five minutes and Herby was puffing like a steam engine. Through the holes in the honey-comb steel plate under his feet, Rod could see that they were now a few hundred feet above ground level.

The conveyor reached the head of a tall tower and dumped its load of ore into the gaping mouths of the screeners. As the rock fell down the tower to ground level again it was sorted for size, and the larger pieces diverted to the jaw crushers which chewed it into fist-size bites.

'See anything?' Herby asked, barely concealing the sarcasm.

Rod grinned at him.

They climbed down the steel ladders that seemed endless. The screeners rattling and the crushers hammering, until Rod's eardrums pleaded for mercy.

At last they reached ground level and went through into the mill room. This was a cavernous galvanized-iron shed the size of a large aircraft hangar. At least one hundred yards long and fifty feet high, it was filled with long rows of the cylindrical tube mills.

Forty of them in all, they were as thick as the boiler of a steam locomotive and about twice as long. Into one end of them was fed the ore which had been reduced in size by the jaw crushers. The tube mills revolved and the loose steel balls within them pounded the rock to powder.

If the noise before had been bad, it was hideous in the mill room. Rod and Herby made no effort to speak to each other until they had walked through into the comparative quiet of the first heavy-media separator room.

'Now,' Herby explained. 'This is where we start worrying.' He indicated the rows of pale blue six-inch piping that came through the wall from the mill room.

'In there is the powdered rock mixed with water to a smooth flowing paste. About forty per cent of the gold is free.'

'No one can get into those pipes and you've checked for any possible leak?' Rod asked. Herby nodded.

'But,' he said, 'have a look here!'

Along the far wall was a series of cages. They were made of heavy steel mesh, the perforations would not allow a man's finger through. The heavy steel doors were barred and locked. Outside each battery of cages stood a Bantu attendant in clean white overalls. They were all concentrating on the manipulation of the turncock that obviously regulated the flow of the powdered ore through the pipes.

Herby stopped at one of the cages.

'Shine!' he pointed. Beyond the heavy guard screen the grey paste of rock powder was flowing from a series of nozzles over an inclined black rubber sheet. The surface of the rubber sheet was deeply corrugated, and in each corrugation the free gold was collecting, held there by its own weight. The gold was thick as butter in a Dagwood sandwich, greasy yellow-looking in the folds of rubber.

Rod laid hold of the steel screen and shook it.

'No,' Herby laughed. 'No one will get in that way.'

'How do you clean the gold off that sheet? Does someone have access to the separator?' Rod asked.

'The separator cleans itself automatically,' Herby answered. 'Look!'

Rod noticed for the first time that the rubber sheet was moving very slowly, it was also an endless belt running round two rollers. As the belt inverted, so fine jets of water washed the gold from the corrugations into a collection tank.

'I'm the only one who has access. We change the collection tanks daily,' said Herby.

It looked foolproof, Rod had to admit.

Rod turned and glanced down the row of four Bantu attendants. They were all intent on their duties, and Rod knew that each of them had a high security rating. They had been carefully selected and screened before being allowed into the reduction works.

'Satisfied?' Herby asked.

'Okay,' Rod nodded, and the two of them went out through the door in the far wall. Locking it behind them.

*   *   *

Immediately they had gone the four Bantu attendants reacted. They straightened up, the scowls of concentration smoothed out to be replaced by grins of relief. One made a remark and they all laughed, and opened the waist bands of their tunics. From inside each trouser leg they drew a length of quarter-inch copper wire and began probing them through the steel screen.

It had taken Crooked Leg, the photographer, almost a year to work out a means of milking gold from the heavily screened and guarded separators. The method which he had discovered was, like all workable plans, extremely simple.

Mercury, quicksilver, absorbs gold the way blotting paper sucks up moisture. It will suck in any speck of gold that comes in contact with it. Mercury has a further property, it can be made to spread on copper like butter on bread. This layer of mercury on copper retains its powers of absorbing gold.

Crooked Leg had devised the idea of coating lengths of copper wire with mercury. The wire could be inserted through the apertures in the steel mesh and the wire laid across the corrugated rubber sheet, where it set about mopping up every speck of gold that flowed over it. The lengths of wire could be quickly slipped down the trouser leg at the approach of an official, and they could be smuggled in and out of the reduction works the same way.

Every evening Crooked Leg retrieved the gold-thickened wire, and issued his four accomplices with newly coated lengths. Every night in the abandoned workings beyond the ridge he boiled the mercury to make it release its gold.

*   *   *

'Now,' Herby could speak normally in the blessed quiet of the cyanide plant, 'we have skimmed off the free gold – and we are left with the sulphide gold.' He offered Rod a cigarette as they made their way between the massive steel tanks that spread over many acres. 'We pump this into the tanks and add cyanide. The cyanide dissolves the gold and takes it into solution. We tap it off and run it through zinc powder. The gold is deposited on the zinc, we burn away the zinc and we are left with the gold.'

Rod lit his cigarette. He knew all this but Herby was giving him a Cooks' tour for visiting V.I.P.s. He flicked his lighter for Herby. 'There is no way anyone could swipe it when it's in solution.'

Herby shook his head, exhaling smoke. 'Apart from anything else, cyanide is a deadly poison.' He glanced at his watch. 'Three-twenty, they'll be pouring now. Shall we go across to the smelt house?'

The smelt house was the only brick building among all the galvanized iron. It stood a little isolated. Its windows were high up and heavily barred.

At the steel door Herby buzzed, and a peephole opened in the door. He and Rod were immediately recognized and the door swung open. They were in a cage of bars which could only be opened once the door was closed behind them.

'Afternoon, Mr Ironsides, Mr Innes.' The guard was apologetic. 'Would you sign, please?' He was a retired policeman with a paunch and a holstered revolver on his hip.

They signed and the guard signalled to his mate on the steel catwalk high above the smelt room floor. This guard tucked his pump action shotgun under one arm, and threw the switch on the walk beside him.

The cage door opened and they went through.

Along the far wall the electric furnaces were set into the brickwork. They resembled the doors of the bread ovens in a bakery.

The concrete floor of the room was uncluttered, except for the mechanical loader that carried the gold crucible in its steel arms, and the moulds before it. The half dozen personnel of the smelt house barely looked up as Rod and Herby approached.

The pour was well advanced, the arms of the loader tilted and a thin stream of molten gold issued from the spout of the crucible, and fell into the mould. The gold hissed and smoked and crackled, and tiny red and blue sparks twinkled on its surface as it cooled.

Already forty or fifty bars were laid out on the rubber-wheeled trolley beside the mould. Each bar was a little smaller than a cigar box. It had the knobby bumpy look of roughly cast metal.

Rod stopped and touched one of the bars. It was still hot and it had the slightly greasy feeling that new gold always has.

'How much?' he asked Herby, and Herby shrugged.

'About a million Rand's worth, perhaps a little more.'

So that's what a million Rand looks like, Rod mused, it's not very impressive.

'What's the procedure now?' Rod asked.

'We weigh it, and stamp the weight and batch number into each bar.' He pointed to a massive circular safe deposit door in the near wall. 'It's stored there over-night, and tomorrow a refinery armoured car will come out from Johannesburg and pick it up.' Herby led the way out of the smelt house. 'Anyway, that's not the trouble. Our leak is sucking off the shine before it ever reaches the smelt house.'

'Let me think about it for a few days,' Rod said. 'Then we'll get together again, try and find the solution.'

*　　*　　*

He was still thinking about it now. Lying in the darkness and smoking cigarette after cigarette.

There seemed to be only one solution. They would have to plant Bantu police in the reduction works.

It was an endless game involving all the mining companies and their reduction plant personnel. An inventive mind would devise a new system of sucking off the shine. The Company would become aware of the activity by comparison of estimated and actual recovery and they would work on the leak for a week, a month, sometimes a year. Then they would break the system. There would be prosecutions, stiff gaol sentences, and the Company would circularize its neighbours, and they would all settle back and wait for the next customer to appear.

Gold has many remarkable properties, its weight, its non-corruptibility and, not least, the greed and lust it conjures up in the hearts of men.

Rod stubbed his cigarette, rolled onto his side and pulled the bed-clothes up over his shoulders. His last thought before sleep was for the major problem that, these days, was never very far from the surface of his mind.

The Delange brothers had driven almost fifteen hundred feet in two weeks. At this rate they would hit the Big Dipper seven weeks from now, then even the theft of gold would pale into insignificance.

48

At the time that Rod Ironsides was composing himself for sleep, Big King was taking a little wine with his business associate and tribal brother Philemon N'gabai, alias Crooked Leg.

They sat facing each other in a pair of dilapidated cane chairs with a lantern and a gallon jug of Jeripigo set between them. The bat stench of the abandoned workings did little to bring out the bouquet of the wine, which was of small concern to either man, for they were drinking not for taste but for effect.

Crooked Leg refilled the cheap glass tumbler that Big King

proffered, and as the wine glug-glugged from the jar he continued his attack on the character and moral fibre of José Almeida, the Portuguese.

'For many months now I have had it in my heart to speak to you of these matters,' he told Big King, 'but I have waited until I could set a deadfall for the man. He is like a lion that preys upon our herds, we hear him roar in the night and in the dawn we see his spoor in the earth about the carcasses of our animals, but we cannot meet him face to face.'

Big King enjoyed listening to the oratory of Crooked Leg and while he listened he drank the Jeripigo as though it were water, and Crooked Leg kept refilling the tumbler for him.

'In counsel with myself I spoke thus: "Philemon N'gabai, it is not enough that thou should suspect this white man. It is necessary also that you see with your own eyes that he is eating your substance".'

'How, Crooked Leg?' Big King's voice was thickening, the level of the jug had fallen steadily and now showed less than half. 'Tell me how we shall take this man.' Big King showed a fist the size of a bunch of bananas. 'I will . . .'

'No, Big King.' Crooked Leg was scandalized. 'You must not hurt the man. How then would we sell our gold? We must prove he is cheating us and show him we know it. Then we will proceed as ever, but he will give us full measure in the future.'

Big King thought about that for some time, then at last he sighed regretfully. 'You are right, Crooked Leg. Still, I would have liked to . . .' He showed that fist again, and Crooked Leg went on hurriedly.

'Therefore, I have sent to my brother who drives a delivery van for S.A. Scale Company in Johannesburg, and he has taken from his Company a carefully measured weight of eight ounces.' Crooked Leg produced the cylindrical metal weight from his pocket and handed it to Big King who examined it with interest. 'Tonight, after the Portuguese has weighed the gold you take to him, you will say, "Now, my friend, please weigh this for me on your scale," and you will watch to see that his scale reads the correct number. Each time in the future he will weigh this on his scale before we sell our gold.'

'Hau!' Big King chuckled. 'You are a crafty one, Crooked Leg.'

* * *

Big King's eyes were smoky and blood-shot. The Jeripigo was a raw rough fortified wine, and he had drunk very nearly a gallon of it. He sat opposite the Portuguese store-keeper in the back room behind the concession store, and watched while he poured the gold dust into the pan of the jeweller's scale. It made a yellow pyramid that shone dully in the light from the single bare bulb above their heads.

'One hundred and twenty-three ounces.' Almeida looked up at Big King for confirmation, a strand of greasy black hair hung onto his forehead. His face was pale from lack of sun so that the blue stubble of beard was in heavy contrast.

'That is right,' Big King nodded. He could taste the liquor fumes in the back of his throat, and they were as strong as his distaste for the man who sat opposite him. He belched.

Almeida removed the pan from the scale and carefully poured the dust back into the screw top bottle.

'I will get the money.' He half rose from his chair.

'Wait!' said Big King, and the Portuguese looked at him in mild surprise.

Big King took the weight from the pocket of his jacket. He placed it on the desk.

'Weigh that on your scale,' he said in Portuguese.

Almeida's eyes flicked down to the weight, and then back to Big King's face. He sank back into his seat, and pushed the strand of hair off his forehead. He began to speak, but his voice cracked and he cleared his throat.

'Why? Is there something wrong?' Suddenly he was aware of the size of the man opposite him. He could smell the liquor on his breath.

'Weigh it!' Big King's voice was flat, without rancour. His face was expressionless, but the smoky red glare of his eyes was murderous.

Suddenly Almeida was afraid, deadly, coldly afraid. He could guess what would happen once the error in his balance was disclosed.

'Very well,' he said, and his voice was forced and off key. The pistol was in the drawer beside his right knee. It was loaded, with a cartridge under the hammer. The safety-catch was on, but that would only delay him an instant. He knew it would not be necessary to fire, once he had the weapon in his hand he would have control of the situation again.

If he did have to fire, the calibre was .45 and the heavy slug would stop even a giant like this Bantu. *Self defence*, he was working it out feverishly. *A burglar*, I surprised him and he attacked. *Self defence*. It would work. They'd believe it.

But how to get the pistol? Try and sneak it out of the drawer, or make a grab for it?

There was a desk between them, it would take a few seconds for the Bantu to realize what he was doing, a few more for him to get around the desk. He would have plenty of time.

He snatched the handle of the drawer, and it flew open. His fingernails scrabbled against the wood work as he clawed for the big black U.S. Navy automatic, and with a surge of triumph his hand closed over the butt.

Big King came over the top of the desk like a black avalanche. The scale and the jar of gold dust was swept aside to clatter and shatter against the floor.

Still seated in his chair, with the pistol in his hand, Almeida was borne over backwards with Big King on top of him. Many years before, Big King had worked with a safari outfit in Portuguese East Africa, and he had seen the effect of gunshot wounds in the flesh of dead animals.

In the instant that he had recognized the weapon in Almeida's hand, he had been as afraid as the Portuguese. Fear had triggered the speed of his reaction, it was responsible for the savagery of his attack as he lay over the struggling body of the Portuguese.

He had Almeida's pistol hand held by the wrist and he was shaking it to force him to drop the firearm. With his right hand he had the Portuguese by the throat, and instinctively he was applying the full strength of his arms to both grips. He felt something break under his right hand, cracking like the kernel of a nut, and his fingers locked deeper into the quivering flesh. The pistol flew from fingers that were suddenly without strength, and skittered across the floor to come up against the far wall with a thump.

Only then did Big King begin to regain the sanity that fear had scattered. Suddenly he realized that the Portuguese was lying quietly under him. He released his grip and scrambled to his knees. The Portuguese was dead. His neck was twisted away from his shoulders at an impossible angle. His eyes were wide and surprised, and a smear of blood issued from one nostril over his upper lip.

Big King backed away towards the door, his gaze fixed in horror on the sprawling corpse. When he reached the door, he hesitated, fighting down the urge to run. He subdued it, and went back to kneel beside the desk. First he picked up the controversial cylindrical weight and placed it in his pocket, then he began sweeping up the scattered gold dust and the shattered fragments of the screw-topped container. He placed them into separate envelopes that he found among the papers on the desk. Ten minutes later he slipped out through the back door of the concession store, into the night.

49

At the time Big King was hurrying back towards the mine hostel, Rod Ironsides thrashed restlessly in a bed in which the sheets were already bunched and damp with sweat. He was imprisoned in his own fantasy, locked in a nightmare from which he could not break away. The nightmare was infinite and green, quivering, unearthly, translucent. He knew it was held back only by a transparent barrier of glass. He cowered before it, and he knew it was icy cold, he could see light shining through it, and he was deadly afraid.

Suddenly there was a crack in the glass wall, a hairline crack, and through it oozed a single drop. A large, pear-shaped drop, as perfect as though it had been painted by Tretchikoff. It glittered like a gemstone.

It was the most terrifying thing that Rod had ever seen in his life. He cried out in his sleep, trying to warn them, but the crack starred further, and the drop slid down the glass, to be followed by another and another. Suddenly a jagged slab of glass exploded out of the wall, and Rod screamed as the water burst through, in a frothing jet.

With a roar the entire glass wall collapsed, and a mountain high wave of green water hissed down upon him, carrying a white plume of spray at its crest.

He awoke sitting upright in his bed, a cry of horror on his

lips and his body bathed in sweat. It took minutes for him to steady the wild racing of his heart. Then he went through to the bathroom. He ran a glass of water and held it up to the light. 'Water. It's there!' he muttered. 'I know it's there!' He drank from the tumbler.

Standing naked, with his sweat drying cold on his body, the tumbler held to his lips, the idea came to him. He had never heard of anyone trying it before, but then nobody he knew would be crazy enough to drive into a death trap like the Big Dipper.

'I'll drill and charge a matt of explosive into the hanging wall of the drive. I'll get the Delange boys on to it right away. Then at any time I choose I can blast the whole bloody roof in and seal off the tunnel.'

Rod was surprised at the strength of the relief that flooded over him. He knew then how it had been worrying him. He went back to the bedroom and straightened out his bedclothes. However, sleep would not come easily to him. His imagination was overheated, and a series of events and ideas kept playing through his mind, until abruptly he was presented with the image of Terry Steyner.

He had not seen her for almost two weeks, not since Manfred Steyner's return from Europe. He had spoken to her twice on the telephone, hasty, confused conversations that left him feeling dissatisfied. He was increasingly aware that he was missing her. His one attempt to find solace elsewhere had been a miserable failure. He had lost interest half way through the approach manoeuvres and had returned the young lady to the bosom of her family at the unheard of hour of eleven o'clock on a Saturday night.

Only the unremitting demands of his new job had prevented him from slipping away to Johannesburg and taking a risk.

'You know, Ironsides, you'd better start bracing up a little, don't lose your head over this woman. Remember our vow – *Never Again!*'

He punched the pillow into shape and settled into it.

* * *

Terry lay quietly, waiting for it. It was after one o'clock in the morning. It was one of those nights. He would come soon now. As never before she was filled with dread. A cold slimy feeling in the pit of her stomach. Yet she had been fortunate. He had not been near her since his return from Paris. Over two weeks, but it could not last. Tonight.

She heard the sound of the car coming up the drive and she felt physically ill. I can't do it, she decided, not any more, not ever again. It wasn't meant to be like this, I know that now. It's not dirty and furtive and horrible, it's like . . . like . . . it's the way Rod makes it.

She heard him in his bedroom, suddenly she sat up in bed. She felt desperate, hunted.

The door of her room opened softly.

'Manfred?' she asked sharply.

'It's me. Don't worry.' He came briskly towards her bed, a dark impersonal shape and he was undoing the cord of his dressing-gown.

'Manfred,' Terry blurted, 'I'm early this month, I'm sorry.'

He stopped. She saw his hands fall back to his sides, and he stood completely still.

'Oh!' he said at last, and she heard him shuffle his feet into the thick pile of the carpet. 'I just came to tell you,' he hesitated, seeking an excuse for his visit, 'that . . . that I'll be going away for five days. Leaving on Friday. I have to go to Durban and Cape Town.'

'I'll pack for you,' she said.

'What? Oh, yes – thank you.' He shuffled his feet again. 'Well, then.' He hesitated, then stooped quickly and brushed her cheek with his lips. 'Good night, Theresa.'

'Good night, Manfred.'

Five days, she lay alone in the darkness and gloated. *Five whole days alone with Rod.*

50

Detective Inspector Hannes Grobbelaar of the South African Criminal Investigation Department sat on the edge of the office chair with his hat tipped onto the back of his head and spoke into the telephone, which he held in a handkerchief-covered hand. He was a tall man with a long sad face and a mournful looking moustache that was streaked with grey.

'Gold buying,' he said into the receiver, and then in reply to the obvious question. 'There's gold dust spilled all over the place and a jeweller's scale, and a .45 automatic with a full magazine and the safety-catch still on, dead man's prints on it.' He listened. 'Ja. Ja. All right, ja. Broken neck, looks like.' Inspector Grobbelaar swivelled his chair and looked down at the corpse that lay on the floor beside him. 'Bit of blood on his lip, but nothing else.'

One of the finger-print men came to the desk and Grobbelaar stood up to give him room to work, the receiver still held to his ear.

'Prints?' he asked in disgust. 'There are finger prints on everything, we have isolated at least forty separate sets so far.' He listened a few seconds. 'No, we will get him, all right. It must be a Bantu mine worker and we have got all the finger prints of the men from outside the Republic. It's just a matter of checking them all out and then questioning. Ja, we'll have him within a month, that's for sure! I'll be back at John Vorster Square about five o'clock, just as soon as we finish up here.' He hung up the receiver, and stood looking down at the murdered man.

'Ugly bastard,' said Sergeant Hugo beside him. 'Asked for it, buying gold. It's as bad as diamonds.' He drew attention to the large envelope he carried in his hand. 'I've got a whole lot of glass fragments. Looks like the container the gold was in. The murderer tried to clean up, but he didn't make a very good job. These were under the desk.'

'Prints?'

'Only one piece big enough. It's got a smeary print on it. Might be of use.'

'Good,' Grobbelaar nodded. 'Get cracking on that, then.'

There was a feminine wail from somewhere in the interior of the building, and Hugo grimaced.

'There she starts again. Hell, I thought she'd exhausted herself. Bloody Portuguese women are the end.'

'You should hear them having a baby,' grunted Grobbelaar.

'Where did you hear one?'

'There was one in the ward next door to my old girl at the maternity home. She nearly brought the bloody roof down.'

Grobbelaar's moustache took on a more melancholy droop as he thought about the work that lay ahead. Hours, days, weeks of questioning and checking and cross-checking, with a succession of sullen and uncooperative suspects.

He sighed and jerked a thumb at the corpse. 'All right, we've finished with him. Tell the butcher boys to come and fetch him.'

51

It had taken Rod almost two days to design his drop-blast matt. The angle and depth of the shot holes were carefully placed to achieve maximum disruption of the hanging wall. In addition he had decided to drill and charge the side walls of the drive with charges timed to explode *after* the hanging wall had collapsed. This would kick in on the rubble filling the tunnel and jam it solid.

Rod was fully aware of the power of water under pressures of 2,000 pounds per square inch and more and he had decided it was necessary to block at least three hundred feet of the tunnel. His matt blast was designed to do so, and yet he knew that this would not seal off the water completely. It would, however, reduce the flow sufficiently to allow cementation crews to get in and plug the drive solid.

The Delange brothers did not share Rod's enthusiasm for the project.

'Hey man, that's going to take three or four days to drill and charge,' Johnny protested when Rod showed him his carefully drawn plan.

'Like hell it will,' Rod growled at him. 'I want it done properly. It will take at least a week.'

'You said ultra fast. You didn't say nothing about drilling the hanging wall with more holes than a cheese!'

'Well, I'm saying it now,' Rod told him grimly. 'And I'm also saying that you will drill, but you won't charge the holes until I come down and make sure that you've gone in as deep as I want them.'

He didn't trust either Johnny or Davy to spend time drilling in twenty feet, when he could go in six feet, charge up and nobody would know the difference. Not until it was too late.

Davy Delange spoke for the first time.

'Will you credit us bonus fathomage while we fiddle around with this?' he asked.

'Four fathoms a shift.' Rod agreed to pay them for the removal of fictitious rock.

'Eight?' said Davy.

'Hell, no!' Rod exclaimed. That was robbery.

'I don't know,' Davy murmured, watching Rod with sly ferrety little eyes. 'Maybe I should talk to Brother Duivenhage, you know, ask his advice.'

Duivenhage was No. 1 shaft shop steward for the Mine Workers' Union. He had driven Frank Lemmer to the edge of a nervous breakdown and was now starting on Rodney Ironsides. Rod was pleading with Head Office to offer Duivenhage a fat job in management to get him out of the way. The last thing in the world that Rod wanted was Brother Duivenhage snooping around his drive on the Big Dipper.

'Six,' he said.

'Well . . .' Davy hesitated.

'Six is fair, Davy,' Johnny interrupted, and Davy glared at him. Johnny had snatched complete victory from his grasp.

'Good, that's agreed.' Quickly Rod closed the negotiations. 'You'll start drilling the matt right away.'

*   *   *

Rod's design demanded nearly twelve hundred shot holes to be filled with two and a half tons of explosive. It was a thousand feet down the drive from the main haulage on 66 level to where the matt began.

The drive now was a spacious, well lit and freshly ventilated tunnel, with the vent piping, the compressed air pipe, and the electrical cable bolted into the hanging wall, and a set of steel railway tracks laid along the floor.

All work on the face ceased while the Delange brothers set about drilling the matt. It was light work that demanded little from the men. As each hole was drilled, Davy would insert his charging rod to check the depth and then plug the entrance with a wad of paper. There was much time for drinking Thermos coffee and for thinking.

There were three subjects that endlessly occupied Davy's mind as he sat at ease, waiting for the completion of the next shot hole. Sometimes for half an hour at a time Davy would hold the image of that fifty thousand Rand in his mind. It was his, tax paid, painstakingly accumulated over the years and lovingly deposited with the local branch of the Johannesburg Building Society. He imagined it bundled and stacked in neat green piles in the Society's vault. Each bundle was labelled 'David Delange'.

Then his imagination would pass automatically on to the farm that the money would buy. He saw how it would be in the evenings when he sat on the wide stoep, with the setting sun striking the peaks of the Swart Berg across the valley, and the cattle coming in from the paddocks towards the homestead.

Always there was a woman sitting beside him on the stoep. The woman had red hair.

*   *   *

On the fifth morning Davy drove home in the dawn, he was not tired. The night's labours had been easy and unexacting.

The door of Johnny and Hettie's bedroom was closed. Davy read the newspapers with his breakfast, as always the cartoon strip adventures of Modesty Blaise and Willie Garvin intrigued him completely. This morning Modesty was depicted in a bikini and Davy studied her comparing her to the big healthy body of his brother's wife. The thought of her stayed with him as he rolled into his bed, and he lay unsleeping, daydreaming an adventure in which Modesty Blaise had become Hettie, and Willie Garvin was Davy.

An hour later he was still awake. He sat up and reached for the towel which lay across the foot of his bed. He wrapped the towel around his waist as he went down the passage to the bathroom. As he reached for the handle of the bathroom door, it opened under his hand and he was face to face with Hettie Delange.

She wore a white lace dressing-gown with ostrich-feather mules on her feet. Her face was innocent of make-up and she had brushed her hair and tied it with a ribbon.

'Oh!' she gasped with surprise. 'You gave me a fright, man.'

146

'I'm sorry, hey.' Davy grinned at her, holding the towel with one hand. Hettie let her eyes run quickly over his naked upper body.

Davy was muscled like a prize fighter. His chest hair was crisp and curly. On both arms the tattoos drew attention to the thickness and weight of muscle.

'Gee, you *are* built,' Hettie murmured in admiration, and Davy sucked in his belly reflexively.

'You think so?' His grin was self-conscious now.

'Yes.' Hettie leaned forward and touched his arm. 'It's hard too!'

The movement had allowed the front of her dressing-gown to gape open. Davy's face flushed as he looked down into the opening. He started to say something, but his voice had dried up on him. Hettie's fingers stroked down his arm, and she was watching the direction of his eyes. Slowly she moved closer to him.

'Do you like me, Davy?' she asked, her voice throaty and low, and with an animal cry Davy attacked her.

His hands ripping at the opening of her gown, pinning her to the wall of the bathroom with his mouth frantically hunting hers. His body pressing hard and urgent, his eyes wild, his breathing ragged.

Hettie was laughing, a breathless gasping laugh.

This was what she loved. When they lost their heads, when they went mad for her.

'Davy,' she said, jerking loose his towel. 'Davy.'

She kept wriggling away from his thrusting hips, knowing that it would inflame him further. His hands were tearing at her body, his eyes were maniacal.

'Yes!' she hissed into his mouth. He threw her off balance and she slid down the wall onto the floor.

'Wait,' she panted. 'Not here – the bedroom.'

But it was too late.

*   *   *

Davy had spent the afternoon locked in his bedroom, lying on his bed in an agony of black all-pervading remorse and guilt.

'My brother,' he kept repeating. 'Johnny is my brother.'

Once he wept, each sob tearing something in his chest. The

tears squeezed out between burning eyelids, leaving him feeling exhausted and weak.

'My *own* brother,' he shook his head slowly in horrified disbelief. 'I cannot stay here,' he decided miserably. 'I'll have to go.'

He went to the washbasin and washed his eyes. Stooping over the basin, water still dripping from his face, he decided.

'I will have to tell him.' The burden of guilt was too heavy. 'I'll write to Johnny. I'll write it all, and then I'll go away.'

Frantically he searched for pen and paper, it was almost as though he could wipe away the deed by writing it down. He sat at the table by the window and wrote slowly and laboriously. When he had finished it was three o'clock. He felt better.

He sealed the four closely written pages into an envelope and slipped it into the inside pocket of his jacket. He dressed quickly, and crept out of the house, fearful of meeting Hettie, but she was nowhere about. Her big white Monaco was not in the garage, and with relief he turned out of the driveway and took the road out to the Sonder Ditch. He wanted to reach the mine before Johnny came off shift.

Davy listened to his brother's voice, as he kidded and laughed with the other off-duty miners in the company change house. He had locked himself in one of the lavatory closets to avoid meeting his brother, and he sat disconsolately on the toilet seat. The sound of Johnny's voice brought his guilt flooding back in its full strength. His letter of confession was buttoned into the top pocket of his overalls, and he took it out, broke open the flap and reread the contents.

'So long, then.' Johnny's voice sang out gaily from the change room. 'See you bastards tomorrow.'

There was an answering chorus from the other miners, then the door slammed.

Davy went on sitting alone for another twenty minutes in the stench of stale bodies and urine, dirty socks and rank disinfections from the foot baths. At last he tucked the letter away in his pocket and opened the closet door.

*   *   *

Davy's gang were at their waiting place at the head of the drive. They were sitting along the bench laughing and chatting.

There was a holiday spirit amongst them for they knew it would be another shift of easy going.

They greeted Davy cheerfully, as he came down the haulage. Both the Delange brothers were popular with their gangs and it was unusual that Davy did not reply to the chorused greeting. He did not even smile.

The Swazi boss boy handed him the safety lamp, and Davy grunted an acknowledgement. He set off alone down the tunnel, trudging heavily, not conscious of his surroundings, his mind encased in a padding of guilt and self-pity.

A thousand feet along the drive he reached the day's work area. Johnny's shift had left the rock drills in place, still connected to the compressed air system, ready for use. Davy came to a halt in the centre of the work area, and without a conscious command from his brain his hands began the routine process of striking the wick of the safety lamp.

The little blue flame came alight behind the protective screen of wire mesh, and Davy held the lamp at eye level before him and walked slowly along the drive. His eyes were watching the flame without seeing it.

The air in the tunnel was cool and refrigerated, scrubbed and filtered, there was no odour nor taste to it. Davy walked on somnambulantly. He was wallowing in self-pity now. He saw himself in a semi-heroic role, one of the great lovers of history caught up in tragic circumstances. His brain was fully occupied with the picture. His eyes were unseeing. Blindly he performed the ritual that a thousand times before had begun the day's shift.

Slowly in its wire mesh cage the blue flame of the safety lamp changed shape. Its crest flattened, and there formed above it a ghostly pale line. Davy's eyes saw it, but his brain refused to accept the message. He walked on in a stupor of guilt and self-pity.

That line above the flame was called 'the cap', it signified that there was at least a five per cent concentration of methane gas in the air. The last shot hole that Johnny Delange's gang had drilled before going off shift, had bored into a methane-filled fissure. For the previous three hours, gas had been blowing out of that hole. The ventilation system was unable to wash the air fast enough and now the gas had spread slowly down the drive. The air surrounding Davy's body was heavy with gas, he had breathed it into his lungs. It needed just one spark to ignite it.

Davy reached the end of the drive and snapped the snuffer over the wick, extinguishing the flame in the lamp.

'All safe,' he muttered, not realizing that he had spoken. He went back to his waiting men.

'All safe,' he repeated, and with the Swazi boss boy leading them the forty men of Davy Delange's gang trooped gaily into the mouth of the drive.

Moodily Davy followed them. As he walked he reached into his hip pocket and took out a pack of Lexington filter tips. He put one between his lips, returned the pack and began patting his pockets to locate his lighter.

Davy went from team to team of his machine boys, directing them in the line and spot to be drilled. Every time he spoke, the unlit cigarette waggled between his lips. He gesticulated with the hand that held his cigarette-lighter.

It took twenty minutes for him to set all his drills to work. And he stood and looked back along the tunnel. Each machine boy and his assistant formed a separate sculpture. Most of them were stripped to the waist. Their bodies appeared to be carved and polished in oiled ebony, as they braced themselves behind the massive rock drills.

Davy lifted his cupped hands, holding the cigarette-lighter near his face and he flicked the cog wheel.

The air in the tunnel turned to flame. In a flash explosion, the flame reached the temperature of a welding torch. It seared the skin from the faces and exposed bodies of the machine boys, it burned the hair from their scalps. It turned their ears to charred stumps. It roasted their eyeballs in their sockets. It scorched their clothing, so as they fell the cloth smouldered and burned against their flesh.

In that instant, as the skin was licked from his face and hands, Davy Delange opened his mouth in a greast gasp of agony. The flame shot down his throat into his gas-drenched lungs. Within the confines of his body the gas exploded and his chest popped like a paper bag, his ribs fanning outward about the massive wound like the petals of a sunflower.

Forty-one men died at the same moment. In the silence after that whooshing, sucking detonation, they lay like scorched insects along the floor of the drive. One or two of them were moving still, an arched spine relaxing, a leg straightening, charred fingers unclenching, but within a minute all was absolutely still.

Half an hour later Doctor Dan Stander and Rodney Ironsides were the first men into the drive. The smell of burned flesh was overpowering. Both of them had to swallow down their nausea as they went forward.

52

Dan Stander sat at his desk and looked out over the car park in front of the mine hospital. He appeared to have aged ten years since the previous evening. Dan envied his colleagues the detachment they could bring to their work. He had never been able to perfect the trick. He had just completed forty-one examinations for issue of death certificates.

For fifteen years he had been a mine doctor, so he was accustomed to dealing with death in its more hideous forms. This, however, was the worst he had ever encountered. Forty-one of them, all victims of severe burning and massive explosion trauma.

He felt washed out, exhausted with ugliness. He massaged his temples as he examined the tray of pathetic possessions that lay on the desk before him. This was the contents of the pockets of the man Delange. Extracting them from the scorched clothing had been a filthy business in itself. Cloth had burned into the flesh, the man had been wearing a cheap nylon shirt under his overalls. The fabric had melted in the heat and had become part of his blistered skin.

There was a bunch of keys on a brass ring, a Joseph Rogers pen-knife with a bone handle, a Ronson cigarette-lighter which had been clutched in the man's clawed and charred right hand, a springbok skin wallet, and a loose envelope with one corner burned away.

Dan had already passed on the effects of the Bantu victims to the agent of the Bantu Recruiting Agency, who would send them on to the men's families. Now he sighed with distaste and picked up the wallet. He opened it.

In one compartment there were half a dozen postage stamps,

and five Rands in notes. The other flap bulged with paper. Dan glanced through salesmen's cards, dry-cleaning receipts, news-paper cuttings offering farms for sale, a folded page from the *Farmers' Weekly* on the planning of a dairy herd, a J.B.S. Savings Book.

Dan opened the Savings Book and whistled when he saw the total. He fanned the remaining pages.

There was a much-fingered envelope, unsealed and tucked behind the cardboard cover of the Savings Book. Dan opened it, and pulled a face. It contained a selection of photographs of the type which one found offered for sale in the dock area of the Mozambique port of Lourenço Marques. It was for this type of material that Dan was searching.

When the man's possessions were returned to his grieving relatives, Dan wanted to spare them this evidence of human frailty. He burned the photographs and the envelope in his ashtray and then crushed the blackened sheets to powder before spilling it into his waste-paper bin.

He went across to the window and opened it to let the smell of smoke escape. He stood at the window and searched the car park for Joy's Alfa Romeo. She had not arrived as yet and Dan returned to his desk.

The remaining envelope caught his eye and he picked it up. There was a smear of blood upon it, and the corner was burned away. Dan removed the four sheets of paper and spread them on the desk:

'Dear Johnny,

When Pa died you were still little – and I always reckoned you were more like my son, you know, than my brother.

Well, Johnny, I reckon now I've got to tell you some-thing . . .'

Dan read slowly, and he did not hear Joy come into the room. She stood at the door watching him. Her expression fond, a small smile on her lips, shiny blonde hair hanging straight to her shoulders. Then she moved up quietly behind his chair and kissed his ear. Dan started and turned to face her.

'Darling,' Joy said and kissed him on the mouth. 'What is so interesting that you ignore my arrival?'

Dan hesitated a moment before telling her.

'There was a man killed last night in a ghastly accident. This was in his pocket.'

He handed her the letter and she read it slowly.

'He was going to send this to his brother?' she asked, and Dan nodded.

'The bitch,' Joy whispered, and Dan looked surprised.

'Who?'

'The girl – it's her fault, you know.' Joy opened her purse and took out a tissue to dab her eyes. 'Damn it, now I'm messing my make-up.' She sniffed, and then went on. 'It would serve her right if you gave that letter to her husband.'

'You mean I shouldn't give it to him?' Dan asked. 'We have no right to play God.'

'Haven't we?' asked Joy, and Dan watched quietly as she tore the letter to tiny shreds, screwed them into a ball, then dropped them into the waste bin.

'You are wonderful,' he said. 'Will you marry me?'

'I've already answered that question, Dr Stander.' And she kissed him again.

53

Hettie Delange was in a turmoil.

It had started with the phone call that had roused Johnny from their bed. He had said something about trouble at the shaft as he pulled on his clothes, but she had come only briefly awake and then drifted off again as Johnny hurried out into the night.

He had come in hours later and sat on the edge of the bed, his hands clasped between his knees and his head bowed.

'What's wrong, man,' she had snapped at him. 'Come to bed. Don't just sit there.'

'Davy's dead.' His voice had been listless.

There was a moment's shock that had convulsed the muscles of her belly, and brought her fully awake. Then, immediately she had felt a swift cleansing rush of relief.

He was dead. It was as easy as that! All day she had worried. She had been stupid to let it happen. Just that moment of weakness, that self-indulgent slip and she had been dreading the consequences all that day. She had imagined Davy trailing after her with puppy eyes, trying to touch her, making it so obvious that even Johnny would see it. She had enjoyed it but just the once was enough. She wanted no repeat performance and certainly no complications to follow the original deed.

Now it was all taken care of. He was dead.

'Are you sure?' she had asked anxiously, and Johnny heard the tone as concern.

'I saw him!' Johnny had shuddered, and wiped the back of his hand across his mouth.

'Gee, that's terrible.' Hettie had remembered her role, and sat up to put her arms about Johnny. 'That's terrible for you.'

She had not slept again that night. Somehow the thought of Davy going directly from her to his violent death was exciting. It was like in the movies, or a book, or something. Like he was an airman and he had been shot down, and she was his girl. Perhaps she was pregnant and all alone in the world, and she would have to go to Buckingham Palace to get his medal for him. And the Queen would say . . .

The fantasies had played out in her mind until the dawn, with Johnny tossing and muttering beside her.

She woke him when it was first light in the room.

'How was he?' she asked softly. 'What did he look like, Johnny?'

Johnny shuddered again, and then he started to tell her. His voice was husky, and the sentences broken and disconnected. When he stumbled into silence, Hettie found herself trembling with excitement.

'How terrible,' she kept repeating. 'Oh, how awful!' And she pressed against him. After a while Johnny made love to her, and for Hettie it was better than she had ever known it to be.

All that morning there were phone calls, and four of her friends came over to drink coffee with her. A reporter and photographer from the *Johannesburg Star* called and asked questions. Hettie was the centre of attraction, and again and again she repeated the story with all its grisly details.

After lunch Johnny came home with a little dark-haired man in a charcoal suit and black Italian shoes, with a matching black briefcase.

'Hettie, this is Mr Boart. He was Davy's lawyer. He's got something to tell you.'

'Mrs Delange. May I convey to you my sincere condolences in the tragic bereavement you and your husband have suffered.'

'Yes, it's terrible, isn't it?' Hettie was apprehensive. Had Davy told this lawyer about them? Had this man come to make trouble?

'Your brother-in-law made a will of which I am the executor. Your brother-in-law was a wealthy man. His estate is in excess of fifty thousand Rand.' Boart paused portentously. 'And you and your husband are the sole beneficiaries.'

Hettie looked dubiously from Boart to Johnny.

'I don't – what's that mean? Beneficiary?'

'It means that you and your husband share the estate between you.'

'I get half of fifty thousand Rand?' Hettie asked in delighted disbelief.

'That's right.'

'Gee,' exulted Hettie. 'That's fabulous!' She could hardly wait for Johnny and the lawyer to go before she phoned her friends again. All four of them returned to drink more coffee, to thrill again and to envy Hettie the glamour and excitement of it.

'Twenty-five thousand,' they kept repeating the sum with relish.

'Hell, man, he must really have liked you a lot, Hettie,' one of the girls commented with heavy emphasis, and Hettie lowered her eyes and contrived to look bereft and mysterious.

Johnny came home after six, unsteady on his feet and reeking of liquor. Reluctantly Hettie's four friends left to rejoin their waiting families, and almost immediately after that a big white sports car pulled up in the driveway and Hettie's day of triumph was complete. Not one of her friends had ever had the General Manager of the Sonder Ditch Gold Mining Company call at their home.

She had the front door open the instant the doorbell rang. Her greeting had been shamelessly plagiarized from a period movie that had recently played at the local cinema.

'Mr Ironsides, how good of you to come.'

When she led Rod through into the over-furnished lounge, Johnny looked up but did not get to his feet.

'Hello, Johnny,' said Rod. 'I have come to tell you that I'm sorry about Davy, and to ...'

'Don't give me that bull dust, Tin Ribs,' said Johnny Delange.

'Johnny,' gasped Hettie, 'you can't talk to Mr Ironsides like that.' And she turned to Rod, laying a hand on his sleeve. 'He doesn't mean it, Mr Ironsides. He has been drinking.'

'Get out of here,' said Johnny. 'Get into the bloody kitchen where you belong.'

'Johnny!'

'Get out!' roared Johnny, rising from his chair, and Hettie fled from the room.

Johnny lurched across to the chrome and glass liquor cabinet that filled one corner. He sloshed whisky into two glasses and handed one to Rod.

'God speed to my brother,' he said.

'To Davy Delange, one of the best rock hounds on the Kitchenerville field,' said Rod, and tossed the drink back in one gulp.

'The best!' Johnny corrected him, and emptied his own glass. He gasped at the sting of the whisky, then leaned forward to speak into Rod's face.

'You've come to find out if I'm game to finish your bloody drive for you, or if I'm going to quit. Davy didn't mean nothing to you and I don't mean nothing to you. Only one thing worrying you – you want to know about your bloody drive.' Johnny refilled his glass. 'Well, hear this, friend, and hear it well. Johnny Delange don't quit. That drive ate my brother but I'll beat the bastard, so you got nothing to worry about. You go home and get a good night's sleep, 'cos Johnny Delange will be on shift and breaking rock tomorrow morning first thing.'

54

A Silver Cloud Rolls Royce was parked amongst the trees in the misty morning. Ahead was the practice track with the white-painted railings curving away towards the willow-lined river. The mist was heavier along the river and the grass was very green against it.

The uniformed chauffeur stood away from the Rolls, leaving

its two occupants in privacy. They sat on the back seat with an angora wool travelling rug spread over their knees. On the folding table in front of them was a silver Thermos of coffee, shell-thin porcelain cups, and a plate of ham sandwiches.

The fat man was eating steadily, washing each mouthful down with coffee. The little bald-headed man was not eating, instead he puffed quickly and nervously at his cigarette and looked out of the window at the horses. The grooms were walking the horses in circles, nostrils steaming in the morning chill, blankets flapping. The jockeys stood looking up at the trainer. They wore hard caps and polo-necked jerseys. All of them carried whips. The trainer was speaking urgently, his hands thrust deep into the pockets of his overcoat.

'It's a very fine service,' said the little man. 'I particularly enjoyed the stop in Rio. My first visit there.'

The fat man grunted. He was annoyed. They shouldn't have sent this agent out. It was a mark of suspicion, distrust, and it would seriously hamper his market operation.

The conference between trainer and jockeys had ended. The diminutive riders scattered to their mounts, and the trainer came towards the Rolls.

'Good morning, sir.' He spoke through the open window, and the fat man grunted again.

'I'm giving him a full run,' the trainer went on. 'Emerald Isle will make pace for him to the five, Pater Noster will take over and push him to the mile, I've Tiger Shark to pace him for the run in.'

'Very well.'

'Perhaps you'd like to keep time, sir.' The trainer proffered a stop-watch, and the fat man seemed to recover his urbanity and charm.

'Thank you, Henry.' He smiled. 'He looks good, I'll say that.'

The trainer was pleased by the condescension.

'Oh! He's red hot! By Saturday I'll have him sharpened down to razor edge.' He stood back from the window. 'I'll get them off, then.' He walked away.

'You have a message for me?' asked the fat man.

'Of course.' The other wriggled his moustache like a rabbit's whiskers. It was an annoying habit. 'I didn't fly all this way out here to watch a couple of mokes trotting around a race-track.'

'Would you like to give me the message?' The fat man hid his affront. What the agent had called a moke was some of the finest horseflesh in Africa.

'They want to know about this gas explosion.'

'Nothing.' The fat man dismissed the question with a wave of his hand. 'A flash explosion. Killed a few men. No damage to the workings. Negligence on the part of the miner in charge.'

'Will it affect our plans?'

'Not one iota.'

The two horses had jumped away from the start, shoulder to shoulder, with the wreaths of mists swirling in their wake. The glossy bay horse on the rails ran with an easy floating action while the grey plunged along beside it.

'My principals are very concerned.'

'Well, they have no need to be,' snapped the fat man. 'I tell you it makes no difference.'

'Was the explosion due to an error of judgement on the part of this man Ironsides?'

'No.' The fat man shook his head. 'It was negligence of the miner in charge. He should have detected the gas.'

'Pity.' The bald man shook his head regretfully. 'We had hoped it was a flaw in the Ironsides character.'

The grey horse was tiring, while the bay ran on smoothly, drawing away from him. From the side rail a third horse came in to replace the grey, and ran shoulder to shoulder with the bay.

'Why should the character of Ironsides concern you?'

'We have heard disturbing reports. This is no pawn to be moved at will. He is taking the job of general manager by the throat. Already our sources indicate that he has reduced running costs on the Sonder Ditch by a scarcely believable two per cent. He seems to be tireless, inventive – a man, in short, to reckon with.'

'Well and good,' the fat man conceded. 'But I still fail to see why your – ah, principals – are alarmed. Do they expect that this man will hold back the flood waters by the sheer force of his personality?'

The second pacemaker was faltering, but still the big bay ran on alone. A far figure in the mist, passing the mile post, joined at last by the third pacemaker.

'I know nothing about horses,' said the bald man watching the two flying forms. 'But I've just seen that one,' he pointed with his cigarette at the far-off bay. 'I've just seen him run the guts out of the other two. One after the other he has broken their hearts and left them staggering along behind him. We would call him an imponderable, one who cannot be judged by normal standards.' He puffed at his cigarette before going on. 'There are men like that also, imponderable. It seems to us that Ironsides is one of them, and we don't like it. We don't like them on the opposing team. It is just possible that he could upset the entire operation, not, as you put it, by sheer force of personality, but by suddenly doing the unexpected, by behaving in a manner for which we have not allowed.'

Both men fell silent watching the galloping horses come round the last bend and hit the straight.

'Watch this.' The fat man spoke softly, and as though in response to his words the big bay lengthened his stride, reaching out, driving strongly away from the other horse. His head was going like a hammer, twin jets of steam shot from wide flaring nostrils, and thrown turf and dirt flew from his hooves. Five lengths clear of the following horse he went slashing past the finish line and the fat man clicked his stop watch.

He scrutinized the dial of the watch anxiously and then chuckled like a healthy baby.

'And he wasn't really being extended!'

He rapped on the window beside him, and immediately the uniformed chauffeur opened the driving door and slid in behind the wheel.

'To my office,' instructed the fat man, 'and close the partition.'

When the sound-proof glass panel had slid closed between driver and passengers, the fat man turned to his guest.

'And so, my friend, you consider Ironsides to be an imponderable. What do you want me to do about him?'

'Get rid of him.'

'Do you mean what I think you mean?' The fat man lifted an eyebrow.

'No. Nothing that drastic.' The bald head bobbed agitatedly. 'You have been reading too much James Bond. Simply arrange it that Ironsides is far away and well occupied when the drive holes through the Big Dipper Dyke, otherwise there is an excellent chance that he will do something to frustate our good intentions.'

'I think we can arrange that,' said the fat man and helped himself to another ham sandwich.

55

As he had promised, Manfred caught the Friday evening flight for Cape Town. On the Saturday night Rod and Terry took a wild chance on not being recognized and spent the evening at the Kyalami Ranch Hotel. They danced and dined in the Africa Room, but were on their way back to the apartment before midnight.

In the dawn a playful slap with the rolled-up Sunday papers which Rod delivered to Terry's naked posterior as she slept triggered off a noisy brawl in which a picture was knocked off the wall by a flying pillow, a coffee table overturned and the shrieking and laughter reached such a pitch that it called down a storm of indignant thumping from the apartment above them.

Terry made a defiant gesture at the ceiling, but they both subsided gasping with laughter back onto the bed to indulge in activity every bit as strenuous if not nearly so noisy.

Later, much later, they collected Melanie and once again spent the Sunday at the stud farm on the Vaal. Melanie actually *rode* a horse, a traumatic experience which bade fair to alter her whole existence. After lunch they launched the speedboat from the boat house on the bank of the river and water-skied down as far as the barrage, Terry and Rod taking turns at the wheel and on the skis. It occurred to Rod that Terry Steyner looked good in a white bikini. It was dark before Rod delivered his sleeping daughter to her mother.

'Who is this *Terry* that Melanie talks about all the time?' demanded Patti, she was still sulking about Rod's promotion. Patti had a memory like a tax collector.

'Terry?' Rod feigned surprise. 'I thought you knew.' And he left Patti glaring after him as he went back down the stairs.

Terry was curled up in the leather bucket seat of the Maserati, just the tip of her nose protruding from the voluminous fur coat she wore.

'I love your daughter, Mr Ironsides,' she murmured.

'It would appear that the feeling is reciprocated.'

Rod drove slowly towards the hillbrow ridge, and Terry's hand came out of the wide fur sleeve and lay on his knee.

'Wouldn't it be nice if we had a daughter of our own one day?'

'Wouldn't it,' Rod agreed dutifully, and then found to his intense amazement that he really meant it.

He was still investigating this remarkable phenomenon as he parked the Maserati in the basement garage of his apartment and went round to open Terry's door.

Manfred Steyner watched Terry climb out of the Maserati and lift her face towards Rodney Ironsides. Ironsides stooped over her and kissed her, then he slammed and locked the door of the Maserati, and arm in arm the two of them crossed to the elevator.

'Peterson Investigations always delivers the goods,' said the man at the wheel of the black Ford parked in the shadows of the garage. 'We will give them half an hour to get settled in comfortably, then we will go up and knock on the door of his apartment.'

Manfred Steyner sat very still and unblinking on the seat beside the private detective. He had arrived back in Johannesburg three hours previously in answer to the summons from the investigation bureau.

'You will leave me here. Drive the Ford out and park at the corner of Clarendon Circle. Wait for me there,' said Manfred.

'Hey? Aren't you going to ... ?' The detective was taken aback.

'Do as I tell you.' Manfred's voice stung like thrown vitriol, but the detective persisted.

'You will need evidence for the court, you need me as a witness ...'

'Get out,' Manfred snapped, and opening the door of the Ford he climbed out and closed the door behind him. The detective hesitated a moment longer, then started the engine and drove out of the garage leaving Manfred alone.

Manfred moved slowly towards the big shiny sports car. From his pocket he took a gold-plated pen-knife and opened the large blade.

He had recognized that the car was of special significance to the man. It was the only form of retaliation he could make at the moment. Until Rodney Ironsides completed the drive on the Big Dipper Dyke, he could not confront him nor Theresa Steyner. He could not let them know he even suspected them.

Such human emotions as love and hate and jealousy Manfred Steyner seldom experienced, except in their mildest manifestions. Theresa Hirschfeld he had never loved, as he had never loved any woman. He had married her for her wealth and station in life. The emotion that gripped him was neither hatred nor jealousy. It was affront. He was affronted that these two insignificant persons should conspire to cheat him.

He would not rush in blindly now with threats of physical violence and divorce. No, he would administer an anonymous punishment that would hurt the man deeply. This would be part payment. Later, when he had served his purpose, Manfred would crush him as coldly as though he were stepping on an ant.

As for the woman, he was aware of a mild relief. Her irresponsible behaviour had placed her completely at his mercy, both legally and morally. As soon as the strike beyond the Big Dipper had made him financially secure and independent, he could throw her aside. She would have served her purpose admirably.

The journey which he had interrupted by this hurried return to Johannesburg was connected with the purchase of Sonder Ditch shares. He was touring the major centres arranging with various firms of stock brokers that on a given date they would commence to purchase every available scrap of Sonder Ditch script.

As soon as he had completed this business he would tell the private detective to drive him out to Jan Smuts Airport where he had a reservation on the night plane to Durban where he would continue his preparations.

It had all worked out very well, he thought, as he slipped the knife blade through the rubber buffer of the triangular side window of the Maserati. With a quick twist he lifted the window catch, and pushed the window open. He reached through and turned the door handle. The door clicked open and Manfred climbed into the driver's seat.

The blade of the pen-knife was razor sharp. He started on the passenger seat and then the driver's seat, ripping the leather upholstery to shreds before moving to the back seat and repeating the process there. He slid the panel that concealed the tray of tools each in their separate foam rubber padded compartment, and selected a tyre lever.

With this he smashed all the dials on the dashboard, broken glass tinkling and falling to the carpeted floor. With the point of the tyre lever he dug into the rosewood panelling and tore out a section, splintering and cracking the woodwork into complete ruin.

He climbed out of the Maserati and struck the windshield with the tyre lever. The glass starred. He rained blows on it, unable to shatter it but reducing it to a sagging opaque sheet.

Then he dropped the tyre lever and groped for his pen-knife again. On his knees he slashed at the front offside tyre. The rubber was tougher than he had allowed. Annoyed, he slashed again. The knife turned in his hand, the blade folding against the blow. It sliced the ball of his thumb, a deep stinging cut. Manfred came to his feet with a cry, clutching his injured thumb. Blood spurted from the wound.

'Mein Gott! Mein Gott!' Manfred gasped, horrified by his own blood. As he staggered wildly from the basement garage, he was wrapping a handkerchief around his thumb.

He reached the waiting Ford, hauled the door open and fell into the front seat beside the detective.

'A Doctor! For God's sake, get me to a Doctor. I'm badly hurt. Quickly! Drive quickly!'

56

Terry's husband is due back in town today, Rod thought, as he sat down at his desk. It was not a thought that gave him strength to work through a day he knew would be filled with hectic activity.

The quarterly reports were due at Head Office tomorrow morning. In consequence the entire administration was in its usual last-minute panic. Already there was a mob in the waiting-room outside his office that Lily Jordan would soon need a stock whip to control. At three o'clock he was due at a consultants' meeting at Head Office, but before that he wanted to go underground to check the drop-blast matt that Johnny Delange had now completed and charged up.

The phone went as Lily led in his first visitor, a tall, thin, sorrowful-looking man with a droopy moustache.

'Mr Ironsides?' said the voice on the phone.

'Yes.'

'Porters Motors here. I've got an estimate on the repairs to your Maserati.'

'How much?' Rod crossed his fingers.

'Twelve hundred Rand.'

'Wow!' Rod gasped.

'Do you want us to go ahead?'

'No, I'll have to contact my insurance company first. I'll call you.' He hung up. That act of unaccountable vandalism still irked him terribly. He realized that he would be reduced to the Company Volkswagen for a further indefinite period.

He turned his attention to his visitor.

'Detective Inspector Grobbelaar,' the tall man introduced himself. 'I am investigating officer in the murder of José Almeida, the concession store proprietor on this mine.'

They shook hands.

'Have you any ideas on who did it?' Rod asked.

'We have always got ideas,' said the Inspector, so sadly that for a moment Rod had the impression that his name was on the list of suspects. 'We believe that the murderer is employed by one of the mines in the district, probably the Sonder Ditch. I have called on you to ask for your co-operation in the investigation.'

'Of course.'

'I will be conducting a great number of interrogations amongst your Bantu employees. I hoped you might find a room for me to use on the premises.'

Rod lifted his phone and while he dialled he told Grobbelaar, 'I'm calling our Compound Manager.' Then he transferred his attention to the mouthpiece. 'Ironsides here. I am sending an Inspector Grobbelaar down to see you. Please see that an office is placed at his disposal and that he receives full co-operation.'

Grobbelaar stood up and extended his hand.

'I won't take up more of your time. Thank you, Mr Ironsides.'

His next visitor was Van der Bergh, his Personnel Officer, brandishing his departmental reports as though they were a winning lottery ticket.

'All finished,' he announced triumphantly. 'All we need is your signature.'

As Rod uncapped his pen, the telephone squealed again.

'My God,' he muttered with pen in one hand and telephone in the other. 'Is it worth it?'

*   *   *

It was well after one o'clock when Rod fled his office, leaving Lily Jordan to hold back the tide. He went directly to No. 1 shaft where he was welcomed like the prodigal son by Dimitri and his old Line Managers. They were all anxious to know who would be replacing him as Underground Manager. Rod promised to find out that afternoon when he visited Head Office, and changed into his overalls and helmet.

At the spot where Davy Delange had died, Rod found a gang fixing a screen of wire mesh over the hanging wall to protect the fuses of his drop-blast. The electric cable that carried the blasting circuit to the surface was covered with a distinctive green plastic coating and securely pegged to the roof of the drive.

In the concrete blast room at the shaft head, his electrician had already set up a separate control for this circuit. It would be in readiness at all times. He could fire it within minutes. Rod felt as though a great weight had been lifted from his shoulders as he passed through the swinging ventilation doors and tramped on up the drive to speak to Johnny Delange.

Half-way to the face he met the gigantic figure of Big King coming back towards him with a small gang of lashing boys under his command. Rod greeted him, and Big King stopped and let his gang go on out of earshot before he spoke.

'I wish to speak.'

'Speak then.' Rod noticed suddenly that Big King's face was gaunt, his eyes appeared sunken and his skin had the dusty greyish look of sickness so evident in an ailing Bantu.

'I wish to return to my wives in Portuguese Mozambique,' said Big King.

'Why?' Rod was dismayed at the prospect of losing such a valuable boss boy.

'My blood is thin.' This was as non-committal an answer as any man has ever received. In essence it meant, 'My reasons are my own, and I have no intention of disclosing them.'

'When your blood is thick again, will you return to work here?' Rod asked.

'That is with the gods.' An answer signifying no more than the one preceding it.

'I cannot stop you if you wish to go, Big King, you know that,' Rod told him. 'Report to the Compound Manager and he will mark your notice.'

'I have told the Compound Manager. He wants me to work out my ticket, thirty-three more days.'

'Of course,' Rod nodded. 'You know that it is a contract. You must work it out.'

'I wish to leave at once,' Big King replied stubbornly.

'Then you must give me your reason. I cannot let you break contract except if there is some good reason.' Rod knew better than to set a dangerous precedent like that.

'There is no reason.' Big King admitted defeat. 'I will work out the ticket.'

He left Rod and followed his gang down the drive. Since the night he killed the Portuguese, Big King had slept little and eaten less. Worry had kept his stomach in a turmoil of dysentry, he had neither danced nor sung. Nothing that Crooked Leg nor the Shangaan Induna could say comforted him. He waited for the police to come. As the days passed, so the flesh melted from his body, he knew that they would come before the thirty-three days of his contract expired.

His approach to Rod had been a last despairing effort. Now he was resigned. He knew that the police were inexorable. One day soon they would come. They would lock the silver chains on his wrists and lead him to the closed van. He had seen many men led away like that and he had heard what happened to them after that. The white man's law was the same as the tribal law of the Shangaans. The taking of life must be paid for with life.

They would break his neck with the rope. His ancestors would have crushed his skull with a war club, it was the same in the end.

*   *   *

Rod found Johnny Delange drinking cold tea from his canteen while his gang barred down the face.

'How's it going?' he asked.

'Now we have finished messing about, it has started moving again.' Johnny wiped cold tea from his lips and recorked the canteen. 'We have broken almost fifteen hundred feet since Davy died.'

'That's good going.' Rod ignored the reference to the methane explosion and the drop-blast matt.

'Would have been better if Davy were still alive.' Johnny disliked Campbell, the miner who had replaced Davy on the night shift. 'The night shift aren't breaking their fair ground.'

'I'll chase them up,' Rod promised.

'You do that.' Johnny turned away to shout an order at his gang.

Rod stood and stared at the end of the drive. Less than a thousand feet ahead lay the dark hard rock of the Big Dipper – and beyond it . . . ? Rod felt his skin creep as he remembered his nightmare. That cold green translucent thing waiting for them beyond the dyke.

'All right, Johnny, you are getting close now.' Rod tore his imagination away from that green horror. 'As soon as you hit the Serpentine rock you are to stop work immediately and report to me. Is that understood?'

'You'd better tell that to Campbell also,' said Johnny. 'The night shift may hit the Big Dipper.'

'I'll tell him,' Rod agreed. 'But you make sure you remember. I want to be down here when we hole through the dyke.'

Rod glanced at his watch. It was almost two o'clock. He had an hour to get to the consultants' meeting at Head Office.

*   *   *

'You are late, Mr Ironsides.' Dr Manfred Steyner looked up from the head of the board-room table.

'My apologies, gentlemen.' Rod took his seat at the long oak table. 'Just one of those days.'

The men about the table murmured sympathetic acknowledgement, and Dr Steyner studied him for a moment without expression before remarking.

'I would be obliged for a few minutes of your time after this meeting, Mr Ironsides.'

'Of course, Dr Steyner.'

'Good.' Manfred nodded. 'Now that Mr Ironsides has graced

the table with his presence, the meeting can come to order.' It was the closest any of them had ever heard Dr Steyner come to making a joke.

It was dark outside when the meeting ended. The participants shrugged on their coats, made their farewells and left Manfred and Rod sitting at the table with its overflowing ash trays and littered pencils and note pads.

Manfred Steyner waited for fully three minutes after the door had closed on the last person to leave. Rod was accustomed to these long intent silences, yet he was uneasy. He sensed a new hostility in the man's attitude. He covered his awkwardness by lighting another cigarette and blowing a series of smoke rings at the portrait of Norman Hradsky, the original chairman of the company. Flanking Hradsky's portrait were two others. One of a slim blond man, with ravaged good looks and laughing blue eyes. The caption read: 'Dufford Charleywood. Director of C.R.C. from 1867–1872.' The other portrait in its heavy gilt frame depicted an impressively built man with mutton-chop whiskers and black Irish features. 'Sean Courtney' said the caption, and the dates were the same as Charleywood's.

These three had founded the Company, and Rod knew a little of their story. They had been as pretty a bunch of rogues as would be found in any convict settlement. Hradsky had ruined the other two in an ingenious bear raid on the stock exchange, and had virtually stolen their shares in the Company.*

We have become a lot more sophisticated since then, thought Rod. He looked instinctively towards the head of the long table and met Dr Steyner's level, unblinking stare. *Or have we?* he wondered. Just what devilment has our friend in mind?

Manfred Steyner was examining Rod with detached curiosity. So remote from any emotional rancour was Manfred, that he intended using the relationship that had developed between this man and his wife to further the instructions he had received that morning.

'How far is the end of the drive from the dyke?' he asked suddenly.

'Less than a thousand feet.'

'How much longer before you reach it?'

'Ten days. No more, possibly less.'

'As soon as the dyke is reached, all work on it must cease

* Read *When the Lion Feeds*

immediately. The timing of this is important, do you under-stand?'

'I have already instructed my miners not to hole through with-out my specific orders.'

'Good.' Manfred lapsed into silence for another full minute. Andrew had called him that morning with instructions from the man. Ironsides was to be well away from the Sonder Ditch when they pierced the dyke. It was left to Manfred to engineer his absence.

'I must inform you, Mr Ironsides, that it will be at least three weeks before I give the order to drill through. When you reach the dyke, it will be necessary for me to proceed to Europe to make certain arrangements there. I will be away for at least ten days during which time no work of any type must be allowed in the drive to the Big Dipper.'

'You will be away over Christmas?' Rod asked with sur-prise.

'Yes,' Manfred nodded, and could read Rod's mind.

Terry will be alone, Rod thought quickly, she will be alone over Christmas. The Sonder Ditch goes onto *essential services only* for a full seven days over Christmas. Just a skeleton crew to keep her going. I could get away for a week, a whole week away together.

Manfred waited until he knew that Rod had reached the decision to which he had been steered, then he asked: 'You understand? You will await my order to hole through. You need not expect that order until the middle of January.'

'I understand.'

'You may go.' Manfred dismissed him.

'Thanks,' Rod acknowledged drily.

*   *   *

There was a coffee bar in the ground-floor shopping centre of Reef Building. Rod beat a bearded hippie to the telephone booth, and dialled the Sandown number. It was safe enough, he had just left Manfred upstairs.

'Theresa Steyner,' she answered his call.

'We've got a week to ourselves,' he told her. 'One whole glorious week.'

'When?' she demanded joyously.

And he told her.

'Where shall we go?' she asked.

'We'll think of somewhere.'

57

At 11.26 a.m. on December 16th, Johnny Delange blasted the face of the drive, and went forward in the fumes and dust.

In the beam of his lantern, the new rock blown from the face was completely different from the blueish Ventersdorp quartzite. It was a glassy, blackish green, veined with tiny white lines, more like marble than country rock.

'We are on the dyke.' He spoke to Big King, and stooped to pick up a lump of the Serpentine rock. He weighed it in his hand.

'We've done it, we've beaten the bastard!'

Big King stood silently beside him. He did not share Johnny's elation.

'Right!' Johnny tossed the lump of rock back onto the pile. 'Bar down, and make safe. Then pull them out of the drive. We are finished here until further orders.'

*　　*　　*

'Well done, Johnny,' applauded Rod. 'Clean her up and pull out of the drive. I don't know how much longer it will be till we get the order to hole through the dyke. But take a holiday in the meantime. I'll pay you four fathoms of bonus a day while you are waiting.' He broke the connection with his finger, keeping the receiver to his ear. He dialled and spoke to the switchboard girl at Head Office. 'Get me Dr Steyner, please. This is Rodney Ironsides.' He waited a few seconds and then Manfred came on the line.

'We've hit the Big Dipper,' Rod told him.

'I will leave for Europe on tomorrow morning's Boeing,' said

Manfred. 'You are to do nothing until I return.' Manfred cradled the receiver and depressed the button on his intercom.

'Cancel all my appointments,' he told his secretary. 'I am unavailable.'

'Very well, Dr Steyner.'

Manfred picked up the receiver of his unlisted, direct-line telephone. He dialled.

'Hello, Andrew. Will you tell him that I am ready to discharge my obligations. We have intersected the Big Dipper.' He listened for a few seconds, then spoke again. 'Very well, I will wait for your reply.'

*   *   *

Andrew replaced the telephone and went out through the sliding glass doors onto the terrace. It was a lazy summer's day, hushed with heat, and the sun sparkled on the crystal clear waters of the swimming-pool. Insects murmured languidly in the massed banks of blooms that surrounded the terrace.

The fat man stood before an artist's easel. He wore a blue beret and a white smock that hung like a maternity dress over his jutting stomach.

His model lay face down on an air mattress by the edge of the pool. She was a dainty, dark-haired girl with a pixy face and a doll-like body. Her discarded bikini lay in a damp bundle on the flags of the terrace. Drops of water caught the sun and bejewelled her creamy buttocks, giving her a paradoxical air of innocence and oriental eroticism.

'That was Steyner,' said Andrew. 'He reports that they have hit the Big Dipper.'

The fat man did not look up. He went on laying paint upon the canvas with complete concentration.

'Please lift your right shoulder, my dear, you are covering that utterly delightful bosom of yours,' he instructed, and the girl obeyed him immediately.

Finally he stepped back and regarded his own work critically.

'You may have a break now.' He wiped his brushes while the naked girl stood up, stretched like a cat and then dived into the pool. She surfaced with the water slicking her short dark hair against her head like the pelt of an otter, and swam slowly to the far end of the pool.

'Cable New York, Paris, London, Tokyo and Berlin the code word "Gothic",' he instructed Andrew. This was the word which would unleash the bear offensive on the financial markets of the world. On receipt of those cables, agents in the major cities would begin to sell the shares of the companies mining the Kitchenerville field, sell them by the millions.

'Then instruct Steyner to get Ironsides out of the way, and hole through the dyke.'

*   *   *

Manfred answered Andrew's return call on the unlisted line. He listened to, and acknowledged, his instructions. Afterwards he sat still as a lizard, running over his preparations. Reviewing them minutely, examining them for flaws. There were none.

It was time to begin the purchase of Sonder Ditch shares. He called his secretary on the intercom and instructed her to place calls to numbers in Cape Town, Durban and Johannesburg itself. He wanted the purchase orders to come through a number of different brokers, so that it would not be obvious that there was only one buyer in the market. There was also the question of credit; he was not covering his purchase orders with Banker's guarantees. The stock brokers were buying for him simply on his name and reputation and position with C.R.C. Manfred could not place too large a buying order with any one firm lest they ask him to provide surety. Dr Manfred Steyner had no surety to offer.

So, instead, he placed moderate orders with dozens of different firms. By three o'clock that afternoon Manfred had ordered the purchase of three quarters of a million Rands' worth of shares. He had no means of paying for those shares but he knew he would never be called upon to do so. When he sold them again in a few weeks' time they would have doubled in value.

A few minutes after his final conversation with the firm of Swerling and Wright in Cape Town, his secretary came through on the intercom.

'S.A.A. have confirmed your reservation on the Boeing to Salisbury. Flight 126 at nine a.m. tomorrow morning. You are booked to return to Johannesburg on the Rhodesian Airways Viking at 6 p.m. tomorrow evening.'

'Thank you.' Manfred grudged this wasted day but it was

imperative that Theresa believed he had left for Europe. She must see him depart on the S.A.A. flight. 'Please get my wife on the phone for me.'

'Theresa,' he told her, 'something important has come up. I have to fly to London tomorrow morning. I am afraid I will be away over Christmas.'

Her display of surprise and regret was unconvincing. She and Ironsides had made their own arrangements for the time he was away, Manfred was convinced of this.

It was all working out very well, he thought, as he cradled the receiver, very well indeed.

58

The Daimler drew up under the portico of Jan Smuts Airport and the chauffeur opened the door for Terry and then for Manfred.

While the porter removed his luggage from the boot of the Daimler, Manfred swept the car park with a quick scrutiny. So early in the morning it was less than half filled. There was a cream Volkswagen with a Kitchenerville number plate parked near the far end. All the line and senior managers of the Sonder Ditch had cream Volkswagens as their official vehicles.

'The bee has come to the honeypot,' thought Manfred, and smiled bleakly. He took Terry's elbow and they followed the porter with the crocodile-skin luggage into the main concourse of the airport.

Terry waited while Manfred went through his ticket and immigration formalities. On the outside she was a demure and dutiful wife, but she also had seen the Volkswagen and inside she was itching and bubbling with excitement. Darting surreptitious glances from behind her sunglasses, looking for that tall broad-shouldered figure among the crowds.

It seemed a lifetime until she stood alone on the observation balcony with the wind whipping her piebald calf-skin coat around her legs, and blowing her hair into a snapping, dancing tangle. The long shark-like shape of the Boeing jet crouched at the far end of the runway and as it started forward Terry turned from the balcony rail and ran back into the main building.

Rod was waiting for her just inside the doors, and he swung her off her feet.

'Gottcha!'

With her feet dangling, she put her arms around his neck and kissed him.

The watchers paused and smiled, and there was a minor traffic jam at the head of the stairs.

'Come on,' she entreated, 'let's not waste a minute of it.'

He put her on her feet, and they ran down the staircase hand in hand. Terry paused only to dismiss the chauffeur, and then they ran through the car park like children let out of school, and clambered into the Volkswagen. Their luggage was on the back seat.

'Go,' she said, 'go as fast as you can!'

Twenty minutes later Rod pulled the Volkswagen to a tyre-squealing halt in front of the hangars at the private airfield.

The twin-engined Cessna stood on the tarmac. Both engines were ticking over in readiness, and the mechanic climbed down from the cockpit when he recognized Terry.

'Hello, Terry, right on time,' he greeted her.

'Hello, Hank. You've got her warmed up already. You are a sweety!'

'Filed your flight plan also. Nothing too good for my most favourite customer.' The mechanic was a chunky grizzled little man, and he looked at Rod curiously.

'Give you a hand with the bags,' he said.

By the time they had the luggage stowed away in its compartment, Terry was in the cockpit speaking to the control tower.

Rod climbed up into the passenger seat beside her.

Terry switched off her radio and leaned over Rod's lap to speak to Hank.

'Thanks, Hank.' She paused delicately, and then went on with a rush. 'Hank, if anyone asks you, I was on my own today, okay?'

'Okay.' Hank grinned at her. 'Happy landings.' And he closed the cockpit door, and Terry taxied out onto the runway.

'Is this yours?' Rod asked. It was a hundred thousand Rands' worth of aircraft.

'Pops gave it to me for my birthday,' Terry replied. 'Do you like it?'

'Not bad,' Rod admitted.

Terry turned upwind and applied the wheel brakes while she ran the engines up to peak revs, testing their response.

Suddenly Rod realized that he was in the hands of a woman pilot. He fell silent and his nerves began to tighten up.

'Let's go,' said Terry and kicked off the brakes. The Cessna surged forward, and Rod gripped the arm rests and froze with his gaze fixed dead ahead.

'Relax, Ironsides,' Terry advised him without taking her eyes off the runway, 'I've been flying since I was sixteen.'

At three thousand feet she levelled out and banked gently onto an easterly heading.

'Now that didn't hurt too much did it?' She smiled sideways at him.

'You are quite a girl,' he told her. 'You can do all sorts of tricks.'

'You just wait,' she warned him. 'You ain't seen nothing yet!'

They flew in silence until the Highveld had fallen away behind them, and they were over the dense green mattress of the Bushveld.

'I'm going to divorce him.' She broke the silence, and Rod was not surprised that they were experiencing the mental telepathy of closely attuned minds. He had been thinking about her husband also.

'Good,' he said.

'You think I'd have a chance with you if I did?'

'If you played your cards right, you might get that lucky.'

'Conceited swine,' she said. 'I don't know why I love you.'

'Do you?' he asked.

'Yes.'

'And I you.'

They relapsed into a contented silence, until Terry put the Cessna in a shallow dive.

'What's wrong?' Rod asked with alarm.

'Going down to have a look for game.'

They flew low over thick olive-green bush broken by vleis of golden brown grass.

'There,' said Rod, pointing ahead. A line of fat black bugs moving across one of the open places. 'Buffalo!'

'And over there.' Terry pointed left.

'Zebra and wildebeeste,' Rod identified them. 'And there is a giraffe.' Its long stalk of a neck stuck up like a periscope. It broke into an awkward stiff-legged run as the aircraft roared overhead.

'We have arrived.' Terry indicated a pair of round granite koppies on the horizon ahead. They were as symmetrical as a young girl's breasts, and as they drew nearer Rod made out the thatched roof of a large building standing in the hollow between the koppies. Beyond it a long straight landing-strip had been cut from the trees, and the fat white sausage of a wind sock flew from its pole.

Terry throttled back and circled the homestead. On the lawns half a dozen tiny figures waved up at the Cessna, and as they watched, two of the figures climbed into a toy Landrover and set off for the landing-strip. A ribbon of white dust blew out from behind it.

'That's Hans,' Terry explained. 'We can go down now.'

She lined the Cessna up for its approach, and then let it sink down with the motors bumbling softly. The ground came up and jarred the undercarriage, then they were taxiing to meet the racing Landrover.

The man who piled out of the Landrover was white-haired, and sunburned like old leather.

'Mrs Steyner!' He was making no attempt to conceal his pleasure. 'It's been much too long. Where have you been?'

'I've been busy, Hans.'

'New York? What the hell for?' said Hans surprisingly.

'This is Mr Ironsides.' Terry introduced them. 'Rod, this is Hans Kruger.'

'Van Breda?' asked Hans as they shook hands. 'You related to the van Bredas from Caledon?'

'I don't think so,' Rod muttered weakly and looked at Terry appealingly.

'He is stone deaf,' Terry explained. 'Both his ear drums blown out by a hangfire in the 1930's. He won't admit it though.'

'I'm glad to hear it,' Hans nodded, happily. 'You always were a healthy girl. I remember when you were a little piccanin.'

'He is an absolute darling though, so is his wife. They look after the shooting lodge for Pops,' Terry told Rod.

'Good idea!' Hans agreed heartily. 'Let's get your bags into the Landrover and go up to the house. I bet Mr van Breda could use a drink also.' And he winked at Rod.

The lodge had thatch and rough-hewn timber roofing, stone-flagged floors covered with cured animal skins and Kelim rugs. There was a walk-in fireplace flanked by gun racks on which were displayed fifty fine examples of the gunsmith's art. The furniture was massive and masculine, leather-cushioned and low. The Spanish plaster walls were hung with trophies, horned heads and native weapons.

A vast wooden staircase led up to the bedrooms that opened off the gallery above the main room. The bedrooms were air-conditioned and after they had got rid of Hans and his fat wife, Rod and Terry tested the bed to see if it was suitable.

An hour and a half later the bed had been judged eminently satisfactory, and as they went down to pass further judgement on the gargantuan lunch that fat Mrs Hans had spread for them, Terry remarked, 'Has it ever occurred to you, Mr Ironsides, that there are parts of your anatomy other than your flanks which are ferrous in character?' Then she giggled and added softly, 'And thank the Lord for that!'

Lunch was an exhausting experience and Terry pointed out that there was little sense in going out before four o'clock as the game would still be in thick cover avoiding the midday heat, so they went back upstairs.

After four o'clock Rod selected a ·375 magnum Holland and Holland rifle from the rack, filled a cartridge belt with ammunition from one of the drawers, and they went out to the Landrover.

'How big is this place?' Rod asked as he turned the Landrover away from the gardens and took the track out into the virgin bush.

'You can drive for twenty miles in any direction and it's all ours. Over there our boundary runs against the Kruger National Park,' Terry answered.

They drove along the banks of the river, skirting sandbanks on which grew fluffy-headed reeds. The water ran fast between glistening black rocks, then spread into slow lazy pools.

They saw a dozen varieties of big game, stopping every few hundred yards to watch some lovely animal.

'Pops obviously doesn't allow shooting here,' Rod remarked, as a kudu bull with long spiral horns and trumpet-shaped ears studied them with big wet eyes from a range of thirty feet. 'The game is as tame as domestic cattle.'

'Only family are allowed to shoot,' Terry agreed. 'You qualify as family, however.'

Rod shook his head. 'It would be murder.' Rod indicated the kudu. 'That old fellow would eat out of your hand.'

'I'm glad you feel like that,' Terry said, and they drove on slowly.

The evening was not cool enough to warrant a log fire in the cavernous fireplace of the lodge. They lit one anyway because Rod decided it would be pleasant to sit in front of a big, leaping fire, drink whisky and hold the girl you love.

59

When Inspector Grobbelaar lowered his teacup, there was a white scum of cream on the tips of his moustache. He licked it off carefully, and looked across at Sergeant Hugo.

'Who have we got next?' he asked.

Hugo consulted his notebook.

'Philemon N'gabai.' He read out the name, and Grobbelaar sighed.

'Number forty-eight, only sixteen more.' The single smeary fingerprint on the fragment of glass from the gold container had been examined by the fingerprint department. They had provided a list of sixty-four names anyone of which might be the owner of that print. Each of them had to be interrogated, it was a lengthy and so far unrewarding labour.

'What do we know about friend Philemon?' Grobbelaar asked.

'He is approximately forty years old. A Shangaan from Mozambique. Height 5' 7½", weight 146 lb. Crippled right leg. Two previous convictions. 1956: 60 days for bicycle theft. 1962: 90 days for stealing a camera from a parked car,' Hugo read from the file.

'At one hundred forty-six pounds I don't see him breaking many necks. But send him in, let's talk to him,' Grobbelaar suggested and dunked his moustache in the tea cup again. Hugo nodded to the African Sergeant and he opened the door to admit Crooked Leg and his escort of an African constable.

They advanced to the desk at which the two detectives sat in their shirt sleeves. No one spoke. The two interrogators subjected him to a calculated and silent scrutiny to set him at as great a disadvantage as possible.

Grobbelaar prided himself on being able to sniff out a guilty conscience at fifty paces, and Philemon N'gabai reeked of guilt. He could not stand still, he was sweating heavily, and his eyes darted from floor to ceiling. He was guilty as hell, but not necessarily of murder. Grobbelaar did not feel the slightest confidence as he shook his head sorrowfully and asked, 'Why did you do it, Philemon? We have found the marks of your hand on the gold bottle.'

The effect on Crooked Leg was instantaneous and dramatic. His lips parted and began to tremble, saliva dribbled onto his chin. His eyes for the first time fixed on Grobbelaar's face, wide and staring.

'Hello! Hello!' Grobbelaar thought, straightening in his chair, coming completely alert. He sensed Hugo's quickening interest beside him.

'You know what they do to people who kill, Philemon? They take them away to . . .' Grobbelaar did not have an opportunity to finish.

With a howl Crooked Leg darted for the door. His crippled gait was deceptive, he was fast as a ferret. He had the door open before the Bantu Sergeant collared him and dragged him gibbering and struggling back into the room.

'The gold, but not the man! I did not kill the Portuguese,' he babbled, and Grobbelaar and Hugo exchanged glances.

'Pay dirt!' Hugo exclaimed with deep satisfaction.

'Bull's eye!' agreed Grobbelaar, and smiled, a rare and fleeting occurrence.

60

'You see it has a little light that comes on to show you where the keyhole is,' said the salesman pointing to the ignition switch on the dashboard.

'Ooh! Johnny, see that!' Hettie gushed, but Johnny Delange had his head under the bonnet of the big glossy Ford Mustang.

'Why don't you sit in her?' the salesman suggested. He was very cute really, Hettie decided, with dreamy eyes and the most *fabulous* side burns.

'Ooh! Yes, I'd love to.' She manoeuvred her bottom into the leather bucket seat of the sports car. Her skirt pulled up, and the salesman's dreamy eyes followed the hem all the way.

'Can you adjust the seat?' Hettie asked innocently looking up at him.

'Here, I'll show you.' He leaned into the interior of the Mustang and reached across Hettie's lap. His hand brushed over her thigh, and Hettie pretended not to notice his touch. He smelled of Old Spice after-shave lotion.

'That's better!' Hettie murmured, and wriggled into a more comfortable position, contriving to make the movement provocative and revealing.

The salesman was encouraged, he lingered with his wrist just touching a sleek thigh.

'What's the compression ratio on this model?' Johnny Delange demanded as he emerged from the engine, and the salesman straightened up quickly and hurried to join him.

An hour later Johnny signed the purchase contract, and both he and Hettie shook the salesman's hand.

'Let me give you my card,' the salesman insisted, but Johnny had returned to his new toy, and Hettie took the cardboard business card.

'Call me if you need anything, anything at all,' said the salesman with heavy significance.

'Dennis Langley. Sales Manager,' Hettie read out aloud. 'My! You're very young to be Sales Manager.'

'Not all that young!'

'I'll bet,' Hettie murmured, and her eyes were suddenly bold. She ran the tip of a pink tongue over her lips. 'I won't lose it,' she promised, and placing the card in her handbag, walked to the Mustang, leaving him with a tantalizing promise and a memory of swaying hips and clicking heels.

*　　*　　*

They raced the new Mustang as far as Potchefstroom; Hettie encouraging Johnny to overtake slower vehicles with inches to spare for oncoming traffic. With horn blaring he tore over blind rises, forking ringed fingers at the protesting toots of other drivers. They had the speedometer registering 120 m.p.h. on the return run, and it was dark as they pulled into the driveway and Johnny hit the brakes hard to avoid running into the back of a big black Daimler that was parked outside their front door.

'Jesus,' gasped Johnny. 'That's Dr Steyner's bus!'

'Who is Dr Steyner?' Hettie demanded.

'Hell, he's one of the big shots from Head Office.'

'You're kidding!' Hettie challenged him.

'Truth!' Johnny affirmed. 'One of the real big shots.'

'Bigger than Mr Ironsides?' The General Manager of the Sonder Ditch was as high up the social ladder as Hettie had ever looked.

'Tin Ribs is chicken feed compared to this joker. Just look at his bus, it's five times better than Tin Ribs' clapped-out old Maserati.'

'Gee!' Hettie could follow the logic of this line of argument. 'What's he want with us?'

'I don't know,' Johnny admitted with a twinge of anxiety. 'Lets go and find out.'

*　　*　　*

The lounge of the Delange home was not the setting which showed Dr Manfred Steyner to best advantage.

He sat on the edge of a scarlet and gold plastic-covered arm-chair as stiff and awkward as the packs of china dogs that stood on every table and shelf of the show cabinet, or the porcelain wild ducks which flew in diminishing perspective along the pale pink painted wall. In contrast to the tinsel Christmas decorations that festooned the ceiling and the gay greeting cards that Hettie had pinned to strips of green ribbon, Manfred's black homburg and Astrakhan-collared overcoat were unnecessarily severe.

'You will forgive my presumption,' he greeted them without rising. 'You were not at home and your maid let me in.'

'You're welcome, I'm sure,' Hettie simpered.

'Of course you are, Dr Steyner,' Johnny supported her.

'Ah! So you know who I am?' Manfred asked with satisfaction. This would make his task much easier.

'Of course we do.' Hettie went to him and offered her hand. 'I am Hettie Delange, how do you do?'

With horror Manfred saw that her armpit was unshaven, filled with damp ginger curls. Hettie had not bathed since the previous evening. Manfred's nostrils twitched and he fought down a queasy wave of nausea.

'Delange, I want to speak to you alone.' He cowered away from Hettie's overwhelming physical presence.

'Sure.' Johnny was eager to please. 'How about you making us some coffee, honey,' he asked Hettie.

*　　*　　*

Ten minutes later Manfred sank with relief into the lush upholstery of the Daimler's rear seat. He ignored the two Delanges waving their farewells, and closed his eyes. It was done. Tomorrow morning Johnny Delange would be on shift and drilling into the glassy green rock of the Big Dipper.

By noon Manfred would own quarter of a million shares in the Sonder Ditch.

In a week he would be a rich man.

In a month he would be divorced from Theresa Steyner. He would sue with all possible notoriety on the grounds of adultery. He no longer needed her.

The chauffeur drove him back to Johannesburg.

61

It began on the floor of the Johannesburg Stock Exchange.

For some months nearly all the activity had been in the industrial counters, centring about the Alex Sagov group of companies and their merger negotiations.

The only spark of life in the mining and mining financials had been Anglo American Corporation and De Beers Deferred rights issues, but this was now old news and the prices had settled at their new levels. So it was that nobody was expecting fireworks when the call over of the gold mining counters began. The brokers' clerks crowding the floor were quietly spoken and behaved, when the first squib popped.

'Buy Sonder Ditch,' from one end of the hall.

'Buy Sonder Ditch,' a voice raised.

'Buy!' The throng stirred, heads turned.

'Buy.' The brokers suddenly agitated swirled in little knots, broke and reformed as transactions were completed. The price jumped fifty cents, and a broker ran from the floor to confer with his principal.

Here a broker thumped another on the back to gain his attention, and his urgency was infectious.

'Buy! Buy!'

'What the hell's happening?'

'Where is the buying coming from?'

'It's local!'

The price hit ten Rand a share, and then the panic began in earnest.

'It's overseas buying.'

'Eleven Rand!'

Brokers rushed to telephone warnings to favoured clients that a bull run was developing.

'Twelve fifty. It's only local buying.'

'Buy at best. Buy five thousand.'

Clerks raced back onto the floor carrying the hastily telephoned instructions, and plunged into the hysterical trading.

'Jesus Christ! Thirteen Rand, sell now. Take your profit! It can't go much higher.'

'Thirteen seventy five, it's overseas buying. Buy at best.'

In fifty brokers' offices around the country, the professionals who spent their lives hovering over the tickers regained their balance and, cursing themselves for having been taken unawares, they scrambled onto the bull wagon. Others, the more canny ones, recognized the makings of a sick run and off-loaded their holdings, selling industrial shares as well as mining shares. Prices ran amok.

At ten-fifteen there was a priority call from the offices of the Minister of Finance in Pretoria to the office of the President of the Johannesburg Stock Exchange.

'What are you going to do?'

'We haven't decided. We won't close the floor if we can possibly help it.'

'Don't let it go too far. Keep me informed.'

Sixteen Rand and still spiralling when at eleven o'clock South African time, the London Stock Exchange came in. For the first fifteen wild minutes the price of Sonder Ditch gold mining rocketed in sympathy with the Johannesburg market.

Then suddenly and unexpectedly the Sonder Ditch shares ran head-on into massive selling pressure. Not only the Sonder Ditch, but all the Kitchenerville gold mining companies staggered as the pressure increased. The prices wavered, rallied a few shillings and then fell back, wavered again, and then crashed downwards, plummeting far below their opening prices.

'Sell!' was the cry. 'Sell at best!' Within minutes freshly-made paper fortunes were wiped away.

When the price of the Sonder Ditch gold mining shares fell to five Rand seventy-five cents, the committee of the Johannesburg Stock Exchange closed the floor in the interests of the national welfare, preventing further trading.

But in New York, Paris and London the investing public continued to beat South African gold mining shares to death.

*   *   *

In the air-conditioned office of a skyscraper building, the little bald-headed man was smashing his balled fist onto the desk top of his superior officer.

'I told you not to trust him,' he was almost sobbing with anger. 'The fat greedy slug. One million dollars wasn't enough for him! No, he had to blow the whole deal!'

'Please, Colonel,' his chief intervened. 'Control yourself. Let us make a fair and objective appraisal of this financial activity.'

The bald-headed man sank back into his chair, and tried to light a cigarette with hands that trembled so violently as to extinguish the flame of his lighter.

'It sticks out a mile.' He flicked the lighter again, and puffed quickly. 'The first activity on the Johannesburg Exchange was Dr Steyner being clever. Buying up shares on the strength of our dummy report. That was quite natural and we expected it, in fact we wanted that to happen. It took suspicion away from us.' His cigarette had gone out, the tip was wet with spit. He threw it away and lit another.

'Fine! Everything was fine up to then. Doctor Steyner had committed financial suicide, and we were on the pig's back.' He sucked at his new cigarette. 'Then! Then our fat friend pulls the big double-cross and starts selling the Kitchenerville shares short. He must have gone into the market for millions.'

'Can we abort the operation at this late date?' his chief asked.

'Not a chance.' The bald head shook vigorously. 'I have sent a cable to our fat friend, ordering him to freeze the work on the tunnel but can you imagine him obeying that order? He is financially committed for millions of dollars and he will protect that investment with every means at his disposal.'

'Could we not warn the management of the Sonder Ditch company?'

'That would put the finger squarely on us, would it not?'

'Hmm!' the chief nodded. 'We could send them an anonymous warning.'

'Who would put any credence on that?'

'You're right,' the chief sighed. 'We will just have to batten down our hatches and ride out the storm. Sit tight and deny everything.'

'That is all we can do.' The cigarette had gone out again, and there were bits of wet tobacco in his moustache. The little man flicked his lighter.

'The bastard, the fat, greedy bastard!' he muttered.

62

Johnny and Big King rode up shoulder to shoulder in the cage. It had been a good shift. Despite the hardness of the Serpentine rock that cut down the drilling rate by fifty per cent, they had been able to get in five blasts that day. Johnny reckoned they had driven more than half-way through the Big Dipper. There was no night shift working now. Campbell had gone back to the stopes, so the honour of holing through would be Johnny's. He was excited at the prospect. Tomorrow he would be through into the unknown.

'Until tomorrow, Big King,' he said as they reached the surface and stepped out of the cage.

They separated, Big King heading for the Bantu hostel, Johnny to the glistening new Mustang in the car park.

Big King went straight to the Shangaan Induna's cottage without changing from his working clothes. He stood in the doorway and the Induna looked up from the letter he was writing.

'What news, my father?' Big King asked.

'The worst,' the Induna told him softly. 'The police have taken Crooked Leg.'

'Crooked Leg would not betray me,' Big King declared, but without conviction.

'Would you expect him to die in your place?' asked the Induna. 'He must protect himself.'

'I did not mean to kill him,' Big King explained miserably. 'I did not mean to kill the Portuguese, it was the gun.'

'I know, my son.' The Induna's voice was husky with helpless pity.

Big King turned from the doorway and walked down across the lawns to the ablution block. The spring and swagger had gone from his step. He walked listlessly, slouching, dragging his feet.

63

Manfred Steyner sat at his desk. His hands lay on the blotter before him, one thumb wearing a turban of crisp white bandage. His only movement was the steady beat of a pulse in his throat and a nerve that fluttered in one eyelid. He was deathly pale, and a light sheen of perspiration gave his features the look of having been sculptured from washed marble.

The volume of the radio was turned high, so the voice of the announcer boomed and reverberated from the panelled walls.

'The climax of the drama was reached at eleven forty-five South African time when the President of the Johannesburg Stock Exchange declared the floor closed and all further trading suspended.

'Latest reports from the Tokyo Stock Exchange are that Sonder Ditch gold mining shares were being traded at the equivalent of four Rand forty cents. This compares with the morning's opening price of the same share on the Johannesburg Stock Exchange of nine Rand forty-five cents.

'A spokesman for the South African Government stated that although no reason for these extraordinary price fluctuations was apparent, the Minister of Mines, Doctor Carel De Wet, had ordered a full-scale commission of enquiry.'

Manfred Steyner stood up from his desk and went through into the bathroom. With his flair for figures he did not need pen and paper to compute that the shares he had purchased that morning had depreciated in value by well over one million Rand at the close of business that evening.

He knelt on the tiled floor in front of the toilet bowl and vomited.

64

The sky was darkening rapidly, for the sun had long ago sunk below a blazing horizon.

Rod heard the whisper of wings, and strained his eyes upwards into the gloom. They came in fast, in vee-formation, slanting down towards the pool of the river. He stood up from the blind and swung the shotgun on them, leading well ahead of the line of flight.

He squeezed off both barrels, Wham! Wham! And the duck broke formation and rocketed upwards, whirring aloft on noisy wings.

'Damn it!' said Rod.

'What's wrong, dead-eye Dick, did you miss?' asked Terry.

'The light's too bad.'

'Excuses! Excuses!' Terry stood up beside him, and Rod pushed a balled fist lightly against her cheek.

'That's enough from you, woman. Let's go home.'

Carrying the shotguns and bunches of dead duck, they trudged along the bank in the dusk to the waiting Landrover.

It was completely dark as they drove back to the lodge.

'What a wonderful day it's been,' Terry murmured dreamily. 'If for nothing else, I will always be grateful to you for teaching me how to enjoy my life.'

Back at the lodge, they bathed and changed into fresh clothes. For dinner they had wild duck and pineapple, with salads from Mrs Fat Hans' vegetable garden. Afterwards, they sprawled on the leopard-skin rugs in front of the fireplace and watched the log fire without talking, relaxed and happy and tired.

'My God, it's almost nine o'clock,' Terry checked her wrist-watch. 'I fancy a bit of bed myself, how about you, Mr Ironsides?'

'Let's hear the nine o'clock news first.'

'Oh Rod! Nobody ever listens to the news here. This is fairyland!'

Rod switched on the radio and the first word froze them both. It was 'Sonder Ditch'.

In horrified silence they listened to the full report. Rod's expression was granite hard, his mouth a tight grim line. When the news report ended, Rod switched off the radio set and lit a cigarette.

'There is trouble,' he said. 'Big trouble. I'm sorry, Terry, we must go back. As soon as possible. I have to get back to the mine.'

'I know,' Terry agreed immediately. 'But Rod, I can't take off from this landing-strip in the dark. There is no flare path.'

'We'll leave at first light.'

Rod slept very little that night. Whenever she woke, Terry sensed him lying unsleeping, worrying. Twice she heard him get up and go to the bathroom.

In the very early hours of the morning she woke from her own troubled sleep and saw him silhouetted against the starlit window. He was smoking a cigarette and staring out into the darkness. It was the first night they had spent together without making love. In the dawn Rod was haggard and puffy-eyed.

They were airborne at eight o'clock and they landed in Johannesburg a little after ten.

Rod went straight to the telephone in Hank's office and Lily Jordan answered his call.

'Miss Jordan, what the hell is happening? Is everything all right?'

'Is that you, Mr Ironsides. Oh! Thank God! Thank God you've come, something terrible has happened!'

65

Johnny Delange blew the face of the drive twice before nine o'clock, cutting thirty feet further into the glassy green dyke.

He had found that by drilling his cutter blast holes an additional three feet deeper, he could achieve a shatter effect on the serpentine rock which more than compensated for the additional drilling time. This next blast he was going to flout standard regulations and experiment with double charging his cutter holes. He would need additional explosives.

'Big King,' he shouted to make himself heard above the roar of drills. 'Take a gang back to the shaft station. Pick up six cases of Dynagel.'

He watched Big King and his gang retreat back down the drive, and then he lit a cigarette and turned his attention to his machine boys. They were poised before the rock face, sweating behind their drills. The dark rock of the dyke absorbed the light from the overhead electric bulbs. It made the end of the drive a gloomy place, filled with a sense of foreboding.

Johnny began to think about Davy. He was aware suddenly of a sense of disquiet, and he moved restlessly. He felt the hair on his forearms come slowly erect, each on a separate goose pimple. *Davy is here.* He knew it suddenly, and surely. His flesh crawled and he went cold with dread. He turned quickly and looked over his shoulder. The tunnel behind him was deserted, and Johnny gave a sickly grin.

'Shaya, madoda,' he called loudly and unnecessarily to his gang. They could not hear him above the roar of the drills, but the sound of his own voice helped reassure him.

Yet the creepy sensation was still with him. He felt that Davy was still there, trying to tell him something.

Johnny fought the sensation. He walked quickly forward, standing close to his machine boys, as though to draw comfort from their physical presence. It did not help. His nerves were shrieking now, and he felt himself beginning to sweat.

Suddenly the machine boy who was drilling the cutter hole in the centre of the face staggered backwards.

'Hey!' Johnny shouted at him, then he saw that water was spurting in fine needle jets from around the drill steel. Something was squeezing the drill steel out of its hole, like toothpaste out of a tube. It was pushing the machine boy backwards.

'Hey!' Johnny started forward and at that instant the heavy metal drill was fired out of the rock with the force of a cannon ball. It decapitated the machine boy, tearing his head from his body with such savagery that his carcass was thrown far back down the drive, his blood spraying the dark rock walls.

From the drill hole shot a solid jet of water. It came out under such pressure that when it caught the machine boy's assistant in the chest it stove in his ribs as though he had been hit by a speeding automobile.

'Out!' yelled Johnny. 'Get out!' And the rock face exploded. It blew outwards with greater force than if it had been blasted with Dynagel. It killed Johnny Delange instantly. He was smashed to a bloody pulp by the flying rock. It killed every man in his gang with him, and immediately afterwards the monstrous burst of water that poured from the face picked up their mutilated remains and swept them down the drive.

*   *   *

Big King was at the shaft station when they heard the water coming. It sounded like an express train in a tunnel, a dull bellow of irresistible power. The water was pushing the air from the drive ahead of it, so that a hurricane of wind came roaring from the mouth of the drive, blowing out a cloud of dust and loose rubbish.

Big King and his gang stood and stared in uncomprehending terror until the head of the column of water shot from the drive, frothing solid, carrying with it a plug of debris and human remains.

Bursting into the T-junction of the main 66 level haulage, the strength of the flood was reduced, yet still it swept down towards the lift station in a waist deep wall.

'This way!' Big King was the first to move. He leapt for the steel emergency ladder that led up to the level above. The rest of his gang were not fast enough, the water picked them up and crushed them against the steel-mesh barrier that guarded the shaft. The crest of the wave burst around Big King's legs, sucking at him, but he tore himself from its grip and climbed to safety.

Beneath him the water poured into the shaft like bath water into a plug hole, forming a spinning whirlpool about the collar as it roared down to flood the workings below 66 level.

66

Leaving Terry at the airfield to solicit transport from Hank, the mechanic, Rod drove directly to the head of No. 1 shaft of the Sonder Ditch. He jumped from the Volkswagen into the clamouring crowd clustered above the shaft head.

Dimitri was wide-eyed and distracted, beside him Big King towered like a black colossus.

'What happened?' Rod demanded.

'Tell him,' Dimitri instructed Big King.

'I was at the shaft with my gang. A river leaped from the mouth of the drive, a great river of water running faster than the Zambesi in flood; roaring like a lion the water ate all the men with me. I alone climbed above it.'

'We've hit a big one, Rod,' Dimitri interrupted. 'It's pouring in fast. We calculate it will flood the entire workings up to 66 level in four hours from now.'

'Have you cleared the mine?' Rod demanded.

'All the men are out except Delange and his gang. They were in the drive. They've been chopped, I'm afraid,' Dimitri answered.

'Have you warned the other mines we could have a burst through into their workings?'

'Yes, they are pulling all their shifts out.'

'Right.' Rod set off for the blast control room with Dimitri trotting to keep up with him. 'Give me your keys, and find the foreman electrician.'

Within minutes the three of them were crowded into the tiny concrete control room.

'Check in the special circuit,' Rod instructed. 'I'm going to shoot the drop-blast matt and seal off the drive.'

The foreman electrician worked quickly at the control panel. He looked up at Rod.

'Ready!' he said.

'Check her in,' Rod nodded.

The foreman threw the switch. The three of them caught their breath together.

Dimitri said it for them: 'Red!'

On the control panel of the special circuit the red bulb glared balefully at them, the Cyclops eye of the god of despair.

'Christ!' swore the foreman. 'The circuit is shot. The water must have torn the wires out.'

'It may be a fault in the board.'

'No.' The foreman shook his head with certainty.

'We've had it,' whispered Dimitri. 'Goodbye the Sonder Ditch!'

Rod burst out of the blast control room into the expectant crowd outside.

'Johnson!' He singled out one of his mine captains. 'Go down to the Yacht Club at the dam, get me the rubber rescue dinghy. Quick as you can, man.'

The man scurried away, and Rod turned on the electrician foreman as he emerged from the control room.

'Get me a battery hand-operated blaster, a reel of wire, pliers, gloves, two coils of nylon rope. Hurry!'

The foreman went.

'Rod.' Dimitri caught his arm. 'What are you going to do?'

'I'm going down there. I'm going to find the break in the circuit and I'm going to blast her by hand.'

'Jesus!' Dimitri gasped. 'You are crazy, Rod. You'll kill yourself for sure!'

Rod completely ignored his protest.

'I want one man with me. A strong man. The strongest there is, we will have to drag the dinghy against the flood.' Rod looked about him. Big King was standing by the banksman's office. The two of them were tall enough to face each other over the heads of the men between them.

'Will you come with me, Big King?' Rod asked.

'Yes,' said Big King.

67

In less than twenty minutes they were ready. Rod and Big King were stripped down to singlets and bathing-trunks. They wore canvas tennis shoes to protect their feet, and the hard helmets on their heads were incongruous against the rest of their attire.

The rubber dinghy was ex-naval disposal. A nine-foot air-filled mattress, so light that a man could lift it with one hand. Into it was packed the equipment they would need for the task ahead. A water-proof bag contained the battery blaster, the reel of insulated wire, the pliers, gloves and a spare lantern. Lashed to the eyelets along the sides of the dinghy were two coils of light nylon rope, a small crowbar, an axe and a razor-sharp machete in a leather sheath. To the bows of the dinghy were fastened a pair of looped nylon towing lines.

'What else will you need, Rod?' Dimitri asked.

Rod shook his head thoughtfully. 'That's it, Dimitri. That should do it.'

'Right!' Dimitri beckoned and four men came forward and carried the dinghy into the waiting cage.

'Let's go,' said Dimitri and followed the dinghy into the cage. Big King went next and Rod paused a second to look up at the sky. It was very blue and bright.

Before the onsetter could close the shutter door, a Silver Cloud Rolls Royce came gliding onto the bank. From the rear door emerged first Hurry Hirschfeld and then Terry Steyner.

'Ironsides!' roared Hurry. 'What the hell is going on?'

'We've hit water,' Rod answered him from the cage.

'Water? Where did it come from?'

'Beyond the Big Dipper.'

'You drove through the Big Dipper?'

'Yes.'

'You bastard, you've drowned the Sonder Ditch,' roared Hurry, advancing on the cage.

'Not yet, I haven't,' Rod contradicted.

'Rod.' Terry was white-faced beside her grandfather. 'You can't go down there.' She started forward.

Rod pushed the onsetter aside and pulled down the steel shutter door of the cage. Terry threw herself against the steel mesh of the guard barrier, but the cage was gone into the earth.

'Rod,' she whispered, and Hurry Hirschfeld put his arm around her shoulders and led her to the Rolls Royce.

*   *   *

From the back seat of the Rolls, Hurry Hirschfeld was conducting a Kangaroo Court Trial of Rodney Ironsides. One by one he called for the line managers of the Sonder Ditch and questioned them. Even those who were loyal to Rod could say little in his defence, and there were others who took the opportunity to level old scores with Rodney Ironsides.

Sitting beside her grandfather, Terry heard such a condemnation of the man she loved as to chill her to the depths of her soul. There was no doubt that Rodney Ironsides, without Head Office sanction, had instituted a new development so risky and contrary to company policy as to be criminal in concept.

'Why did he do it?' muttered Hurry Hirschfeld. He seemed bewildered. 'What could he possibly achieve by driving through the Big Dipper. It looks like a deliberate attempt to sabotage the Sonder Ditch.' Hurry's anger began to seethe within him. 'The bastard! He has drowned the Sonder Ditch and killed dozens of men.' He punched his fist into the palm of his hand. 'I'll make him pay for this. I'll break him, so help me God, I'll smash him! I'll bring criminal charges against him. Malicious damage to property. Manslaughter. Culpable homicide! By Jesus, I'll have his guts for this!'

Listening to Hurry ranting and threatening, Terry could keep silent no longer.

'It wasn't his fault, Pops. Truly it wasn't. He was forced to do it.'

'Ha!' snorted Hurry. 'I heard you at the pithead a few minutes ago. Just what is this man to you, Missy, that you spring to his defence so nobly?'

'Pops, please believe me.' Her eyes were enormous in her pale face.

'Why should I believe you? The two of you are obviously up to mischief together. Naturally you will try and protect him.'

'Listen to me at least,' she pleaded, and Hurry checked the run of his tongue and breathing heavily he turned to face her.

'This better be good, young lady,' he warned her.

In her agitation she told it badly, and half-way through she realized that she wasn't even convincing herself. Hurry's expression became more and more bleak, until he interrupted her impatiently.

'Good God, Theresa, this isn't like you. To try and put the blame for this onto your own husband! That's despicable! To try and switch the blame for this . . .'

'It's true! As God is my witness.' Terry was almost in tears, she was tugging at Hurry's sleeve in her agitation. 'Rod was forced to do it. He had no option.'

'You have proof of this?' Hurry asked drily, and Terry fell silent, staring at him dumbly. What proof was there?

68

The cage checked and slowed as it approached 65 level. The lights were still burning, but the workings were deserted. They lugged the dinghy out onto the station.

They could hear the dull waterfall roar of the flood on the level below them. The displacement of huge volumes of water disturbed the air so that a strong cool breeze was blowing up the shaft.

'Big King and I will go down the emergency ladder. You will lower the dinghy to us afterwards,' Rod told Dimitri. 'Make sure all the equipment is tied into it.'

'Right.' Dimitri nodded.

All was in readiness. The men who had come down with them in the cage were waiting expectantly. Rod could find no reason for further delay. He felt something cold and heavy settle in his guts.

'Come on, Big King.' And he went to the steel ladder.

'Good luck, Rod.' Dimitri's voice floated down to him, but Rod saved his breath for that cold dark climb downwards.

All the lights had fused on 66 level, and in the beam of his lamp the water below him was black and agitated. It poured into the mouth of the shaft, bending the mesh barrier inwards. The mesh acted as a gigantic sieve, straining the floating rubbish from the flood. Amongst the timber and planking, the sodden sacking and unrecognizable objects, Rod made out the waterlogged corpses of the dead pressed against the wire.

He climbed down and gingerly lowered himself into the water. Instantly it dragged at his lower body, shocking in its power. It was waist deep here, but he found that by bracing his body against the steel ladder he could maintain his footing.

Big King climbed down beside him, and Rod had to raise his voice above the hissing thunder of water.

'All right?'

'Yes. Let them send down the boat.'

Rod flashed his lamp up the shaft, and within minutes the dinghy was swaying slowly down to them. They reached up and guided it right side up to the surface of the water, before untying the rope.

The dinghy was sucked firmly against the wire mesh, and Rod checked its contents quickly. All was secure.

'Right.' Rod tied a bight of the nylon rope around his waist, and climbed up the wire mesh barrier until he could reach the roof of the tunnel. Behind him Big King was paying out the nylon line.

Rod leaned out until he could get his hands on the compressed air pipes that ran along the roof of the tunnel. The pipes were as thick as a man's wrist, bolted securely into the hanging wall of the drive they would support a man's weight with ease. Rod settled his grip firmly on the piping and then kicked his feet free from the barrier. He hung above the rushing waters, his feet just brushing the surface.

Hand over hand, swinging forward with his feet dangling, he started up the tunnel. The nylon rope hung down behind him like a long white tail. It was three hundred feet to where the water boiled from the drive into the main haulage, and Rod's shoulder muscles were shrieking in protest before he reached it. It seemed that his arms were being wrenched from their sockets, for the weight of the nylon rope that was dragging in the water was fast becoming intolerable.

There was a back eddy in the angle formed by the drive and the haulage. Here the flood swirled in a vortex, and Rod lowered himself slowly into it. The water buffeted him, but again he was able to cower against the side wall of the haulage and hold his footing. Quickly he began tying the rope onto the rawlbolts that were driven into the sidewall to consolidate the rock. Within minutes he had established a secure base from which to operate, and when he flashed his lamp back down the haulage he saw Big King following him along the compressed air piping.

Big King dropped into the waist deep water beside Rod, and they gripped the nylon rope and rested their burning arm muscles.

'Ready?' asked Rod at last, and Big King nodded.

They laid hold of the rope that led back to the dinghy and hauled upon it. For a moment nothing happened, the other end might just as well have been anchored to a mountain.

'Together!' grunted Rod, and they recovered a foot of rope.

'Again!' And they drew the dinghy inch by inch up the haulage against the rush of water.

Their hands were bleeding when they at last pulled the laden dinghy up to their own position and anchored it to the rawlbolts beside them. It bounced and bobbed with the water drumming against its underside.

Neither Rod nor Big King could talk. They hung exhausted on the body lines with the water ripping at their skin and gasped for breath.

At last Rod looked up at Big King, and in the lamp light he saw his own doubts reflected in Big King's eyes. The drop-blast matt was a thousand feet up the drive. The strength and speed of the water in the drive was almost double what it was in the haulage. Could they ever fight their way against such primeval forces as these that were now unleashed about them?

'I will go next,' Big King said and Rod nodded his agreement.

The huge Bantu drew himself up the rope until he could reach the compressed air pipe. His skin in the lamplight glistened like that of a porpoise. Hand over hand he disappeared into the gaping black maw of the drive. His lamp threw deformed and monstrous shadows upon the walls of rock.

When Big King's lamp flashed the signal to him, Rod climbed

up to the pipe and followed him into the drive. Three hundred feet later he found Big King had established another base. But here they were exposed to the full force of the flood, and they were pulled so violently against the body lines that the harsh nylon smeared the skin from their bodies. Together they dragged the dinghy up to them and anchored it.

Rod was sobbing softly as he held his torn hands to his chest and wondered if he could do it again.

'Ready?' Big King asked beside him, and Rod nodded. He reached up and placed the raw flesh of his palms onto the metal piping, and felt the tears of pain flood his eyes. He blinked them back and dragged himself forward.

Vaguely he realized that should he fall, he was a dead man. The flood would sweep him away, dragging him along the jagged side walls of the drive, ripping his flesh from the bone, and finally hurling him against the mesh surrounding the shaft to crush the life from his body.

He went on until he knew he could go no farther. Then he selected a rawlbolt in the side wall and looped the rope through it. And they repeated the whole heart-breaking procedure. Twice as he strained against the dinghy rope Rod saw his vision explode into stars and pinwheels. Each time he dragged himself back from the brink of unconsciousness by sheer force of will.

The example that Big King was setting was the inspiration which kept Rod from failing. Big King worked without change of expression, but his eyes were bloodshot with exertion. Only once Rod heard him grunt like a gut-shot lion, and there was bright blood on the rope where he touched it.

Rod knew he could not give in while Big King held on.

Reality dissolved slowly into a dark roaring nightmare of pain, wherein muscles and bone were loaded beyond all endurance, and yet continued to function. It seemed that for all time Rod had hung on arms that were leadened and slow with exhaustion. He was inching his way along the compressed air pipe for yet another advance up the drive. Sweat running into his eyes was blurring his vision, so at first he did not credit what he saw ahead of him in the darkness.

He shook his head to clear his eyes, and then squinted along the beam of his lamp. A heavy timber structure was hanging drunkenly from the roof of the drive. The bolts that held it were resisting the efforts of the water to tear it loose.

Rod realized abruptly that this was what remained of the frame which had held the ventilation doors. The doors were gone, ripped away, but the frame was still in position. He knew that just beyond the ventilation doors the drop-blast matt began. They had reached it!

New strength flowed into his body and he swung forward along the pipe. The timber frame made a fine anchor point and Rod secured the rope to it, and flashed back the signal to Big King. He hung in the loop of rope and rested awhile, then he forced himself to take an interest in his surroundings. He played the beam over the distorted timber frame and saw instantly why the blasting circuit had been broken.

In the lamp light the distinctive green plastic-coated blasting cable hung in festoons from the roof of the drive, clearly it had become entangled in the ventilation doors and been severed when they were ripped away. The loose end of the cable dangled to the surface of the racing water. Rod fastened his eyes on it, drawing comfort and strength from the knowledge that they would not have to continue their agonized journey down the drive.

When Big King came up out of the gloom, Rod indicated the dangling cable.

'There!' he gasped, and Big King narrowed his eyes in acknowledgement; he was unable to speak.

It was five minutes before they could commence the excruciating business of hauling the dinghy up and securing it to the door frame.

Again they rested. Their movements were slowing up drastically. Neither of them had much strength left to draw upon.

'Get hold of the end of the cable,' Rod instructed Big King, and he dragged himself over the side of the dinghy and lay sprawled full-length on the floor boards.

His weight forced the dinghy deeper, increasing its resistance to the racing water, and the rope strained against the wooden frame. Rod began clumsily to unpack the battery blaster. Big King stood waist-deep clinging with one arm to the wooden frame, reaching forward with the other towards the end of the green-coated cable. It danced just beyond his finger tips, and he edged forward against the current, steadying himself against the timber frame, placing a greater strain on the retaining bolts.

His fingers closed on the cable and with a grunt of satisfaction he passed it back to Rod.

Working with painstaking deliberation, Rod connected the crocodile clips from the reel of wire to the loose end of the green cable. Rod's plan was for both he and Big King to climb aboard the dinghy and, paying out the nylon rope, let themselves be carried back down the drive. At the same time they would be letting the wire run from its reel. At a safe distance they would fire the drop-blast matt.

Rod's fingers were swollen and numbed. The minutes passed as he completed his preparations and all that while the strain on the wooden frame was heavy and consistent.

Rod looked up from his task, and crawled to his knees.

'All right, Big King,' he wheezed as he knelt in the bows of the dinghy and gripped the wooden frame to steady the dinghy. 'Come aboard. We are ready.'

Big King waded forward and at that instant the retaining bolts on one side of the heavy timber frame gave way. With a rending, tearing sound the frame slewed across the tunnel. The beams of timber crossed each other like the blades of a pair of gigantic scissors. Both Rod's arms were between the beams. The bones in his forearms snapped with the loud crackle of breaking sticks.

With a scream of pain Rod collapsed onto the floorboards of the dinghy, his arms useless, sticking out at absurd angles from their shattered bones. Three feet away Big King was still in the water. His mouth was wide open, but no sound issued from his throat. He stood still as a black statue and his eyes bulged from their sockets. Even through his own suffering Rod was horrified by the expression on Big King's contorted features.

Below the surface of the water the bottom timber beams had performed the same scissor movement, but this time they had caught Big King's lower body between them. They had closed across his pelvis and crushed it. Now they held him in a vicelike grip from which it was not possible to shake them.

The white face and the black face were but a few feet apart. The two stricken companions in disaster, looked into each other's eyes and knew that there was no escape. They were doomed.

'My arms,' whispered Rod huskily. 'I cannot use them.' Big King's bulging eyes held Rod's gaze.

'Can you reach the blaster?' Rod whispered urgently. 'Take it and turn the handle. Burn it, Big King, burn it!'

Slow comprehension showed in Big King's pain-glazed eyes.

'We are finished, Big King. Let us go like men. Burn it, bring down the rock!'

Above them the rock was sown with explosive. The blaster was connected. In his agitation Rod tried to reach out for the blaster. His forearm swung loosely, the fingers hanging open like the petals of a dead flower, and the pain checked him.

'Get it, Big King,' Rod urged him, and Big King picked up the blaster and held it against his chest with one arm.

'The handle!' Rod encouraged him. 'Turn the handle!'

But instead Big King reached into the dinghy once more and drew the machete from its sheath.

'What are you doing?' Rod demanded, and in reply Big King swung the blade back over his shoulder and then brought it forward in a gleaming arc aimed at the nylon rope that held the dinghy anchored to the wooden frame. Clunk! The blade bit into the wood, severing the rope that was bound around it.

Freed by the stroke of the machete, the dinghy was whisked away by the current. Lying in the dancing rubber dinghy, Rod heard a bull voice bellow above the rush of the water.

'Go in peace, my friend.'

Then Rod was careening back along the drive, a hell ride during which the dinghy spun like a top and in the beam of his lamp the roof and walls melted into a dark racing blur as Rod lay maimed on the floor of the dinghy.

Then suddenly the air jarred against his ear drums, a long rolling concussion in the confines of the drive and he knew that Big King had fired the drop-blast matt. Rodney Ironsides slipped over the edge of consciousness into a soft warm dark place from which he hoped never to return.

69

Dimitri squatted on his haunches above the shaft at 65 level. He was smoking his tenth cigarette. The rest of his men waited as impatiently as he did, every few minutes Dimitri would cross to the shaft and flash his lamp down the hundred foot hole to 66 level.

'How long have they been gone,' he asked, and they all glanced at their watches.

'An hour and ten minutes.'

'No, an hour and fourteen minutes.'

'Christ, call me a liar for four minutes!'

And they lapsed into silence once more. Suddenly the station telephone shrilled, and Dimitri jumped up and ran to it.

'No, Mr Hirschfeld, nothing yet!'

He listened a moment.

'All right, send him down then.'

He hung up the telephone, and his men looked at him enquiringly.

'They are sending down a policeman,' he explained.

'What the hell for?'

'They want Big King.'

'Why?'

'Warrant of arrest for murder.'

'Murder?'

'Ja, they reckon he murdered that Portuguese storekeeper.'

'Jeez!'

'Big King, is that so!' Delighted to have found something to pass the time, they fell into an animated debate.

The police inspector arrived in the cage at 65 level, but he was disappointing. He looked like a down-at-heel undertaker, and he replied to their eager questions with a sorrowful stare that left them stuttering.

For the fifteenth time Dimitri went to the shaft and peered down into it. The blast shook the earth around them, a long rumbling that persisted for many seconds.

'They've done it!' yelled Dimitri, and began to caper wildly. His men leapt to their feet and began beating each other on the back, shouting and laughing. The police inspector alone took no part in the celebrations.

'Wait,' yelled Dimitri at last. 'Shut up all of you! Shut up! Damn it! Listen!'

They fell silent.

'What is it?' someone asked. 'I can't hear anything.'

'That's just it!' exulted Dimitri. 'The water! It has stopped!'

Only then did they become aware that the dull roar of water

to which their ears had become resigned was now ended. It was quiet; a cathedral hush lay upon the workings. They began to cheer, their voices thin in the silence, and Dimitri ran to the steel ladder and swarmed down it like a monkey.

From thirty feet up Dimitri saw the dinghy marooned amongst the filth and debris around the shaft. He recognized the crumpled figure lying in the bottom of it.

'Rod!' he was shouting before he reached the station at 66 level. 'Rod, are you all right?'

The floor of the haulage was wet, and here and there a trickle of water still snaked towards the shaft. Dimitri ran to the stranded dinghy and started to turn Rod onto his back. Then he saw his arms.

'Oh, Christ!' he gasped in horror, then he was yelling up the ladder. 'Get a stretcher down here.'

*   *   *

Rod regained consciousness to find himself covered with blankets and strapped securely into a mine stretcher. His arms were splinted and bandaged, and from the familiar rattle and rush of air he knew he was in the cage on the way to the surface.

He recognized Dimitri's voice raised argumentatively.

'Damn it! The man is unconscious and badly injured, can't you leave him alone?'

'I have my duty to perform,' a strange voice answered.

'What's he want, Dimitri?' Rod croaked.

'Rod, how are you?' At the sound of his voice Dimitri was kneeling beside the stretcher anxiously.

'Bloody awful,' Rod whispered. 'What does this joker want?'

'He's a police officer. He wants to arrest Big King for murder,' Dimitri explained.

'Well, he's a bit bloody late,' whispered Rod, and even through his pain this seemed to Rod to be terribly funny. He began to laugh. He sobbed with laughter, each convulsion sending bright bursts of pain along his arms. He was shaking uncontrollably with shock, sweat pouring from his face, and he was laughing wildly.

'He's a bit bloody late,' he repeated through his hysterical laughter as Dr Dan Stander pushed the hypodermic needle into his arm and shot him full of morphine.

70

Hurry Hirschfeld stood in the main haulage on 66 level. There was bustle all around him. Already the crews from the cementation company were manhandling their equipment up towards the blocked drive.

These were specialists from an independent contracting company. They were about to begin pumping thousands of tons of liquid cement into the rock jam that sealed the drive. They would pump it in at pressures in excess of 3000 pounds per square inch, and when that concrete set it would form a plug that would effectively seal off the drive for all time. It would also form a burial vault for the body of Big King, thought Hurry, a fitting monument to the man who had saved the Sonder Ditch.

He would arrange to have a commemorative plaque placed on the outer wall of the cement plug with a suitable inscription describing the man and the deed.

The man's dependants must be properly taken care of, perhaps they could be flown down for the unveiling of the plaque. Anyway he could leave that to Public Relations and Personnel.

The haulage stank of wetness and mud. It was dank and clammy cool, and it would not improve his lumbago. Hurry had seen enough; he started back towards the shaft. Faintly he was aware of the muted clangour of the mighty pumps which in a few days would free the Sonder Ditch of the water that filled her lower levels.

The laden stretchers with their grisly blanket-covered burdens stood in a row under the hastily rigged electric lights along one wall of the tunnel. Hurry's expression hardened as he passed them.

'I'll have the guts of the man responsible for this,' he vowed silently as he waited for the cage.

*   *   *

Terry Steyner rode in the rear of the ambulance with Rod. She wiped the mud from his face.

'How bad is it, Dan?' she asked.

'Hell, Terry, he'll be up and about in a few days. The arms of course are not very pretty, that's why I'm taking him directly to Johannesburg. I want a specialist orthopaedic surgeon to set them. Apart from that he is suffering from shock pretty badly and his hands are superficially lacerated. But he will be fine.'

Dan watched curiously as Terry fussed ineffectually with the damp hair of the drugged man.

'You want a smoke?' he asked.

'Light me one, please Dan.'

He passed her the cigarette.

'I didn't know that you and Rod were so friendly,' he ventured.

Terry looked up at him quickly.

'How very delicate you are, Dr Stander,' she mocked him.

'None of my business, of course.' Hurriedly Dan withdrew.

'Don't be silly, Dan. You're a good friend of Rod's and Joy is mine. You two are entitled to know. I am desperately, crazily in love with this big hunk. I intend divorcing Manfred just as soon as possible.'

'Is Rod going to marry you?'

'He hasn't said anything about marriage but I'll sure as hell start working on him,' Terry grinned, and Dan laughed.

'Good luck to you both, then. I'm sure Rod will be able to get another job.'

'What do you mean?' Terry demanded.

'They say your grandfather is threatening to fire him so high he'll be the first man on the moon.'

Terry relapsed into silence. Proof was what Pops had asked for, but what proof was there?

*　　*　　*

'They'll be waiting on the X-Ray reports.' Joy Allbright gave her opinion. Since her engagement to Dan, Joy had suddenly become something of a medical expert. She had rushed down to the Johannesburg Central Hospital at Dan's hurried telephonic request. Dan wanted her to keep Terry company while she waited for Rod to come out of emergency. They sat together in the waiting-room.

'I expect so,' Terry agreed. Something Joy had just said had jolted in her mind, something she must remember.

'It takes them twenty minutes or so to expose the plates and develop them. Then the radiologist has to examine the plates and make his report to the surgeon.'

There, Joy had said it again. Terry sat up straight and concentrated on what Joy had said. Which word had disturbed her?

Suddenly she had it.

'The report!' she exclaimed. 'That's it! The report, that's the proof.'

She leapt out of her chair.

'Joy! Give me the keys of your car,' she demanded.

'What on earth?' Joy looked startled.

'I can't explain now. I have to get home to Sandown urgently, give me your keys. I'll explain later.'

Joy fished in her handbag and produced a leather key folder. Terry snatched it from her.

'Where are you parked?' Terry demanded.

'In the car park, near the main gate.'

'Thanks, Joy.' Terry dashed from the waiting-room, her high heels clattered down the passage.

'Crazy woman.' Joy looked after her bewildered.

Ten minutes later Dan looked into the waiting-room.

'Rod's fine now. Where's Terry?'

'She went mad —' And Joy explained her abrupt departure. Dan looked grave.

'I think we'd better follow her, Joy.'

'I think you're right, darling.'

'I'll just grab my coat,' said Dan.

*   *   *

There was only one place where Manfred would keep the geological report on the Big Dipper that Rod had told her about. That was in the safe deposit behind the panelling in his study. Because her jewellery was kept in the same safe, Terry had a key and the combination to the lock.

Even in Joy's Alfa Romeo, taking liberties with the traffic regulations, it was a thirty-five minute drive out to Sandown. It was after five in the evening when Terry coasted down the long driveway and parked before the garages.

The extensive grounds were deserted, for the gardeners finished at five, and there was no sign of life from the house. This was as it should be, for she knew Manfred was still in Europe. He was not due back for at least another four days.

Leaving the ignition keys in the Alfa, Terry ran up the pathway and onto the stoep. She fumbled in her handbag and found the keys to the front door. She let herself in, and went directly to Manfred's study. She slid the concealing panel aside and set about the lengthy business of opening the steel safe. It required both key and combination to activate the mechanism, and Terry had never developed much expertise at tumbling the combination.

Finally, however, the door swung open and she was confronted by the voluminous contents. Terry began removing the various documents and files, examining each one and then stacking them neatly on the floor beside her.

She had no idea of the shape, size nor colour of the report for which she was searching, it was ten minutes before she selected an unmarked folder and flicked open the cover. 'Confidential Report on the geological formations of the Kitchenerville gold fields, with special reference to those areas lying to the east of the Big Dipper Dyke.'

Terry felt a wonderful lift of relief as she read the titling for she had begun doubting that the report was here. Quickly she thumbed through the pages and began reading at random. There was no doubt.

'This is it!' she exclaimed aloud.

'*I'll take that, thank you.*' The dreaded familiar voice cut into her preoccupation, and Terry spun around and came to her feet in one movement, clutching the file protectively to her breast. She backed away from the man who stood in the doorway.

She hardly recognized her own husband. She had never seen him like this. Manfred was coatless, and his shirt was without collar or stud. He appeared to have slept in his trousers, for they were rumpled and baggy. There was a yellow stain down the front of his white shirt.

His scanty brown hair was dishevelled, hanging forward wispily onto his forehead. He had not shaved, and the skin around his eyes was discoloured and puffy.

'Give that to me.' He came towards her with hand outstretched.

'Manfred.' She kept moving away from him. 'What are you doing here? When did you get back?'

'Give it to me, you slut.'

'Why do you call me that?' She asked, trying for time.

'Slut!' he repeated, and lunged towards her. Terry whirled away from him lightly.

She ran for the study door, with Manfred close behind her. She beat him into the passage and raced for the front door. Her heel caught in one of the persian carpets that covered the floor of the passage, and she staggered and fell against the wall.

'Whore!' He was on her instantly trying to wrestle the report out of her hands, but she clung to it with all her strength. Face to face they were almost of a height, and she saw the madness in his eyes.

Suddenly Manfred released her. He stepped back, bunched his fist and swung it round-armed into her cheek. Her head jerked back and cracked against the wall. He drew back his fist and hit her again. She felt the quick warm burst of blood spurt from her nose, and staggered through the door beside her into the dining-room. She was dizzy from the blows and she fell against the heavy stinkwood table.

Manfred was close behind her. He charged her, sending her sprawling backwards onto the table. He was on top of her, both his hands at her throat.

'I'm going to kill you, you whore,' he wheezed. His thumbs hooked and pressed deep into the flesh of her throat. With the frenzied strength of despair, Terry clawed at his eyes with both hands. Her nails scored his face, raking long red lines into his flesh. With a cry Manfred released her, and backed away holding both hands to his injured face, leaving Terry lying gasping across the table.

He stood for a moment, then uncovered his face and inspected the blood on his hands.

'I'll kill you for that!'

But as he advanced towards her, Terry rolled over the table.

'Whore! Slut! Bitch!' he screamed at her, following her around the table. Terry kept ahead of him.

There were a matched pair of heavy Stuart crystal decanters on the sideboard, one containing port, the other sherry. Terry snatched up one of them and turned to face Manfred. She hurled the decanter with all her remaining strength at his head.

Manfred did not have time to duck. The decanter cracked against his forehead, and he fell backwards, stunned. Terry snatched up the report and ran out of the dining-room, down the passage, out of the front door and into the garden. She was running weakly, following the driveway towards the main road.

Then behind her she heard the engine of an automobile roar into life. Panting wildly, holding the report, she stopped and looked back. Manfred had followed her out of the house. He was behind the steering wheel of Joy's Alfa Romeo. As she watched he threw the car into gear and howled towards her, blue smoke burning from the rear tyres with the speed of the acceleration. His face behind the windscreen was white and streaked with the marks of her nails, his eyes were staring, insane, and she knew he was going to ride her down.

She kicked off her shoes and ran off the driveway onto the lawns.

*   *   *

Crouched forward in the driver's seat of the Alfa, Manfred watched the fleeing figure ahead of him.

Terry ran with the full-hipped sway of the mature woman, her long legs were tanned and her hair flew out loosely behind her.

Manfred was not concerned with the return of the geological report, its existence was no longer of significance to him. What he wanted was to completely destroy this woman. In his crazed state, she had become the symbol and the figurehead of all his woes. His humiliation and fall were all linked to her, he could exact his vengeance by destroying her, crushing that revolting warm and clinging body, bruising it, ripping it with the steel of the Alfa Romeo's chassis.

He hit second gear and spun the steering-wheel. The Alfa swerved from the driveway, and as its rear wheels left the tarmac, they skidded on the thick grass. Deftly Manfred checked the skid and lined up on Terry's running back.

Already she was among the protea bushes on the lower terrace. The Alfa buck-jumped the slope, flying bird-free before crashing down heavily on its suspension. Wheels spun and bit, and the sleek vehicle shot forward again.

Terry looked back over her shoulder, her face was white and her eyes very big and fear-filled. Manfred giggled. He was aware of a sense of power, the ability to dispense life or death. He steered for her, reckless of all consequences, intent on destroying her.

There was a six-foot tall protea bush ahead of him, and Manfred roared through it, bursting it asunder. Scattering branches and leaves, giggling again, he saw Terry directly ahead of him. She was still looking back at him, and at that moment she stumbled and fell onto her knees.

She was helpless. Her face streaked with tears and blood, her hair falling forward in wild disorder, kneeling as though for the headsman's stroke. Manfred felt a flood of disappointment. He did not want it to end so soon, he wanted to savour this sadistic elation, this sense of power.

At the last possible moment he yanked the wheel over and the car slewed violently. It shot past Terry with six inches to spare, and its rear wheels pelted her with clods of turf and thrown dirt.

Laughing aloud, wild-eyed, Manfred held the wheel hard over, bringing the Alfa around in a tight skidding circle, crackling sideways through another protea bush.

Terry was up and running again. He saw immediately that she was heading for the change rooms of the swimming-pool among the trees on the bottom lawn and she was far enough ahead to elude him, perhaps.

'Bitch!' he snarled, and crash-changed into third gear, with engine revs peaking. The Alfa howled in pursuit of the running girl.

Had Terry thrown the bulky report aside, she might have reached the brick change rooms ahead of the racing sports car, but the report hampered and slowed her. She still had twenty yards to cover, she was running along the paved edge of the swimming-pool, and she sensed that the car was right on top of her.

Terry dived sideways, hitting the water flat on her side, and the Alfa roared past. Manfred trod heavily on the brakes, the Michelin metallic tyres screeched against the paving stones, and Manfred was out of the driver's seat the moment the Alfa stopped.

He ran back to the pool side. Terry was floundering towards the far steps. She was exhausted, weak with exertion and terror. Her sodden hair streamed down over her face, and she was gasping open-mouthed for air.

Manfred laughed again, a high-pitched, almost girlish giggle, and he dived after her, landing squarely between Terry's shoulder blades with his full weight. She went under, sucking water agonizingly into already aching lungs, and when she surfaced she was coughing and gagging, blinded with water and her own wet hair.

Almost immediately she felt herself seized from behind and forced face down into the water. For half a minute she struggled fiercely, then her movements slowed and became weaker.

Manfred stood over her, chest deep in the clear water, gripping her around the waist and by a handful of her sodden hair, forcing her face deep below the surface. He had lost his spectacles, and he blinked owlishly. The wet silk of his shirt clung to his upper body, and the water had slicked his hair down.

As he felt the life going out of her, and her movements becoming sluggish and slow, he began to laugh again. The broken, incoherent laughter of a madman.

* * *

'Dan!' Joy pointed off through the trees. 'That's my car down there, parked by the swimming-pool!'

'What the hell is it doing there?'

'There's something wrong, Terry wouldn't drive through her beloved garden, unless there was!'

Dan braked sharply and pulled his Jaguar to the side of the driveway.

'I'm going to take a look.' He slid out of the car and started off across the lawns. Joy opened her own door and trotted after him.

Dan saw the man in the water, fully dressed, intent on what he was doing. He recognized Manfred Steyner.

'What the hell is he up to?' Dan started running. He reached the edge of the pool, and suddenly he realized what was happening.

'Christ! He's drowning her,' he shouted aloud, and he sprang into the water.

He did not waste time struggling with Manfred. He hit him a great open-handed, round-armed blow, that cracked against the side of Manfred's head like a pistol shot and sent him lurching sideways, releasing his grip on Terry.

Ignoring Manfred, Dan picked Terry from the water like a drowned kitten and waded to the steps. He carried her out and laid her face down on the paving. He knelt over her and began applying artificial respiration. He felt Terry stir under his hands, then cough and retch weakly.

Joy came up at the run and dropped on her knees beside him.

'My God, Dan, what happened?'

'That little bastard was trying to drown her.'

Dan looked up from his labours without interrupting the rhythm of his movement over Terry. She spluttered and retched again.

On the far side of the pool Manfred Steyner had dragged himself from the pool. He was sitting on the edge with his feet still dangling into the water, his head was hanging and he was fingering the side of his face where Dan had hit him. On his lap he held a wet pulpy mess that had been the geological report.

'Joy, can you take over here? Terry's not too far gone, and I want to get my hands on that little Hun.'

Joy took Dan's place over Terry's prostrate form, and Dan stood up.

'What are you going to do to him?' Joy asked.

'I'm going to beat him to a pulp.'

'Good show!' Joy encouraged him.' 'Give him one for me.'

Manfred had heard the exchange and as Dan ran around the edge of the pool he scrambled to his feet, and staggered to the parked Alfa. He slammed the door and whirred the engine to life. Dan was just too late to stop him. The car shot forward across the lawns, leaving Dan running, futile, behind it.

'Look after her, Joy!' Dan shouted back.

By the time Dan had run up the terrace to his Jaguar and reversed it to point in the opposite direction, the Alfa had disappeared through the white gates with a musical flutter of its exhaust.

'Come on, girlie,' Dan spoke to his Jaguar. 'Let's go get him.'

The rear wheels spun as he pulled away.

*   *   *

Without his spectacles Manfred Steyner's vision was blurred and milky. The outlines of all objects on which he looked were softened and indistinct.

He instinctively checked the Alfa at the stop street at the bottom of the lane. He sat undecided, water still streaming from his clothing, squelching in his shoes. Beside him on the passenger seat lay the sodden report, its pages beginning to disintegrate from its soaking and the rough handling it had received.

He had to get rid of it. It was the shred of incriminating evidence. That was the only clear thought Manfred had. For the first time in his life the crystalline clarity of his thought processes was interrupted. He was confused, his mind jerking abruptly from one subject to another, the intense pleasure of inflicting hurt on Terry mingled with the sting and smart of his own injuries. He could not concentrate on either sensation for overlying it all was a sense of fear, of uncertainty. He felt vulnerable, hunted, hurt and shaken. His brain flickered and wavered as though a computer had developed an electrical fault. The answers it produced were nonsensical.

He looked in the rear view mirror, saw the Jaguar glide out between the white gates and turn towards him.

'Christ!' he panicked. He rammed his foot down on the accelerator and engaged the clutch. The Alfa screeched out into the main highway, swerved into the path of a heavy truck, bounded over the far kerb and swung back into the road.

Dan watched it tear away towards Kyalami.

He let the truck pass and then swung into the traffic behind it. He had to wait until the road was clear ahead before he could overtake the truck, and by that time the Alfa was a dwindling cream speck ahead of him.

Dan settled back in the leather bucket seat, and gave the Jaguar its head. He was furious, outraged by the treatment he had seen Manfred meting out to Terry. Her swollen and bruised face had shocked him and his feet were firmly set upon the path of vengeance.

His hands gripped the steering-wheel fiercely, he was muttering threats of violence as the speedometer moved up over the hundred mile per hour mark and he began relentlessly overhauling the cream sports car.

Steadily he moved up behind the Alfa until he was driving almost on its rear bumper. The Alfa was held up by a green school bus. Dan could not pass, however, for there was a steady stream of traffic coming in the opposite direction.

He fastened his attention on the back of Manfred's head, still fuming with anger.

Dan dropped down a gear, ready to pull out and overtake the Alfa when the opportunity arose. At that moment Manfred looked up into his rear view mirror. Dan saw the reflection of his white face with disordered damp hair hanging onto the forehead, saw his expression change immediately he recognized Dan and the Alfa shot out into the face of the approaching traffic.

There was the howl and blare of horns, vehicles swerved to make way for Manfred's wild rush. Dan glimpsed frightened faces flicking past, but the Alfa had squeezed around the green bus and was speeding away.

Dan dropped back, then sent the Jaguar like a thrown javelin through the gap between bus and kerb, overtaking on the wrong side and ignoring the bus driver's yell of protest.

The Jaguar had a higher top speed, and on the long straight Pretoria highway Dan crept up steadily on the cream Alfa.

He could see Manfred glancing repeatedly into his driving-mirror, and he grinned mirthlessly.

Ahead of them the highway rose and then dipped over a low rounded ridge. A double avenue of tall blue gum trees flanked each side of the road.

Travelling in the same direction as the two high performance sports cars was a mini of a good vintage year. Its elderly driver was triumphantly about to overtake an overloaded vegetable truck. Neck and neck they approached the blind rise at twenty-five miles per hour, between them they effectively blocked half the road.

The horn of the Alfa wailed a high-pitched warning, and Manfred pulled out to overtake both slower vehicles. He was level with them, well out over the white dividing line, when a cement truck popped up over the blind rise.

Dan stood on his brake pedal with all the strength of his right leg, and watched it happen.

The cement truck and the Alfa came head on towards each other at a combined speed of well over a hundred miles per hour. At the last moment the Alfa began to turn away but it was too late by many seconds.

It caught the heavy cement truck a glancing blow and was hurled across the path of the two slower vehicles, miraculously touching neither of them; it skidded sideways leaving reeking black smears of rubber on the tarmac, and hurdled the low bank. It struck one of the blue gums full on, with a force that shivered the giant tree trunk and brought down a rain of leaves.

Dan pulled the Jaguar into the side of the road, parked it, and walked back.

He knew there was no hurry. The drivers of the mini and the vegetable truck were there before him. They were attempting to talk each other down, both of them excited and relieved by their own escapes.

'I'm a doctor,' said Dan, and they fell back respectfully.

'He doesn't need a doctor,' said one of them. 'He needs an undertaker.'

One look was sufficient. Dr Manfred Steyner was as dead as Dan had ever seen anybody. His crushed head was thrust through the windscreen. Dan picked up the sodden bundle of paper from the seat beside the huddled body. He was aware that some particular importance was attached to it.

Dan's anger had evaporated entirely, and he felt a twinge of pity as he looked into the wreckage at the corpse. It appeared so frail and small – of such little consequence.

71

The sunlight was sparkling bright, broken into a myriad eye-stinging fragments by the rippling surface of the bay.

The breeze was strong enough for the Arrow class yachts to fly their spinnakers as they came down on the wind. The sails bulged out blue and yellow and bright scarlet against the sombre green of the great whale-back bluff above Durban Bay.

Under the awning on the afterdeck of the motor yacht it was cool, but the fat man wore only a pair of white linen slacks with his feet thrust into dark blue cloth espadrilles.

Sprawled in a deck-chair, his belly bulged smooth and hard over the waistband of his slacks; he was tanned a dark mahogany colour and his body-hair grew thick and curly from chest to navel.

'Thank you, Andrew.' He extended his empty glass, and the younger man carried it to the open-air bar. The fat man watched him as he mixed another Pimms No. 1 cup.

A white-clad crew member clambered down the companion way from the bridge. He touched his cap respectfully to the fat man.

'Captain's respects, sir, and we are ready to sail when you give the order.'

'Thank you. Please tell the captain we will sail as soon as Miss du Maine comes aboard.' And the crew man ran back to the bridge.

'Ah!' The fat man sighed happily as Andrew placed the Pimms in his out-stretched hand. 'I have really earned this break. The last few weeks have been nerve-racking, to say the least.'

'Yes, sir,' Andrew agreed dutifully. 'But, as usual, you snatched victory from the ashes.'

'It was close,' the fat man agreed. 'Young Ironsides gave us all a nasty fright with his drop-blast matt. I was only just able to make good my personal commitments before the price shot up again. The profit was not as high as I had anticipated, but then I have never made a habit of peering into the mouths of gift-horses.'

'It was a pity that our associates lost all that money,' Andrew ventured.

'Yes, yes. A great pity. But rather them than us, Andrew.'

'Indeed, sir.'

'In a way I am glad it worked out as it did. I am a patriotic man, at heart. I am relieved that it was not necessary to disrupt the economy of the country to make our little profit.'

He stood up suddenly, his interest quickening as a taxi cab came down onto the Yacht Club jetty. The cabby opened a rear door and from it emerged a very beautiful young lady.

'Ah, Andrew! Our guest has arrived. You may warn the captain that we will be sailing within minutes; and send a man to fetch her luggage.'

He went to the entry port to welcome the young lady.

72

In mid-summer in the Zambesi Valley the heat is a solid white shimmering thing. In the noon day nothing moves in the merciless sunlight.

At the centre of the native village grew a baobab tree. A monstrous bloated trunk with malformed branches like the limbs of a polio victim. The carrion crows sat in it, black and shiny as cockroaches. A score of grass huts ringed the tree, and beyond them lay the tilled fields. The millet stood tall and green in the sun.

Along the rude track towards the village came a Landrover. It came slowly, lurching and jolting over the rough ground, its motor growling in low gear. Printed in black on its sides were the letters A.R.C., African Recruiting Corporation.

The children heard it first, and crawled from the grass huts. Naked black bodies, and shrill excited voices in the sunlight.

They ran to meet the Landrover and danced beside it, shrieking and laughing. The Landrover came to a halt in the meagre shade under the baobab tree. An elderly white man climbed from the cab. He wore khaki safari clothes and a wide-brimmed hat. Complete silence fell, and one of the oldest boys fetched a carved stool and placed it in the shade.

The white man sat on the stool. A girl came forward, knelt before him and offered a gourd of millet beer. The white man drank from the gourd. No one spoke, none would disturb an honoured guest until he had taken refreshment, but from the grass huts the adult members of the village came. Blinking into the sunlight, winding their loin clothes about their waists. They came and squatted in a semi-circle before the white man on his stool.

He lowered the gourd and set it aside. He looked at them.

'I see you, my friends,' he greeted them, and the response was warm.

'We see you, old one,' they chorused, but the expression of their visitor remained grave.

'Let the wives of King Nkulu come forward,' he called. 'Let them bring each their first-born son with them.'

Four women and four adolescent boys left the crowd and came shyly into the open. For a moment the white man studied them compassionately, then he stood and stepped forward. He placed a hand on the shoulder of each of the two eldest lads.

'Your father has gone to *his* fathers,' he told them. There was a stirring, an intake of breath, a startled cry, and then, as was proper, the eldest wife let out the first sobbing wail of mourning.

One by one each wife sank down onto the dry dusty earth and covered her head with her shawl.

'He is dead,' the white man repeated against the background of their keening lament. 'But he died in such honour as to let his name live on forever. So great was his dying that for all their lives money will each month be paid to his wives, and for each of his sons there is already set aside a place at the University that each may grow as strong in learning as his father was in body. Of Big King there will be raised up an image in stone.

'The wives of Big King and his sons will travel in a flying machine to I'Goldi, that their eyes also may look upon the stone image of the man who was their husband and their father.' The white man paused for breath, it was a lengthy speech in the midday heat of the valley. He wiped his face and then tucked the handkerchief into his pocket.

'He was a lion!'

'Ngwenyama!' whispered the sturdy twelve-year-old boy standing beside the white man. The tears started from his eyes and greased down his cheeks. He turned away and ran alone into the millet fields.

73

Dennis Langley, the Sales Manager of Kitchenerville Motors who were the local Ford agents, stretched his arms over his head luxuriously. He sighed with deep contentment. What a lovely way to spend a working day morning.

'Happy?' asked Hettie Delange beside him in the double bed. In reply Dennis grinned and sighed again.

Hettie sat up and let the sheet fall to her waist. Her breasts were big and white, and damp with perspiration. She looked down on his naked chest and arm muscles approvingly.

'Gee, you're built nicely.'

'So are you,' Dennis smiled up at her.

'You're different from the other chaps I've gone out with,' Hettie told him. 'You speak so nicely – like a gentleman, you know.'

Before Dennis Langley could decide on a suitable reply, the front door bell shrilled, the sound of it echoing through the house. Dennis shot into an upright position with a fearful expression on his face.

'Who's that?' he demanded.

'It's probably the butcher delivering the meat.'

'It may be my wife!' Dennis cautioned her. 'Don't answer it.'

'Of course I've got to answer it, silly.' Hettie threw back the sheet, and rose in her white and golden glory to find her dressing-gown. The sight was enough to momentarily quiet Dennis Langley's misgivings, but as she belted her gown and hid it from view he urged her again.

'Be careful! Make sure it's not her before you open the door.'

Hettie opened the front door, and immediately drew her gown more closely around her with one hand, while with the other she tried to pat her hair into a semblance of order.

'Hello,' she breathed.

The tall young man in the doorway was really rather dreamy. He wore a dark business suit and carried an expensive leather briefcase.

'Mrs Delange?' he inquired. He had a nice soft dreamy voice.

'Yes, I'm Mrs Delange.' Hettie fluttered her eyelashes. 'Won't you come in?'

She led him through to the lounge, and she was pleasantly aware of his eyes on the opening of her gown.

'What can I do for you?' she asked archly.

'I am your local representative of the Sanlam Insurance Company, Mrs Delange. I have come to express my company's condolences on your recent sad bereavement. I would have called sooner, but I did not wish to intrude on your sorrow.'

'Oh!' Hettie dropped her eyes, immediately adopting the role of the widow.

'However, we hope we can bring a little light to disperse the darkness that surrounds you. You may know that your husband was a policy-holder with our Company?'

Hettie shook her head, but watched with interest while the visitor opened his briefcase.

'Yes, he was. Two months ago he took out a straight life policy with double indemnity. The policy was ceded to you.' The Insurance man extracted a sheaf of papers from his case. 'I have here my company's cheque in full settlement of all claims under the policy. If you will just sign for it, please.'

'How much?' Hettie abandoned the role of the bereaved.

'With the double indemnity, the cheque is for forty-eight thousand Rand.'

Hettie's eyes flew wide with delight.

'Gee!' she gasped. 'That's *fabulous*!'

74

Hurry's original intentions had expanded considerably. Instead of a plaque on the cement plug at 66 level, the monument to Big King had become a life-sized statue in bronze. He sited it on the lawns in front of the Administrative offices of the Sonder Ditch on a base of black marble.

It was effective. The artist had captured a sense of urgency, of vibrant power. The inscription was simple, just the name of the man – 'King Nkulu' – and the date of his death.

Hurry attended the unveiling in person, even though he hated ceremonies and avoided them whenever possible. In the front row of guests facing him his granddaughter sat beside Doctor Stander and his very new blonde wife. She winked at him and Hurry frowned lovingly back at her.

From the seat beside Hurry, young Ironsides stood up to introduce the Chairman. Hurry noted the expression on his granddaughter's face as she transferred all her attention to the tall young man with both his arms encased in plaster of Paris and supported by slings.

'Perhaps I should have fired him, after all,' thought Hurry. 'He is going to cut one out of my herd.'

Hurry glanced sideways at his General Manager, and decided with resignation, 'Too late'. Then went on to cheer himself. 'Anyway he looks like good breeding stock.'

His line of thought switched again. 'Better start making arrangements to transfer him up to Head Office. He will need a lot of grooming and polishing.'

Without thinking he fished a powerful-looking cigar from his breast pocket. He had it half-way to his mouth when he caught Terry's scandalized glare. Silently her lips formed the words: 'Your doctor!'

Guiltily Hurry Hirschfeld stuffed the cigar back into his pocket.

PRODUCTION
EDITO-SERVICE S.A., GENEVA

PRINTED IN SWITZERLAND

27/7